my mother's lovers

WESTERN LITERATURE SERIES

books by joy passanante

Sinning in Italy (poetry), 1999
My Mother's Lovers, 2002

For dear Summer
in life-long
friendship
and with
love, Joy

my mother's lovers

joy passanante

university of nevada press
reno and las vegas

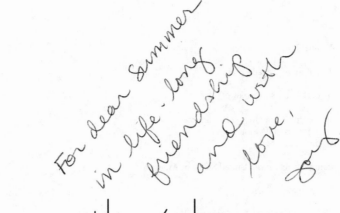

Joy Passanante
The Breakfast Club
Moscow, Idaho
March 6, 2003

Western Literature Series

University of Nevada Press,

Reno, Nevada 89557 USA

Manufactured in the United States of America

Design by Carrie House

Library of Congress Cataloging-in-Publication Data

Passanante, Joy, 1947–

My mother's lovers / Joy Passanante.

p. cm. — (Western literature series)

ISBN 0-87417-495-3 (pbk. : alk. paper)

1. Aircraft accident victims' families — Fiction.

2. Hippies — Family relationships — Fiction. 3. Italian

American families—Fiction. 4. Mothers and

daughters

—Fiction. 5. Children of artists—Fiction. 6. Saint

Louis (Mo.) — Fiction. 7. Jewish families —Fiction.

8. Young women — Fiction. 9. Idaho —Fiction.

I. Title. II. Series.

PS3616.A85 M9   2002

813'.6—dc21   2001005958

FIRST PRINTING

11   10   09   08   07   06   05   04   03   02

5   4   3   2   1

This book is for Gary Williams,
who helped me give birth to my three dreams.

When my mother dies, I will feel her slip into me gentle as breath, opening like the petals of a flower somewhere deep within me, and then I will carry my mother inside my body. She will live in me like a small pebble, like a pearl in a pomegranate, a kernel in a nut. We will share my body then, the one she gave me, and I will feed her as she fed me.

CYNTHIA KIMBALL

contents

acknowledgments

I am particularly grateful to Gary Williams and Kenny Marotta, who spent uncountable hours helping me revise this novel; to Cynthia Kimball, who imagined Wilders Ferry with me and constantly encouraged me to write; to Sally Brady and Barbara Hogenson, who made wise suggestions on earlier drafts; to those who gave me information—David Goldring, Karl Dye, Glenda Deitrick, Vanessa Graham, Joe Colburn, Jan Vogtman, Jan Abrams, Sam Ham, Bennett Lumber Products, Inc., and especially Cathy Goldstein; to the Idaho Commission on the Arts, for partially funding my work on this project; to the University of Idaho, particularly the Department of English and Larry Merk of the Center for Business Development and Research, for giving me time to write; to June and Harvey Whitten, for giving me a place to write; to those who helped me prepare the manuscript—Kim Sarff, Louise Hecht, Karen Gillespie, Marjory Whitten, Tisha Egashira, and especially Yvonne Sertich; to Monica Miceli, Trudy McMurrin, Jan McInroy, Sara Vélez Mallea, and Christine Campbell, who ushered this book through to publication; to the teachers who had early faith in me—Helen Hollander, William Heyde, Kenneth Weber, and Esther Doyle; to Roger Zehntner, for his excellent legal advice; and, most of all, to my extraordinary family, who inspired this book in more ways than even I know—my husband, Gary Williams; my sisters, Judy and Jean Passanante; my daughters, Liza and Emily Williams; my mother, Alberta Passanante; and especially my father, Bart Passanante—physician, gardener, pianist, painter, diarist—who wrote my name in crocuses.

first revelation

Secrets were encoded in the blood of the women in my family. And like an addict, I returned to their revelations again and again. The day I disappeared with my mother I discovered the first fragile layer of all the secrets that would be revealed to me. And even before I began to peel back more and more toward the core, and feel helpless against its gravity, I knew they had already changed my life forever.

It was the day that was to be my first at school. Even in my sleep startled by her presence, I jerked awake. I squinted out my oval window at the glow on the gray horizon. Mimi swept me up from my maple bed.

"Let's disappear. Just fly away together, what do you say?" she whispered, holding a finger to her lips. I glanced toward the room she shared with my father. Before I could answer, she said, already pulling open the drawers to my dresser, "Shhh. Don't wake him. It'll be our secret. Too much time inside will warp your mind."

"Will we be back in time for school?" I asked.

"We always have time for learning," she offered cryptically. She pulled my tie-dyed shirt over my head, the shirt her friend Jillian had made me as a birth gift, then helped me into a pair of floral print overalls, which she rolled at the cuffs.

We tiptoed down the stairs and into the kitchen. I stared at her back as she tossed apples, cheese, and a small knife into a paper bag and scooped from a clear jar a handful of sunflower seeds, which she shoved into the pocket of her blue backpack. Then she stooped and pulled out a bag of M&M's from a soup pot in the cupboard. I gasped. Sugar was one of the bourgeois pleasures that, as far as Mimi was concerned, was beneath us. She caught my expression and winked. She grabbed her backpack, shoved the handle of her metal paint box into my hand, and left the screen to the front door flapping. Somewhat breathless, I followed her out to our 1963 VW, a robin's-egg blue. She lifted me onto the ripped upholstery in the front seat and, belting out "The Times They Are a-Changin'," her head bobbing over the steering wheel as she dodged potholes, she careened along the logging road that took us deep into the woods at the edge of Wilders Ferry.

She pulled up at a stump, set up our food and her paint supplies, her easel next to it. Then she led me by the hand to a young tamarack, and we waltzed around it. We waved our hands in front of us to clear an area of gossamer to give us plenty of room. We hummed tunes we made up ourselves while we whirled, our heads thrown back, gazes fixed on the rising sun, and then fell laughing to the ground.

Later, we sucked on sunflower seeds in silence. "Sometimes it's better not to talk, Lake. Talk is cheap." She unpacked her silver tubes of oils and her brushes, which fanned out of her backpack like peacock feathers, and changed into her paint-stained workshirt embroidered with a fir tree and a sickle moon. She placed a ceramic bell in my hand.

"I made this at college, back East, and brought it with me all the way to Idaho," she said.

"Just for me?" I asked.

"Just for you today," she said and closed my fingers around it.

She lifted a canvas to the easel. "Dance," she said, and I looked up to see if she would join me, but her back was already to me.

I carried the earth-colored bell in both hands, proffering it like a gift, and then I rang it, tentatively at first, then louder, tolling it randomly as I skipped from log to log and as Mimi stroked the blank canvas and painted to a rhythm of her own. Offering a tuneless song to the ospreys in their messy nests, I orbited her easel. When the sun was an apricot-colored disk spiked by the tops of the tamaracks, she put down her brush and wiped her hands with an oily rag, digging under her short finger-nails. "Hungry?" she asked. Before I could answer, she continued, "While we eat I want to introduce you to some of my best friends." Her arm swept over the wildflowers, the sweep of a princess over her subjects.

"I thought Dyl was your best friend." Dyl was Jillian's husband, but Mimi always called him her best friend.

"I said *some*. This sweet soul, for example," she said pointing to a moun-tain lady's slipper, "is Maryellen Shortstem, and I'd like you to meet . . ." (this time flicking the small stem of an owl's clover) "Licoriceleaf." We giggled, we ran our fingers along the edges of petals, we rolled in the pine needles.

I spent the rest of the day in my own reverie while she focused on the distance, studying the mountains, the peaks of the Cabinets rising up from a meadow, where a white-tailed doe sprang through the Indian paintbrush and shooting star. Mimi slashed her canvas and stroked it lovingly in turns. It wasn't until the sun dipped behind the tallest peak that she sighed and said, gently, "It's time." On the way home, as the roll-ing of the VW lulled me to sleep, I cupped the ceramic bell in my palm.

As we entered the house, she was whistling, something I recognized from one of her Joan Baez records. I looked up at her. Her arms were scratched by brambles; her cheeks ruddy from the sun and sheer exhila-ration; her workshirt, slung over an arm, reddened and yellowed and oranged. And then I glanced almost shyly at her canvas. I wanted to see what images she had used to commemorate our flight together. But when I saw it, my eyes must have widened or my upper lip quavered, because she quickly lifted the canvas and set it on a high shelf, one I couldn't see. The rest of the evening she barely glanced at me.

The painting was of a nude woman, the setting a room with wallpaper and a chandelier.

After that Mimi often disappeared for entire days, but always alone; she never invited me again. And each time, she returned with a sketch or the beginning of a painting of a nude woman, always indoors. I don't mean to suggest that Mimi painted the same picture every time; I know she would have been offended if any of us she allowed into her life had implied such a thing. In fact, although the settings were similar, the bodies and faces were all different. She rendered all her interiors in voluptuous colors with a predilection for the tropical. The nude was consistently posed in front of some exotic wallpaper, or on a brocade couch, or on a patterned carpet, or facing heavy drapes looking weighted down by the gargantuan hibiscus and birds-of-paradise printed into the fabric. All the action was in the perception. The women always appeared to be doing nothing at all. Sometimes they had brown hair, sometimes blue hair. They had thighs shaped like lodgepole pines, they had wrists small enough to loop your thumb and forefinger around, they had strands of lace around their necks, they had toenails painted carmine and fuchsia to highlight the blossoms in the background, they had noses as prominent as those of Roman sculptures, and lips as thin as society matrons'. Some of these features I recognized from the college-era photos she kept in well-ordered albums on the lacquered pine shelves Dyl had built for her room; a few I recognized from people we passed on the street—waitresses who served ice cream sodas at the Hoot Owl Drug counter; the woman with enormous breasts that rested on her waist, who took our change at the gas station and printed us receipts in dark, block letters. All the others—that is, save one unforgettable one—remained a mystery the rest of my life.

the blaze struggling up

I don't blame Wilders Ferry for all that happened between my family and me, at least not exclusively. I loved the mountains in the morning and just before night, the Selkirks in their half-circle on the horizon, the Cabinets sloping into the lake, making the north country look as layered and shadowy as my life. And I liked the lake itself, the way it glittered at noon and drew the heat from my body in July and made me numb, but mostly its shape—a spiral that led to somewhere else.

In the summers, beginning as soon as I was old enough to carry a pack and throughout my elementary school years, we spent long week-ends camping or backpacking in the Selway wilderness or the Sawtooth Mountains with Dyl, Jillian, and their daughter, Paris, who was about nine months my junior. The rest of the year we ate dinner with them once a week, almost religiously, the music, from opera to sixties rock, blaring from the tape player on the floor. They owned an alternative food store they called Satellite Health, and I saw at least one of them there midweek, when Mimi would send me out for groceries. I loved looking at Jillian, especially her lavish hair, which covered her slender shoulders and back like a gold cloak. The hairs on her arms and legs were wispy and blond, nearly invisible. Her floral skirts and long-fringed shawls decorated the otherwise drab space. At home, I liked to watch her work with a needle or at her blond loom, to study her graceful fingers. Her work was incessant and meticulous. Her face was impassive, cool, at least until Paris appeared in the periphery of her vision. Then the warmth would return to her cheeks, and the long fingers would stroke Paris's head. Even though we saw Jillian and Dyl frequently, both at our house and theirs, Jillian was different at the Satellite. There, I caught some glint from another life, far removed from ours, one, I imagined, of sophistication and wealth.

Paris had buttercup-hued hair, which Jillian parted in the middle and wove into long braids every day, and pink, chubby cheeks "just like a Boucher painting," Mimi said nearly every time Paris crossed her line of sight. Mimi pronounced it "Booshay" and explained each time that that was how the French would say it.

They lived at the edge of town, a short walk from school, and when we were both in the lower grades, Paris used to invite me over for what Jillian called "luncheon" at least once a week. Jillian would greet us at the door, her voice tinkling like a bracelet of tiny silver bells. She moved like a dancer, and in fact, in warmer months, wore ballet slippers around the house and even in the Satellite. There was something delicate about her; in Paris the same features looked coarse and cloddy.

The luncheon table would already be laid with a pitcher of lunaria or foxglove, cotton place mats, and gingham napkins rolled into interesting shapes in our water glasses. China plates of food would be waiting for us. Jillian had already scooped the melons into balls and carved the pineapple slices into the shapes of stars and snowflakes. She'd cut the sandwiches into diamonds and trimmed the crusts for Paris, and placed something pretty in the middle of the plate, a radish carved to look like a rose, or three cherries in a column lanced with a plumed toothpick. In a glass pitcher of iced juice spiked with a little sparkling soda, she floated strawberries. She never sat down with us, but perched on a stool in the corner and sipped tea with honey. She would unfasten her hair from the tortoiseshell combs, and it would cascade down her back. She'd keep it loose until Dyl entered, and then, almost unconsciously, she'd gather it up again.

When Mimi, Dad, and I ate alone, the kitchen echoed, and the scraping of silverware on the clunky ceramic plates would set my teeth on edge. Increasingly, Dad brought a book to the table. One evening, while we were eating one of Mimi's brown rice casseroles in silence, Dad finished a book and sighed as he shoved it toward the center of the table.

"That's why I dropped out of school," he said.

Mimi placed her fork deliberately on her napkin. "You dropped out because the Movement needed you," she said. There was an edge to her voice; I knew it was no reminder. "And anyway, your parents were dead. What were you going to do without a job in the middle of the city, New York University not about to give you any help?" She made it sound like New York University had given him no choice but to drop out.

"Tell me about how your parents died," I said to Dad, trying to change the subject.

Mimi sighed. "They were visiting their friends—"

"Like Jillian and Dyl—" I interrupted. Mimi shook her head; she rarely engaged in or approved of a ritual that she was not a part of.

"Yes, like Jillian and Dyl," he said.

"They were their bridge partners, for God's sake; not at all like Dyl," Mimi interrupted again.

Dad went on as if she hadn't spoken. "—visiting them upstate and the fire began . . ."

I added my part: "Before dawn—"

". . . and so they all died and—"

"The blaze struggled up and viciously licked the last grays of the lingering twilight away." It was Mimi's voice. I shot her a glare.

"You never let him tell it his way," I said, looking down at my cracked plate, but he went on as if he had heard neither of us.

"And I dropped out of school. And there you pretty much have it." He ate the rest of his dinner in a distracted silence and then, just as he was scooting back his chair, said, "So anyway, the reason I dropped out was so that no one would tell me what to read."

He did indeed love all books indiscriminantly, even children's books and romances. At least he'd start them, or plow into a section at random in the middle. He simply liked the way they looked and smelled, their glossy jacket covers and the noise they made when he cracked open each virgin copy. Dad used to get so excited in bookstores when he went to Spokane or Seattle that he would feel pressure in his bowels and have to flee in pursuit of a bathroom. When he opened his own store, he called it Left Bank Books West, after the St. Louis store Mimi had told him about, conceived and christened by some student radicals at Washington University. He sent a Grand Opening announcement, which Mimi designed, to his St. Louis counterpart, but received no response.

While Mimi spent more and more time on her painting excursions, I would stay with my father and read his books by the living room bay window. As far back as memory takes me, I liked the weight and tug of a hardbound in my hand. I developed muscles in the loop of skin between my thumb and forefinger just from holding these hefty tomes. I soaked up whatever language was offered, from the jacket cover to the last quotes from *Publishers Weekly* and *Kirkus Review,* every word. One day I said, in response to my parents' bickering, "Pray tell, why do you have to be so contentious?" They laughed, forgetting about the conversational bone they were gnawing on, and after that I used as many polysyllabic words as I could.

By the time I was six, Dad had read me most of *The Inferno, The Iliad, Jane Eyre,* and samplings of Dickens and Shakespeare, though in patches and out of order. I was reading with Dad one day when Mimi handed me a book on botany. It was jacketless; its cover faded and slightly warped; the stitching on its binding loose. I opened it and read on the inside of the front cover the name "Vincent Rose." I looked up at her quizzically.

She shrugged. "That's my father. Your grandfather." I stared at her in shock. I suppose I had thought that her parents had died, too. We never heard from them, and she had never mentioned them. I was about to ask questions, but she was already out the door, and every time I tried to find out about him after that, she changed the subject.

Until I started school, I had no idea what a freak all this had made me.

dame's rocket and primrose

From as far away as Yellow Creek, which wound around the back of our property, I could see my room window above the hawthorn branches. Dad and Dyl had cut the window, according to Mimi's design, under the slants of the back gable. They'd used wedding money to order glass with a beveled rim from Seattle. Its shape made it look like a mouth, perpetually open in surprise.

The dining room had a bay window, beneath which outside Mimi had planted bleeding hearts and columbines. But, in the middle of the room, the place where what I considered "normal" people served steaming vegetables and golden turkey dinners, she had placed her canvases and stretchers. Often, right in the center, was her old metal paint box, which looked like the tackle boxes of the mill workers who fished on their weekend vacations from lifting and lugging. Her actual studio, upstairs, was generally empty. In the furnitureless living room, instead of on chairs we sat on cushions, which dotted the pine floors. Each Christmas Jillian gave us a new pillow cover, one she'd woven or embroidered.

The kitchen table was dwarfed by the woodstove, which stood in the center of the room, surrounded by a tiled hearth. The tiles, handmade, had been bought at the Renaissance Fair one hundred miles south in Moscow.

One day I was lying on the cool hearth, running my hand over the shimmering chips of mica, when she said, "How would you like to hear the story of the tiles?"

Before I could answer, she began. "Those two did it for me. You know, as a surprise."

"Which two?"

She looked down at me as if she were surprised that I was there. "Dyl and Dad. They were going to do it as a joint project, have the tile all laid and polished, all that mica shining like white freckles, and I was supposed to walk right in and have it flash at me in the face. Just like that. And I might have stepped on it and felt it beneath my bare toes, but I would notice it in a fantastic way. You know?" She didn't wait for me to answer. "They asked me to keep Jillian company at the store, and I went without suspecting, and you know how Jillian is, she tells very little, not even about her own life, so I really would have been surprised."

She paused for a moment, retreating deeper into a time before I was born. "But when I walked in the door, I almost stumbled over Dyl, who was alone on his hands and knees." Now a faint smile. "Bits of grout stuck to his sleeves and the ends of his hair. Sloppy rags and a metal bucket were next to him. He grinned up at me and was so . . . and did it so . . ." (she paused for a word) "so *compellingly* that I threw down my backpack and joined him on the floor."

She looked down at me, snapped back to reality. "And then your father, who had gone out hours before to get more grout, returned from god knows where . . ."

For a while she studied the grout, then said, "It must be time to get more wood. The pile's down." And she walked out of the house.

For wood we relied on Karl, a young logger. It wasn't until I was close to puberty that it struck me how odd this was. Every other family in Wilders Ferry owned a chain saw. And Dyl, who had every other piece of woodworking equipment imaginable, must have had one, too. Dad could have borrowed anyone's. I can still see Mimi, perched on the back of his truck, watching Karl as he bore his axe down on the cords he brought us every September. An orange paisley scarf is wrapped around her head; her dangly turquoise earrings glitter in the sun. He splits all the wood and piles it in two stacks that tower over me. She leaves for a few minutes to drive his truck to Boone Foods to buy him beer and holds it for him, taking slow sips from the can, while he hefts that axe, and its steady chopping sound rings out most of the afternoon. When he stops, the veins in his arms an azure blue, ovals of sweat darkening his flannel shirt, she hands the can to him. I never saw her drink beer inside the house. Sometimes Karl would change the oil in the VW. I can still see the worn soles of his shoes, his silver boot toes pointing toward the clouds.

The first time I became aware of other people's perceptions of us was the day I began to ride the yellow bus to school. Since ours was the last house on the narrow road around the lake, the bus had to pass our house and then keep going about a half a mile beyond it before our road met a logging road and the bus had room to turn around. Then it would come back for me. The first day I climbed up the steps and as the bus driver, Maybelle Purdy, cranked it into second gear, a boy in the front called out, "Hey, look at that stupid hippie house. And check out that weird bus in the backyard!"

Slinking to the back of the vehicle, I sneaked a peek out the window at the bus in the back. Mimi and Dad had driven it from the East when they moved to Idaho, a few weeks before, Mimi liked to tell me, the election of Tricky Dick. On one side was painted an evergreen forest and on the other a sun rising from a lake, the rays rounding the top and continuing onto the roof. Superimposed on the sun was a scarlet peace sign. On the back, a pointy-toothed dragon with brown eyes the size of baseballs and hooded by droopy lids. His serrated tail wound over and under the rest of him and whipped up to pierce the sunrise on the top. The paint was faded and chipped.

As I hunkered down in the last seat in the back, I heard a whisper, "My mother says her family's going to ruin the town."

When I came home that afternoon, Mimi was pouring dried fruits and nuts into an empty honey jar. "Why do we have to live in a purple house?" I asked.

Mimi laughed; her breath smelled like Red Zinger tea. She leaned toward me as if to embrace me, but I pulled away. Startled, she stiffened and withdrew. "Lake, what happened today?" The alarm in her voice made me nervous, and I said nothing, just studied the open shelves, their cabinet doors having been removed, and the wrinkled bags of dried beans and jars of bamboo shoots.

After a while she touched my shoulder lightly, as if she were afraid I'd recoil again. "It's not purple. The walls are the color of dame's rocket, and the trim is primrose. Don't ever let anyone tell you anything different."

Each day I rode the bus I worried more and more that the children would see into our house from the road. My body would stiffen when Maybelle would take the turn, especially in the winter and early spring, because we had no curtains on our windows and the mountain ash offered no leaves or berries or blossoms to obscure Mimi's image from the critical gazes behind the windows of the bus. I wondered how they would react to the sight of her trophies from the sixties—a hashish pipe the size and shape of a tin of chewing tobacco and carved with daisies; a bronze peace-symbol medallion the size of a salad plate, on a leather thong. I knew what they thought of her unshaven legs: they pointed at them and snickered as they passed us on Main Street.

As I grew older, everything beautiful seemed increasingly far away. Back in 1938, when Thornycroft Lumber had hoisted up and nailed down its branded-wood sign, the mill had logged the area nearest town. It was a greedy move, this first taking of the pristine timber, the prime pine and spruce and tamarack, in nearly concentric circles around the town, the mill itself an ostentatious centerpoint. The signs of barrenness scarred the landscape. The hills around Wilders Ferry that escaped being shaved were covered with scraggly-looking huckleberry, and when I was a child buckbrush tangled thick as a jungle over my head. To walk through it, I'd have to part the stout wood with my hands carefully so I wouldn't have to touch the white foam of the spit bugs that dotted the branches.

While other children were busy playing basketball and dolls, Old Maid and Monopoly, riding bikes and selling lemonade, I spent entire afternoons by myself, skipping stones into the lake or reading on the beach. Sometimes, I'd laze away mornings playing with Paris in the tree house Dyl had made her, or pretending that the trees were our friends. But more and more often, especially when I was bored or upset, I'd walk along the dock and imagine the path of the ferry one hundred years ago, how it would cross and recross the lake, parting the water, the sun on the waves performing its diamond-dance. The boards of the dock were uneven, and I'd stride to the end as if walking a plank and abut my toes with the last board. It was only half a board really. The end was worn water-smooth, the splinters long since removed by time and the water's temperament. I'd lift up on my toes like the ballerinas I'd seen in the glossy renditions of Degas paintings in Mimi's books. Balanced on the brink of the lake like that, I'd search beyond the cedar posts standing like seasoned sentinels at the dock and long to float across that spiral of water to the mountains beyond.

visits

From the first moment I saw my mother's "baby" sister, DeeDee, I thought she might be a beacon lighting the way out of my lonely life. She flew up from San Francisco, and my father drove all the way to the airport in Spokane to meet her. She walked through the front door calling my name. She was bundled in a beaver coat, and as she embraced me, her kisses indenting my cheeks, her tears matted the fur. "Lake Rose Davis," she said, this time more softly. "Nine years old already. Thank God we finally met." Emotion choked her voice.

Mimi pecked her cheek and said pointedly, "You could have come anytime."

Out of her purse Aunt DeeDee took a tape and searched the room for something to play it on. "It's Saturday night, time for a little fever." When we stared blankly, she added, "Don't you just love John Travolta?" Mimi spun around, walked up to her studio, and quietly closed the door, and Aunt DeeDee led me by the hand upstairs to unpack. In my room Aunt DeeDee picked me up, plopped me onto the bed, and produced a bulging shoebox; in it were two objects wrapped in green tissue. One was a Barbie doll; the other a conch.

"These are from your grandparents," she said. My eyes bugged. I saw a flash of that elegant penned signature in the botany book. "They told me to tell you they love you and hope they will be allowed to see you someday. Now. Let's begin making up for lost time."

The next morning, when Mimi saw me playing with the Barbie doll, her face clouded. "This is from my grandmother," I said.

"Uh-huh," she said.

"Why don't we ever talk to them?" I asked.

"We don't have a telephone."

"Why can't they come to see us?"

She twirled a strand of her long hair around her forefinger. "I'm sure DeeDee will tell you." Then she walked away.

Soon after Aunt DeeDee's first visit I received a postcard from Sanibel Island. It said, "Having fun in Florida. Wish you were here. Love, GranVinny and GranPearl." When Mimi handed it to me, she sniffed, "Still vacationing in all the right places apparently," but her gaze lingered over the loopy script.

Despite the tension she seemed to generate, Aunt DeeDee's presence in our house was a relief to me. Everything about DeeDee spelled city, from her pearl rings to her hair tinted increasingly dark shades every visit, sprayed at the roots so that it stood up before fanning down around her heart-shaped face. I suspected that she made her hair erect like that to give herself another inch or two. She always walked in spike heels, never tottering, and the muscles in her calves bulged from her breakneck strides. Pulled over that muscle, her skin was white, almost transparent, and sometimes she wore shimmery nylons. I loved looking at her smooth legs, my mother's bearish ones were so increasingly at the root of my humiliation.

The following summer, DeeDee arrived carrying shopping bags stuffed with clothes, some of which she left with us as if she were on a mission of goodwill: gold-threaded scarves, patent-leather pocketbooks, fluffy white muffs with triangles of fur the color of chocolate, vests of brocade or paisley. Nothing practical, nothing patched. Mimi frowned as soon as she spotted the bags, even though she was hugging Aunt DeeDee hello at the time, her arms hesitant around one of Aunt DeeDee's white coats. Paris and I spent hours trying on all of the clothes and experimenting with her makeup, and Aunt DeeDee emceed our fashion shows. I suspected that Aunt DeeDee was rich, but once when I asked Mimi about it, she responded cryptically, "People are starving in Appalachia."

The only times I took the Barbie doll off my bureau were when Aunt DeeDee came to see us. One afternoon when we were playing with it— my aunt was in charge of hairdos, and I was in charge of outfits—I asked, "What happened between Mimi and my grandparents?"

My aunt was clearly caught off guard. She put Barbie down, removed her compact from her pocketbook, and fussed with her own hair. "Just between us," she said, as if I talked to anyone else, "nothing happened. You know how your mother is." I nodded. I didn't know what she was referring to, but I didn't want to seem ignorant of the obvious. "It's just that your GranPearl had such high hopes for Mimi. She was so smart, and she really was pretty when she fixed herself up. And then she just started to let herself go. GranPearl didn't say much at first, but before we knew it Mimi's hair dripped down to her shoulders in no style at all and started to stick out with all those waves the way it does, and Mama begged her to have it straightened, at least have it styled, but of course Mimi wouldn't compromise one bit. In fact, she even started wearing blue jeans instead of all the expensive clothes your GranPearl bought her. Blue jeans—every single day." I looked up at her expectantly, still waiting for the point.

Aunt DeeDee curled Barbie's saffron-bleached hair around her pinkie. "If Mimi hadn't been so stubborn, things would have been much better. Know what I mean? Anyway, after a big fight your GranPearl packed all Mimi's clothes and her curlers in a trunk in the basement. Mimi made it a much bigger deal than it needed to be. Overreacted, as she always does. Mama always wanted what was best for her." She shut her compact and put it away. "I'll never forget Papa's face the day she left for Poughkeepsie—for that hoity-toity college she insisted on going to. And the day she moved to Idaho . . ." Her voice trailed off, and she clicked her tongue against the roof of her mouth. "That was the day we thought she would break his heart."

I took all this in, feeling somehow betrayed. I wanted badly to find a good reason to have been kept from my grandparents, but could see none. "Selfish," DeeDee said, and at first I thought she was talking about me. "Mimi always accused *me* of being selfish, but if *that* isn't selfish I don't know what is." I, at age ten, was already beginning to see what she meant.

The following year, when I was at the brink of puberty, Aunt DeeDee stayed for two weeks. One afternoon Mimi sequestered herself in her room with the flu, and Aunt DeeDee met me in the upstairs hall with a large rubber-banded manila envelope clutched to her breast. She put her finger to her lips. "We wouldn't want to disturb your mother," she said, and she took me by the hand and led me down the stairs. She reached into a kitchen cabinet, took out a chipped saucer, and opened the door to the cellar. A single bulb hung from the ceiling with a string tied to it with a loop on its end, like a small noose. I hooked my thumb into the loop and yanked. The cellar was long and morguelike, lined with unfinished pine shelves sagging slightly under the weight of quart jars of peaches, crab apples, pickled tomatoes, green beans.

She dug in her skirt pocket and removed a red candle and a matchbook that read, "The Fairmont." Then she crouched down on the cement and put the saucer on the floor, placed the candle on the saucer, and struck a match. When she touched it to the wick, the scent of strawberry tickled my nose. "Click the light again, Sugarbabe," she said. "We've brought our own."

I yanked the loop again and stood awaiting her instructions.

"Down, down," she said, gesturing as if I were a cocker spaniel, or deaf. This gesture gave me some relief; it seemed so matter-of-fact and uncomplicated. I sat, Indian style, wishing my pants were longer because the draft seemed to circle around my exposed ankles, where my corduroys didn't quite reach my socks.

Aunt DeeDee's earrings bounced candlelight my way as she leaned over to hand me the packet. As I opened it, she searched my face. Inside were a pearl-handled letter opener and a bunch of odd-sized envelopes.

"Here are the responses," she said, raising her perfectly plucked eyebrows in tandem. "*You* know." I hadn't the slightest idea what she was talking about. Even then, she seemed to think my sensibility was stamped with the same grooves as the record of her own life. "From our ad."

I nodded. The ad had seemed so like an activity in itself, I had forgotten, or maybe I had never realized, that it was merely the trigger in the process. We had composed the ad during a previous visit, and it was printed in the *San Francisco Bay Guardian,* in the "Relationships" section. Even Mimi had helped. Aunt DeeDee had gotten the idea that she would never meet a man on her own, at least not one she would want to marry. She'd had suitors, plenty of them, but found them somehow all unsuitable. One was twenty or so years older than she was (at least that's how much older he was willing to admit). Another one had been a law student at San Francisco State. Very promising prospect, Dad and Mimi thought, but Aunt DeeDee objected to his taste in present-giving: for her birthday he gave her a toolbox, we supposed because she would always call him in the middle of the night when she let her paranoia about her apartment wiggle under her skin, and she'd extract groggy promises from him to tighten the washers in her bathroom sink, or screw the bolt onto her balcony railing.

At first Mimi did not take the crucial undertaking of writing the ad seriously enough for her sister. She suggested beginning thus: "Quivering mass of unrequited libido seeks insatiable hunk . . . knowledge of English, toilet training, and table manners negotiable."

After Mimi finally calmed her sister down, she lured her back into the kitchen with the promise of her most earnest attention; and four or five cups of tea and uncountable pistachio nuts later, we all came up with the following: "Peppy, petite professional, liberal lover of life, wants laid-back man to share on-the-go lifestyle. Ethnic and age differences inconsequential."

DeeDee seemed a bit edgy about the political reference, but was willing to compromise for the sake of sisterly support and just plain having it over with.

Now, in the basement, Aunt DeeDee's cattail-colored eyes seemed to flare as she gesticulated with the envelopes. "Look at all these, Gorgeous. They liked our ad. All these guys! Just look at all our possibilities."

There didn't seem to be all that many, given Aunt DeeDee's track record for speed, but I didn't want to quibble.

"Look at this one," she said after shuffling the letters a bit, pulling one out of the deck like a seasoned dealer and slitting it expertly with the letter opener. It was thick. Aunt DeeDee was impressed by bulk. She handed me the envelope, and as I reached for the letter, she withdrew it slightly, and said, "Read between the lines."

I accepted the letter as if it were the original manuscript of the Declaration of Independence.

"Go on. Read it," she commanded, and as my eyes looked down, she said, "No. Out loud."

"Dear Peppy, I'm an AM meditator, who is 40-ish but looks 35 in the face and 25 in the body (thanks to a well-disciplined diet of fish and fowl, fresh fruits and vegetables, if possible organically grown, and vitamin therapy). By the way, I consider myself 19 in spirit."

"I don't think this is the guy for you, Aunt DeeDee," I sighed, hating to disappoint her so soon.

"Why not?"

"He says he's an AM meditator. You wouldn't want to meditate in the morning—would you?—when you like to get your 'beauty sleep.'" "Beauty sleep" was one of Aunt DeeDee's favorite expressions. Her laughter almost made me crunch the letter. Sometimes her laugh was like a burst of thunder in the desert; sometimes a release like a thousand red and yellow balloons, funneling from a single source, shot into the sky.

"AM doesn't mean 'morning' in this biz, Babydoll; it means 'Asian Male.'"

She handed me another fat envelope. The letter inside read: "I'm president of my own company and live on 40 acres of property laid out much like a country club or golf course. I own 400 trees including evergreens and oak. One of the buildings on the estate houses a swimming pool with two diving boards, a slide, a Jacuzzi (for more intimate gatherings), and a sauna. Adjacent to the pool building is a basketball court that doubles as a heliport, tennis court, ice-skating and roller-skating rink, and go-cart racetrack. The outside toys include a dune buggy, a dirt bike, toboggan, tractors, and a new deluxe 27-foot motor home with built-in color TV. The main house is brick with 12 rooms and vaulted ceilings. We can watch *The Love Boat* and *Dallas* on the 6 1/2-foot big-screen TV hooked up to 4-foot speakers from the comfort of a kidney-shaped water-bed couch." My eyes popped, and I could almost feel the luxurious bounces of that water-filled heaven. We didn't even have a TV, and these temptations were sweetened by my vision of Mimi tsk-tsking with disapproval. Aunt DeeDee and I exchanged round-eyed glances, and I continued reading: "You would live here with free room and board. In return I would expect about 40 hours a week assistance with diverse tasks such as typing, answering the telephone, filing, accounting, cleaning, cooking, laundry, and care for my four- and six-year-old daughters every other weekend." DeeDee grabbed the letter, balled it up, and sent it spinning into the dark.

Later I merely skimmed the epistles, reading aloud telling phrases like "I have a 30-inch waistline and a 10 1/2-inch shoe"; "I believe in spending quality time with pets"; "I embrace Tao Chi Chuan, Wu-Shu (Kung Fu), Jujitsu, and sushi"; "I am marooned in an ecstasy of waiting to hear from you"; "My heart has a lot of bigness to it and longs to fill you up with its big, big love"; and finally, "Prior to coming to prison I was in the United States Navy." My eyes widened.

Some of them made specific requests: for example, "My gal will know how to orgasm in magnificent multiples, preferably with me."

"Is 'orgasm' a verb?" Aunt DeeDee asked. I quickly assured her it was, though I had never heard the word "orgasm" before.

My voice was croaking with exhaustion as I read the following: "Darling #1166F, Staying awake many full moon nights, I have caught the softest of the moon beams, and I have made a secret pathway with them for you to travel. Fear not, my darling love-flower, the journey is swift, for we shall travel on the chariot of desire. Galloping past the clouds, and the moon, we will enter the land of rainbows and there, keeping you on my lap, I shall teach your body stories of love. Should you protest, oh my petite beauty, I shall seal thy lips with mine. Offering to be your ideal lover, Abdul."

"Well?" she asked, closing her left eye around a contact lens and massaging it with her finger. "What do you think?"

I thought it might be clear what I thought given the way I had read it, but she looked so eager for my praise that I said something noncommittal like, "Sounds like a nice guy," and she took the letter from me almost tenderly and tucked it into her pocket.

I was beginning to think the dog-eared manila envelope was like the car in the circus from which clown after clown just kept coming. She searched in her purse and pulled out a notepad the size of a Hershey bar, in a jeweled cover. "Use this," she said. "It'll help you think better." I stared at the notepad; a two-inch gold pen was hooked to its side.

"Go ahead," she said. "Rank them." I got to work, reviewing the letters, making piles on the cold cement, covering most of the pages in the notepad. First I established categories: one, I have to admit, based solely on appearance, one on intelligence (although intelligence was not Aunt DeeDee's top priority), and one on something I called at the time "coolness." Then I rated each candidate within each list, carefully printing phone numbers next to each name. When I looked up, stretched my arms and shoulders, which were stiff from my having been hunkered down on the floor, the candle had turned into a small red pond rippling out from the center of the saucer. The flame was flickering weakly, and my coconspirator was gone.

If Mimi had learned of this episode, she might have thought three or four times about leaving me alone with Aunt DeeDee again. But when Jillian was asked by a friend from college, who now worked for a magazine in the Northwest, to review the Seattle Opera and for payment received four free tickets, she invited my parents along. Paris went, too, of course, and Aunt DeeDee volunteered to stay with me. As my parents carried their duffel bag and backpacks out the door, Aunt DeeDee called back, "One more thing. Does Lake eat . . . well, meals?"

Mimi put the suitcase down and stood looking at her sister.

"You know." Aunt DeeDee tried again. "A fruit, a vegetable, a starch. That sort of thing."

I was afraid Mimi would turn around and stay, so I chimed in, "We'll be fine. We'll figure it out. Just leave."

And finally they did. As the VW pulled onto the road, Aunt DeeDee draped her arm around my shoulder and said, "I've got an idea. You cook." Then she laughed, and we rummaged through the house to amass our cash to spend on junk food at Boone Foods.

While my parents were gone, Aunt DeeDee arranged to have a telephone installed. Thereafter, between visits she would call at odd hours. I was so excited to have a telephone that I was always the one to answer it—and in any case, my mother's fury upon returning to discover this electronic intruder implanted in her hitherto pristine domain modulated, after a while, into a steady refusal to acknowledge its presence. It was in the upstairs hall, and when it rang in the middle of the night, I knew who it would be. Sometimes she'd call early in the morning, just as the rosy light brought the mountains into shadow. Either way, I'd run to catch the phone on its first ring and pant hello. I'd smile as soon as I heard her voice. "I didn't wake you, did I?" she'd begin. "I just noticed what time it is." After we'd talked for an hour or so she'd say, "Is your mother there?" and I'd whisper, "She's asleep."

"Don't bother her then. Just give her all the news." And from the oval window I'd watch the fog thin and the mountains darken against the backdrop of the luminous sky.

The "news" was inevitably a new man. If her voice was hearty, perhaps tinged with hysteria, I knew right away she had just met someone; if it was barely audible, I knew he had failed to make the commitment we were both certain would have been the commitment of his dreams. Whatever the case, the details she gave me—the jackets and silk ties they wore to concerts, the ordering they did for her from menus with prices only for the men, the pinstripes in their charcoal suits, the leather briefcases they carried to their glassed-in offices—kept me awake with an unidentified yearning all night. And a few hours later, when I'd enter Wilders Ferry Central School and watch all the older boys in their frayed shirts and ragged jeans, their chins and noses and foreheads acne-pocked, the small hairs fuzzy around their ears, arms dangling, spittle collecting in the corners of their mouths and reflecting light no matter how dim the dingy mustard-colored paint over the gray lockers made the halls, when I'd hear the smacking of gum and the snickering as they'd say my name—I wished I had a private genie in a brass lamp, so I could be with my aunt, where I was increasingly certain I belonged.

hair art

One June morning two years later, Mimi walked into my room and announced, "Your Aunt DeeDee wants us to choose her a hair stylist before she visits next month." My jaw dropped. I couldn't imagine my perfectly coiffed, waved, dyed, and blow-dried aunt in any hair salon in Wilders Ferry. Mimi shrugged. "She must be slumming."

By this time the last thing I wanted to do was spend time alone with Mimi. It was a few weeks after my thirteenth birthday, and my body had changed shape out of all proportion with those of the other girls my age. Paris especially seemed to be unaffected by these growths and eruptions of the flesh. Behind each swelling of my new breasts, I became aware of an ache, deeper than just under the skin. I sneaked the silver-backed mirror Mimi had borrowed from Jillian into my room and spent hours with my door closed.

But I suppose I must have seen this as an opportunity to demonstrate my loyalty to Aunt DeeDee, because I grudgingly agreed. For a town of 400 some-odd, Wilders Ferry had a surprising number of beauty places. Mimi insisted we hit all five of them.

Our first stop was Rhonda's Beauty Room, which doubled for the breakfast nook in a clapboard house. Mimi asked questions gently, confidently, as if she knew she had every right to any shred of information. She had a knack for getting people to talk about themselves, and in a few minutes, she and Rhonda were talking like sisters—at least the sort of sisters I knew about from reading books, not like Mimi and DeeDee, the only actual sisters I knew well. In spite of myself, I watched Mimi listen, noted the sympathetic knitting of her brow, as Rhonda described how her daughter spent every hour of her life sitting under the dryer and hallucinating—the linoleum floor waving like the ocean, the dropped curls squirming like snakes. I waited for Mimi to ask about the styling services for my aunt, but she never did.

As soon as we were out the door I asked, "So you must think this one would be all right for Aunt DeeDee." She stared at me as if I had asked for a permanent and a manicure.

"Oh, man, Lake." She tried to rumple my hair, but I ducked. "Rhonda's isn't quite what we're looking for."

The second contender, Sue, from Cuttin' Up, motioned with shiny scissors for me to take her chair. I shook my head. She was pregnant, she said, a phenomenon that we'd have to have been blind not to perceive. She wore white nurse's shoes, and her ankles swelled above the tops of her rolled-down socks. The veins, nearly popping out of her skin, ran up her legs and stopped in little blue knots, like a follow-the-dot picture that someone just couldn't finish. Without any prodding, she listed for us all the names and ages and hair and eye color of her four children and was launching into a catalog of her brothers' children when I saw Mimi stifle a yawn. When Mimi interrupted to inquire about the circumstances of her first pregnancy, Sue answered, "Regular way, I suppose."

The door was still swinging shut when Mimi, sounding annoyed, as if this were a personal affront, said, "Boring."

We hurried by Boone Foods and Hoot Owl Drug, women on a mission. As we passed the Short Branch Saloon, Mimi slowed her pace. She peered in the window; although it was midday, a few fishermen still in their hip boots straddled the barstools, and a cowboy tipped his white hat. I elbowed past Mimi and walked a few feet ahead. By now it was becoming clear to me that she intended to select Aunt DeeDee's hairdresser not on her cosmetological competence at all, but simply on the basis of the degree of pathos in her life.

At Sydney's Salon, Sydney chain-smoked Virginia Slims and flicked the ash each time a split second before it fell onto the damp crown of her customer. I thought I would gag on the ammonia and stale smoke smell that permeated the room. Usually Mimi made it a point to cough when she entered a smoky room, but she showed remarkable restraint. Sydney's own hair, dyed the color of persimmons, was piled on her head in loops that met in the center of her scalp. Her eyebrows were plucked and penciled in the shape of half-moons, and when she talked, she raised them at the end of her sentences, as if for punctuation.

By nodding, Mimi elicited details about Sydney's obsession with a trucker who had a tattoo of the Snake River encircling his private parts. I was itching to ask her how she knew it was the Snake, but this omission didn't seem to concern Mimi. When Sydney described how he had promised to marry her and had even placed a cigar ring on her finger, Mimi's expression reflected joy. Then Sydney took the cigarette from between her teeth and stubbed it out.

"After I made him a fried chicken dinner one night he licked his fingers and told me he was married and hoped that Jesus would forgive me for all that fornication."

I couldn't believe it, but Mimi had real tears in her eyes. The more emotion she expressed, the more I wanted to be home reading.

The woman at Hair by Millie looked like she had been starving herself for the past year. Her chin jutted out, the bones pulling the thin skin back so it appeared the color of skim milk. Her eyes looked sunken, and as she drank from a waxed-paper cup, her cheeks drawn in to suck from the straw, her face might have been a skull.

As Mimi talked to her, I studied the mirror at her station. It was plastered with photos and mementos, and magazine clippings (one was headlined RICHARD GERE SIZZLES AS BOTH OFFICER AND GENTLEMAN; another, TOM CRUISE—THE BRIGHTEST STAR OF TOMORROW?), so that there was only a circle of mirror space left for the clients to see their reflections. A yearbook page ripped from the seam showed a row of mug shots, all smiling as if in desperation. There was an 8 × 10 glossy of a robust girl in a thigh-length green-and-brown pleated skirt. (I recognized the colors of the Wilders Ferry Central School cheering squad—green and brown representing the evergreen forests that had made the town.) The cheerleader was performing a perfect split high in the air and touching her toes, mouth open in a big O and head high.

Millie's voice startled me. "That's me."

"Where?" I asked, still scanning the crowd for something familiar.

She laughed. "You know, front and center. I was something back then," she added wistfully, as if "back then" were more than a few years. "Prom queen. Class secretary. Every girl's dream." I knew without looking at her that Mimi wouldn't find this story fascinating enough, but I was surprised when as we left she touched Millie's arm and Millie said, "Thank you."

I told Mimi that I was going to walk home. Fealty to my aunt or no, she could finish by herself. But she bribed me with a stop at Satellite Health, where I could buy some yogurt-covered raisins and visit Jillian. So it was midafternoon by the time we entered Alice's Hair Art. This was a place I knew. I'd ducked in many a time during those awful coincidences when I was on my way to the Satellite and spotted some of the boys who rode the school bus. I'd loiter near the window and pick up one hair spray after another until they were out of sight. I could read their lips through the glass, forming the words "Lake the Flake."

"Hello," Mimi called in what I considered was a fakey singsong voice.

"Shhh," I said.

As we entered, a cowbell clanged, and we heard two voices arguing in the back. A squat woman with a beehive hairdo and breasts that seemed to be supported only by the shelf of her waist came out from the back room wiping her hands on a towel. "Did you have an appointment?" she asked.

"Not yet," Mimi said. "We're just shopping around for someone to take care of my sister when she arrives from California." I slumped into a red-plastic upholstered chair. "Are you Alice?"

"The very one." Her voice had an impatient edge.

As Mimi launched into her routine, the phantom other person from the back entered the room, and I couldn't stop looking at her. Unlike the other stylists, her hair hung straight down, cut blunt at the neck. It was black and shiny as the bark of the honey locusts after a rainstorm. Her skin had a sheen to it, as if it had been rubbed with oil, and though she stared into my face, she didn't smile. Her eyes were gray with a flash of hazel in the right one only. The left eye was cloudy. Her smooth face had a coppery cast and a slightly flat nose. She had big bones, judging from the size of her wrists and her shoulders. I fingered the plastic bottles on the counter and furtively studied her. She moved with the grace of the horses in the fields, not a movement wasted, and it seemed incongruous that those movements consisted of taking a plastic dustpan and sweeping up hair from the yellowing linoleum. A silver ring snaked up her middle finger. Its eye was a chip of garnet.

Mimi and Alice chatted, but there were pauses between questions. "Mimi must be tired," I thought. Or perhaps she was unable to squeeze any juice out of the hard-boiled Alice.

When the woman with the coppery skin turned and walked toward the back room, Mimi suddenly said, "May I talk with your assistant?"

Alice guffawed. "Assistant? Oh, you mean Graceanne. Sure. Help yourself. Here—use the back room. Don't mind me." And she sauntered to the front desk and picked up the phone.

"You're from out of town, aren't you?" Mimi asked as they walked toward the back.

"How'd you know?"

Mimi turned to gaze full into her face, studied it before she answered, "I would have noticed you."

the winning story

Here is the story I used to imagine Graceanne told Mimi the day she was chosen.

––––––––––––

Her mother was a full-blooded Nez Perce; her father, the only white teacher on the reservation. Her mother was his shyest student, but a willing one. She wore the same gingham dress every day, freshly washed and pressed, and carried boiled potatoes and cornbread in her lunch bag. She never raised her hand to be called on, but whenever he asked her a question, no matter if the answer was "hypotenuse" or "1776" or "carbon dioxide," she always uttered the proper words.

Every day he had her read out loud. He began with a few sonnets from Shakespeare, then added soliloquies. Then on to stanzas from Marvell and Milton, cantos from Spenser, and she read them dutifully, her voice as clear as the ping of a silver knife struck against a crystal bell. And then he added Yeats and Brontë and

Auden and Joyce, and still she read the words, organized into lines and stanzas, sentences and paragraphs, and hesitated only where the text indicated, at the commas and the end-stops and the chapter closes, and caught the current of the iambic and paused at the caesuras. And he heard in her words the voice of a god he had traveled to Idaho and the Natives to seek, and thought she was reading them only for him.

He came to her home and brought presents wrapped in tissue paper and ribbon for her mother and older brothers and younger sisters, and next time, he joined her father under the rusted-out belly of a truck and tinkered with the universal joint and then helped her mother scrape the carrots for the pie. And the next time, he took a sickle and hacked away at the bindweed that was choking the prune trees in the back. And the next time, he mowed the lawn. All the while in class giving her more to read out loud, now adding Plath and Glück and Roethke and W. S. Merwin. So when he asked her father if he could marry her, her father wiped his hands on a greasy rag and said he saw no reason why not.

She was only twelve. Within a year she died in childbirth, leaving a gray-eyed infant who entered the world from the death throes of her mother silently, in spite of the midwife's efforts to flick and smack her into screaming. The teacher named the baby after the grace of God, who had given him his bride, and for his mother, Anne.

Since she never cried, he sometimes forgot she needed taking care of, and as she grew, Graceanne took over the care of her father. She bought and made him food, sewed on his buttons, balanced his checkbook, and read to him, and they lived quietly in a tract home on the Camas Prairie. It was hard being the schoolteacher's daughter, and a half-breed at that, and she came home every day right from school to wash clothes and get dinner, and he stayed behind to plan his lessons. Once on her way home, a gang of boys followed her, whistling and spitting and calling out, "Half-breed! Half-breed!" and threw stones. She had a swelling on the side of her temple where a sharp edge had caught her, and she packed it with ice wrapped in a dish towel and held it for two hours until the teacher came home, so that he wouldn't be able to tell; she knew it would hurt him.

After high school she worked as a waitress in a café in Grangeville. She drove the truck down every morning and stayed until the café closed at ten. The work was slow, mostly people on their way from Boise to points north or south, and a few regulars, who asked her questions at first, but when she gave monosyllabic answers, stopped trying. One Friday just after she tied on her apron and washed her hands, a man with a blond beard, a red baseball cap, tennis shoes, and brand-new jeans came in and smiled at her. Every time she brought him coffee, filled his water glass, or offered him more pie, he smiled at her again.

And she found herself speaking to him. "Just passing through?"

"Uh-huh. Heading over toward Salmon."

"Oh?" she said, instantly hating herself. She wasn't used to making conversation. Most people she met just needed an "Oh" or a "Is that right?" to keep them going. But for the first time she felt inadequate, as if her tongue had been numbed and she had no way to tell it what to do.

"Why don't you sit down and visit with me before I go?"

She looked down at herself and saw her big feet peek out; her skirt looked so threadbare it shone, and her hands were chapped from dishwater. She slipped them into her apron pockets.

"If you don't sit down and talk to me, I'll keep ordering until you run out of food, and then you'll have to close the place anyway." She stared at him as if he were from Pluto. "I'd get so full I'd burst through my pants and knock over the counter, and throw all your nice dishes on the floor and might not fit through the door. I might even start to oink."

She grinned. She might have laughed, but no man had told a joke to her before, and she wasn't sure what the proper response was. She sat and did what she was best at, listened. He loved her for this talent, and said, "You should do this for a living," and at first she thought he meant waiting tables.

"No. I mean listening."

He'd spent his life on the stretch of land between two crossroads river towns in the mountains. In the winter he was a hunting guide. He led pack trips of attorneys and accountants and executives up into the Yellowjacket Mountains, where there were no dictaphones or tape decks or pinstripes or BMW's.

But now the man would ride the River of No Return for as

many months during the summer as the river would take him.
He'd put in at North Fork on the other side of the mountains and
ride the rafts to Riggins in five days, where his partner would meet
him, load the rafts onto his truck, and drive them back through
Montana to North Fork, first heading north along the Lower
Salmon, up the Whitebird Hill, to her. He'd always stop in
Grangeville, and around May she would start combing her hair,
and even put on a little eye shadow that the nice lady in the drugstore showed her, and she'd peer out the window with the white,
ruffled café curtains and keep those curtains open from May
through September, so she would see him when he returned before
he saw her, so she could comb her hair and put on the eye shadow
and lick her lips so that they were shiny. And when he walked
through that door, her heart would beat like a loose window
flapping in a hurricane. He'd saunter right up to the screen door
and grin in at her and yell, "Come out here!"

And she'd run out the door, and he'd hold out his arms, and she
would spring into them and wrap her strong thighs around his
waist, and he'd twirl her around in the middle of the road until he
was as breathless as she was when she saw his truck pull up in
front of the café.

He said, "Let me take you with me on the river."

But her father objected. "You'll always be an outcast," he said.
"He lives for spring when the waters are wildest." Somewhere
along the line, her father had begun to talk like an Indian in a
fifties western.

Still a good child, she thought about what her father had said.
"But I want him."

Her father tried not to know what she meant, apparently having
forgotten his own kind of yearning for the shy student in his class.

So she told the river-runner, "Next time. You can take me next
time." That would give her time to think and her father time to remember his yearning.

When the river-runner was about to leave, she put her hand to
her lower belly and rubbed in circles. It had already begun to swell
a bit with the river-runner's child. He glanced down at the place
she was rubbing and looked sad. When he left, he gave her a ring, a
silver ring coiled like a rattlesnake, a garnet chip for its eye.

"Will you come back this way?"

"It depends," he said, taking out his pocketknife and opening and shutting it. He kissed her good-bye, but something in the way he held her told her his heart was already upriver, riding the rapids.

When he didn't return in April, then not in May, and her clothes pinched around her waist, and she had to eat saltines every morning to keep the room from spinning, she fought a passionless desire to stay in bed until he returned.

Her father began to notice something was wrong. "Where is your river-runner?" he asked, too late. She shrugged.

"I hope you have nothing else to tell me," he said.

She shook her head. "What else could there be?"

The next evening after she drove home from the café, she cleared his dishes and started to write a note on a brown bag from the market. But as usual, she didn't know what to say.

She left on foot, hitching rides north, taking food from small stores along the way—not sneaking it out, just taking it, in plain daylight, walking right out with it and looking the owner or the cashier in the eye on the way out the door. By this time she was bulging out of her clothes, and a shopkeeper followed her out proffering a tent dress, roomy enough for the river-runner's child. She followed the rivers far up in Idaho, asking about the river-runner whenever she thought she could smell him in the air, or where she saw a truck like his. And then she went to the northernmost lake, and Wilders Ferry . . . and stopped. It was time for the child to arrive, and besides, she was running out of rivers. It arrived on Labor Day, the day he traded waters for packhorses. She named it Whitewater, but no one took that name seriously.

The baby was born without hands. Otherwise it laughed and cooed, spit and sucked, smiled when it had gas . . .

———————

And here's where I always got stuck, though I knew how it ended. It wasn't enough to be abandoned, to have a baby alone, a baby without hands. It was the baby that drew Mimi to Graceanne, but something more powerful was needed to tighten the bond that held them together. The baby drowned, suffocation by water. But I didn't know how the baby she called Whitewater and swaddled tight in a thunderhead blanket she took from the Indian store in Plummer got near the water that took its life. I thought all of the following possibilities: (1) she carried it to the river as a matter of ritual, communion with the vanished river-runner, and the water itself simply took the child; (2) she was driven in a fever to immerse it in the river as a sort of solitary baptism to give it the spirit of its father; (3) she gave it to the river because she knew it would always be an outcast or because it would never stop reminding her that *she* would always be an outcast.

There were many other versions of this story, but this is the only one I've ever written down. When I saw Graceanne years later, I had this particular rendition like a scroll in my fist and planned to give it to her, whether as some sort of token of affection, memory of her hours with us, or just to see if I got anything at all right, I don't know. But when I saw her that last time, her hair chopped at odd angles and her lips chalky and dry, I just couldn't.

graceanne

One afternoon, as the time approached for Aunt DeeDee's summer visit, I slouched into the house, and as soon as I crossed the threshold of the kitchen and peered into the dining room, I knew that something was wrong—as the phrase goes—with this picture. There was always something wrong with the pictures I saw; just when I thought I would get it right—all the parts predictable and matching, the conventions securely in place—the rules were revoked.

I flashed onto the first time I saw a Magritte painting. It was in one of Mimi's Metropolitan Museum books—a deceptively simple rendition of the torso and head of a conservatively dressed man, the only backdrop a blue sky tinted slightly with the suggestion of undifferentiated clouds. Everything in order—tie, derby, suit jacket, pressed collar. Everything, that is, except the face, which was obscured save for the left ear, by a white dove, wings angled up in full flight. The first time I was tested at school, they showed me a picture that they must have had archived from the fifties. The picture depicted a nuclear family: the mother in high heels, full skirt, and scalloped apron, wiping her hands on a dish towel and standing in the hallway; a blond preschooler playing with a toy train in the middle of the floor; and, in a ponytail tied with a ribbon, a teenaged girl seated on a sofa and watching a small television topped by an antenna. Sitting in an overstuffed chair and smoking a pipe was a fish, resting his fins on the coffee table. "What's wrong with this picture?" the teacher asked. I smiled. "Nothing. Nothing's wrong," I said, thinking, Mimi will be proud of me.

Now, the scene in the dining room entered my consciousness in fragments, the composition fixed in mid-movement. In the center of the otherwise empty room, where Mimi's canvases and stretchers just that morning had still been stacked and balanced, Mimi was seated in a chair. Her hands looked uncharacteristically demure in her lap; a dish towel was curved around her neck like a bib. Her upturned lips were frozen open, as if she had been laughing when I'd entered. In a dark halo around her on the oak floor were spread curlicues of her hair. A single lock stood straight up from the center of her scalp and was held aloft by two long fingers. A pair of scissors were half closed, poised to take the curl between their teeth. The skin of the hand that held the scissors was a couple of shades deeper than the skin of Mimi's forehead, and from the ring finger something that I was too far away to see flashed silver. The arm connected to the hand was bare to the shoulder, and the face looked at me in shock. At first it seemed like a mask, a face I couldn't place, and then it changed into facile flesh, and I recognized it: the wide-boned woman with the smooth skin, whose hair was black and shiny as the bark of the honey locusts after a rainstorm. I thought of how as a child I had played with those young waves and watched my father snip at the split ends with his clippers. I felt an odd sense of loss. This is the haircut that is etched into my memory; I can't recall the one Graceanne must have given Aunt DeeDee a few days later.

The day before Aunt DeeDee arrived, Dad gave Mimi a gift: a rabbit, a lop-eared black-and-white. Gift-giving was unusual for either of my parents. Mimi sometimes gave Dad books for his birthday, and once he gave her hand-gilded wrapping paper that he'd bought at a craft fair in Hope—nothing wrapped in it; just the paper. She danced him around the room, she was so excited. She said it was her favorite gift ever and that she planned never to use it. "Beauty with no purpose," she called it.

He put the rabbit in her arms just as she was about to leave the house, and she nearly dropped it. "Wow!" she said. "Incredible! So what's the occasion?"

He shrugged sheepishly. "She'll remind you of the civil rights movement."

"It's not like I have to be reminded," she said, but she had already begun to stroke its ears, which looked like skin, and when my face was close to them I realized I could see through them. The rabbit held them down, as a beagle does.

"So? Should I call it Medgar Evers? Dr. King?"

"Actually I was thinking George Washington Carver or Othello, but it's a girl," Dad said, and she flipped the rabbit to examine its underside. He laughed. "I thought she could keep you company when your sister's not around." She seemed to look hard for irony, but apparently found none.

"Okay then. Her name is Georgia, as in Georgia O'Keeffe."

Humming "Georgia on My Mind," Dad plopped the rabbit onto Mimi's head. The rabbit squirmed, and she eased it down to the wood floor and walked away; it followed her from room to room, loping along on its oversized back paws, into the kitchen, where she offered it slices of banana and scraps of lettuce.

"Smells like a 4-H project," I called after them. I think I was already feeling a bit jealous. "What will Aunt DeeDee think?"

Mimi peeked around the door and smiled almost gleefully.

The day Aunt DeeDee arrived, I was feeling unsettled. Something didn't seem right. To intensify my discomfort, it seemed as if my aunt had suddenly shrunk; when she pulled me into her silky red dress, my breasts smashed against her collarbone.

My father lugged a large carton into the house, and she directed traffic.

"Just put it over there." She turned a critical eye on the furnitureless spaces. "Or somewhere else." He practically dropped it on one of the floor cushions. Aunt DeeDee stopped dead and sniffed the air. Then she fished in her purse, extracted one of her perfume samples, and sprayed liberally, while my father cleared his throat and Mimi made a show of holding her nose.

"Aren't people supposed to keep their rabbits in hutches, or eat them with wine sauce, or something?" my aunt said, not quite rhetorically. I couldn't argue with her there. The more Mimi made snide faces at her sister, the closer I drew to my aunt. Things were feeling right again.

"Guess what this is, Sugarspoon? It's something special—all for my favorite person."

The carton came up to her chin. I slit open the taped cardboard with Mimi's palette knife and lifted out a Victorian dollhouse. Gingerbread lined its gables; the shutters were hand-carved. The three stories of rooms rattled, and as we pulled the house from its container, three minute sofas, a canopy bed, and a copy of a Van Gogh painting the width of DeeDee's wrist clattered to the floor.

Unsure how to respond, I glanced at Mimi in alarm. "DeeDee, don't you think Lake's a bit old for a dollhouse?" she said. Aunt DeeDee's face clouded, and I rushed to her defense.

"Oh, man," I said, echoing Mimi in her more gracious moments, "the perfect gift. Now Georgia has a place to sleep." Mimi silently left the room.

I cleared the little mock house of furniture (DeeDee had piled it in) and coaxed the rabbit into the living room, where it crouched, leaving fur on the tiny built-in sconces and looking even blacker and certainly foreboding, like a tar-colored shadow looming over the wallpaper glued to the miniature rooms.

"Whatever," Aunt DeeDee shrugged, and she steered me upstairs. As soon as we were in my room, she shut the door and took a blue velvet box from between her clothes folded in tissue.

"Voila! From your grandparents," she said. Her brown eyes softened with tears, and I opened the box carefully. Inside was a silver locket with my name inscribed. Aunt DeeDee wedged her fingernail between the halves of the locket to open it and revealed a photo of what I thought must be a mansion. It had giant trees in front and a flagstone walk lined with flowers; a stone tower loomed up from one side.

"Home sweet home. That's where GranVinny wanted them to get married, you know," she said, already hanging up her clothes. "But she refused. Lord knows why." She sighed. "At least they agreed to do it in St. Louis. The *first* time, that is." She nodded in my direction as if she expected me to nod back.

I recalled the photos I'd seen in my parents' albums of the wedding in the woods at the edge of Wilders Ferry. The cambric shirt and dress Jillian had made as a nuptial gift for her husband's best friends. Off-white, the color of the bleached stones on the shore. Braided bear grass and lady fern encircling their necks like leis. Mimi's hoop earrings so large they made her look like Minnie Mouse. The domelike cake Dyl had baked in a metal bowl, swathed in ivory frosting—a bit of it clung to his beard in one of the pictures—and decorated with rings of dandelions stuck in up to the blossom. Punch served in a spaghetti pot with a soup ladle.

"The first time?" I asked, askance.

"They didn't tell you about the *real* wedding? The one in St. Louis?" She sounded as incredulous as I felt. She tsk-tsked. "Mama and Papa rented the Starlight Roof of the Chase-Park Plaza Hotel. People are still talking about it. Believe you me. Your GranPearl had a flowered *chuppah* made just for them. Orchids and daisies."

"What's a *chuppah*?"

She sounded almost angry. "Doesn't your mother tell you anything? A *chuppah* is a canopy used at Jewish weddings."

"They had a Jewish wedding?" I couldn't keep the shock from my voice.

She studied me. "Not exactly, Lover. Only half Jewish. Like us." She laughed, a real thunderboom. "The Sicilians treated themselves to mini-bagels and lox; the Jews, to toasted ravioli. It worked out. And we all had caviar—smack-dab in the center of each table; molded into a sturgeon. What a crowd there was around the hors d'oeuvres tables. Your grand-mother had them strewn with rose petals."

"There were a lot of people there?"

She nodded seriously. "Three hundred guests. We danced until mid-night, too. I fox-trotted my little tootsies off. Box-stepped even. Did the hora. There was a mirror ball revolving from the ceiling and lighting up the dance floor."

"What did you do, Aunt DeeDee?"

"I was maid of honor, of course. I wore a yellow taffeta dress. Had spike heels dyed to match. I nearly broke the big toe of my second cousin when I leaped for the bouquet. Your grandparents had a special savings account for your mother's wedding to pay for all this extravagance, you know. But still . . ." She started to fill the bureau top with plastic bottles. "Then she had to ruin it all by getting married again. Two thousand miles away. In bare feet, no less. Wedding Number Two, she calls it."

I searched my memory for a shot of DeeDee in the photos I'd seen, but found none.

"I missed the whole thing," she said, as if she could read my thoughts. "At first I decided not to go; I mean, I didn't want to be disloyal to Mama and Papa. But when push came to shove I just didn't feel right not being a part of things. Problem was, I had to be routed the long way, got fogged in in Seattle. She didn't even invite them." She shook her head, examined her shiny nails. "Still, that wasn't what hurt them most. Not by a long shot."

I waited for her conclusion. She cast me a knowing glance. I was beginning to think that I had two realities. I was swimming in my own thoughts when she leaned toward me and whispered into my ear, as if anyone else could hear. A whiff of her perfume whooshed in my face, overpowering for a second her words. "It was the secret; that's what hurt them." She raised her eyebrows. They were shaped like upside-down U's. "You know." At that moment the door opened and Mimi walked in, wearing a black leotard and holding the trembling rabbit on her shoulder. I started, as if I had been caught in a suspicious act.

"I think Georgia looks just like her Auntie Diane, don't you, Lake?" Mimi said. But Aunt DeeDee did not rise to the bait. She simply continued to gleam at me knowingly, as if she and I, sharing something truly significant, were above bantering. I don't know whether my aunt meant to tell me this secret then and there or not, or if she assumed I already knew it, as she did about so many of the facts of her life. But something about her tone, something about the oversweet scent of her perfume, prevented me from bringing it up again.

When Mimi left the room, Aunt DeeDee grabbed me by the elbow. "C'mon, Sweet Patootie. I brought you some new magazines." We spent the rest of the day lying on my bed, leafing through *Glamour* and *Modern Romance*.

When it was time for Aunt DeeDee to leave us again, Mimi filled in the empty spaces in her sister's shopping bags with jars of her homemade plum jam. Then, as they usually did, as part of their ritual, my aunt clutched both Mimi and me to her chest and cried. I noticed how there was something held back when Mimi kissed her baby sister good-bye, in that quick, dry pressure to the side of the lips, in the arms held at bay around the back, no response to the tears.

On the long drive to the airport in Spokane, DeeDee talked to Dad, and neither he nor I said much of anything. On the way home he said, "They aren't much alike, are they?"

I opened the glove compartment. "Don't you sometimes wish they were?" I asked, peering into the gaping space as if I were searching for something.

He turned toward me as if he had never thought of this before and kept on driving. As soon as we arrived at the purple house, I got out of the car first and walked fast toward the front door. But as I approached the house, I saw a familiar figure through the living room bay window. Graceanne sat on the floor and balanced a coffee cup on the sill. She looked ensconced, like she belonged.

I pivoted on my heel, and as Dad was still fiddling with the car, I took the road out of town, dodging the wide boat trailers throwing dust from the road onto the fireweed sprayed the color of rust. I stomped away from the grit and the noise from the sawmill, its towering kiln belching out smoke, the flames blackening its wire dome. I headed north, and when I saw the green, oblong sign that spelled CANADA, I yearned to keep on going.

That evening, I watched Mimi wash the cups and saucers and the dessert plates that she'd used to serve Graceanne carrot cake. While she dried each piece, she hummed a tune I didn't recognize, and she paused every now and then to study the scalloped edge of the plates.

Dad hung back, watching her, then picked up a saucer and asked, "What did you do this afternoon?"

"Not much," she said. I waited for her to tell him about what she and Graceanne talked about, to narrate and embellish, as she did about so many other significant events of her life. But she put away the rest of the dishes and resumed humming.

"Get anything done?" he interrupted.

"Uh-huh," she said. I glanced at her for signs of irritation, but she left the room, almost floated from it—smiling, as I recall it now, like the Mona Lisa.

Every morning and three afternoons a week, Graceanne stooped over the wives of the mill owners and managers and deck men and sawyers and separators and listened to them, but sometimes in the late afternoons she was Mimi's.

Usually she would let herself in the back door, and Georgia would sniff the air, twitching her nose and wiggling those whiskers as if they were antennae. Graceanne wasn't much on greetings the way Aunt DeeDee was, who insisted on the ceremony of good nights and good mornings and hellos every day. When Graceanne visited us in the evenings, as soon as she strode toward the house, Dad would call out, "Mimi, Graceanne's here," and, having done his duty, retire to another room. Graceanne would simply walk to the cushions in the bay window and position herself among them. Before long it seemed as if that place, which she so completely filled and made her own, had been built especially for her.

Often she'd bring her own thermos of coffee, pour herself a cup, put it down on the floor or on the sill, and stare out the window moodily. The first time she offered me some I was startled at her voice. Not only at its presence in the house, but at its sound. Her voice resonated with the undercurrent of a waterfall, the sound under the sound that enters through the skin and stays there, long after the vision of beauty—the white cascade, the spray refracting the light into pale colors, the sheer height of the drop—has disappeared from the inside of your eyelids.

Mimi liked to have Graceanne relay the stories her customers told while they were having their hair stripped and dyed, or curled or straightened. She and Mimi laughed at the folly of these women, who wanted something society had yet to give them—attention, status, mostly a man. They told Graceanne everything while she was rolling their wet hair with spiked plastic rollers and while she was bending over them in the basin. And these people, who unloaded on her the minutiae of their lives and the lives of their neighbors like so many garbage bags full of unwanted hair, didn't recognize her on the streets when she wasn't wearing her pumpkin-colored uniform. For us, she detailed every story in a linear fashion as if reading it from a TelePrompTer. And Mimi listened, the way Graceanne had listened to all of them. I often wondered what Mimi confided to Graceanne.

In some ways, though, Graceanne was more of a presence in our house when she wasn't there at all. Her visits were erratic, patternless, but after she left, I still felt her in the room.

Whenever Graceanne arrived, Mimi always closed the door to her studio, then yelled down, "Hi, Graceanne." Sometimes she didn't come downstairs for an hour or more. Graceanne would never ask again for her, or venture upstairs to fetch her.

"Why don't you let Graceanne see your paintings?" I asked one evening after Graceanne left.

"I want them to be a surprise. Anyway, she does watch me work sometimes."

These statements seemed contradictory to me, but I wasn't interested enough in her work or her life apart from mine to ask more about it.

When Mimi joined Graceanne by the bay window, she would get

Graceanne something to eat with her coffee, a piece of fresh bread, or sometimes huckleberry pie. Graceanne took whatever was offered, even if she left most of it on her plate. She seemed to like having something in front of her, as if she were an actor and whatever-it-was were a prop.

And they'd sit there in the bay and watch the sun or the moon, whichever. Sometimes they would laugh; I was never sure at what. Sometimes Graceanne would leave when Mimi was in the bathroom or taking the cup and saucer to the sink.

Dad had a sixth sense about when to resurface. "Is the coast clear?" he'd ask, to irritate Mimi.

Although she seldom responded with words, she would sequester herself in her studio until after we both went to bed.

Once I woke up in a sweat over a nightmare I couldn't remember: just images of faceless men in helmets and combat fatigues, hovering together like bloody clouds over an ocean. And when I realized where I was, I thought I heard muted giggling, and, half-asleep, mumbled, "It's just Graceanne."

When Graceanne was in the house, it had a focus for activity, and as much as I scorned her curious relationship with Mimi, I found myself drawn to them. I often invented excuses to get something downstairs just to catch snippets of their conversations. I was beginning to feel that Graceanne was the fourth wheel and we were aligned and balanced only when she was near us. Without her we spun on separate axes. Sometimes I think she was a cipher, a fill-in-the-blank test for Mimi to complete and call her own. With Dad and me, Mimi pretended to know everything about her. Mimi wove into the most casual conversation phrases like "Graceanne doesn't like raisins in her pie" and "Graceanne prefers Modigliani to Picasso" and "Graceanne never voted in an election" and "Graceanne supports separate tribal education." I wondered if Graceanne knew or professed to know so much about herself. But, of course, she had told Mimi her story, the story that had brought her into our life, the way stories often do. And who knew what knowledge, what truth, Mimi really had access to?

I was on my way upstairs one Saturday afternoon, and as I passed the two of them in the living room, Mimi put her Sony on the floor and plugged it in, saying, "Graceanne, it's time to meet Puccini." Graceanne raised her dark brows and settled into the corner. Mimi cranked up the volume and a familiar aria filled the room; I thought I saw the glass in the bay tremble. From a safe distance I watched Mimi watch Graceanne swivel her coffee with her index finger, her head tipped barely to the side as if she could take in more sounds that way. Then as the soprano crescendoed to the heights, Mimi grabbed Georgia from under the chair, whirled her around and swayed with her as if she were an unwilling partner in a dance, the silken ears back and terror in the eyes. Graceanne laughed, bending over so far that the blunt ends of her hair nearly scraped the floor.

Suddenly Jillian stood in the middle of the room. Mimi stopped short and yanked the plug from the socket so fast she nearly dropped the rabbit. The immediate silence stunned our ears.

"I knocked, but . . . " Jillian said softly. She gestured in the air. And then she spotted Graceanne. "Oh," Jillian said. Graceanne nodded imperceptibly, edged farther into the corner, and gazed at the clouds outside. I moved slightly away. "Sorry. I didn't mean to interrupt." She smiled a little and turned to leave.

"Please stay," Mimi said, panting a little. "Here, let me put on some tea. Sleepytime or Orange Pekoe?"

"Dylan and Paris went garnet hunting and won't be back 'til after dinner. I just stopped by . . . " Jillian often let her sentences trail off. "How are you, Lake? We haven't seen you much these days. Paris says you haven't been feeling very well." I winced, wondering if either Paris or she believed that.

"I'm better. Much better. Thanks."

"Maybe you'll come have luncheon with us next week then. Paris would like that."

And then no one said anything. Jillian pretended to listen to the sounds of Mimi in the kitchen. Graceanne made no pretense whatsoever.

Mimi returned with Jillian's tea, offered more coffee to Graceanne, and took the cushion that she had been sitting on, near Graceanne, to another corner. And there we were, the only women in Wilders Ferry I ever really talked to, now in one room, in all four corners of that room, silent.

"Jillian makes such beautiful things," Mimi said suddenly, running her finger along the earth-toned wool of the cushion that Jillian had woven for her last Christmas. She tried to catch Graceanne's eye. "Someday I wish she'd make me a magic carpet. I've always wanted to fly." She smiled ephemerally, quite taken with her singular reverie, so that for a moment the tension in the room dissipated.

In the charged silence that followed, I watched Jillian's hands, how rigid they were in her lap, saw how Graceanne averted her eyes when Jillian spoke, how Mimi insisted on pretending that these particular people were capable of exchanging thoughts and engaging in dialogue and that she wasn't straining to pluck conversation from the air.

Jillian stood. "I'd better get back."

No one protested, and when the door clicked shut, our bodies let down.

Something in the slope of her shoulders brought me back to what was, though I didn't suspect it then, the last time Jillian made lunch for Paris and me. As we'd walked away from their house that afternoon, I'd glanced back through the lattice window into their living room. Jillian had already taken her place at the blond loom, was arched over it slightly as if it were a harp and she were playing celestial music, so unworldly not even Paris could be privy to it. I'd thought even then of *The Odyssey*, the lines Dad had read to me again and again, of Penelope, waiting and scheming.

boredom

Over the course of the next year, we saw Jillian rarely. I steered clear of Satellite Health, but when I had to pass it on my way to somewhere else and caught a glimpse of her from the window, I tried not to meet her eye. Dyl still dropped by the purple house, but he usually stayed outside, chatting with Mimi at the back door. And I avoided Paris at school.

One day as I walked into the house, it struck me that it seemed unusually empty. I tried not to think that it might be Graceanne's and Mimi's absence that made the place seem rambling, but as I walked into the dining room, I thought I had entered the wrong room. The space appeared huge in its new emptiness, and I wondered if it would echo. "Testing one, two, three," I called out, and immediately felt foolish. All the canvases that had been stacked in the room and leaned against the window ledge had been removed. The only evidence of their having been there was oblong patterns in the dust. I climbed the stairs and tried the knob of the studio door three times before I realized it was locked. After that, I tried at odd hours to open the door, but the knob would never turn.

Mimi spent increasing time in her studio when she wasn't simply "out." I waited for her to explain herself, but she never did. Once I came home from school, and no one answered when I called Mimi's name. I went upstairs, and when I tried the knob to the studio, I thought I heard whispering, and I tiptoed away.

A few weeks later, hearing Graceanne's husky mimic, I lingered in the doorway. "She was a separator's wife, y'know, just had to do somethin' but wants to wait for the right moment, y'know. Had enough of his boozin' and knockin' around, so she waits till he's out at the Short Branch after a Friday at the mill, backs a furniture truck from Spokane up to their cabin, and when he comes rollin' in stinkin' drunk all that's there to greet him is the moosehead mounted on the wall. On the antlers she's balanced a can of beer and hung his jockstrap." Graceanne and Mimi laughed so uproariously at this that they didn't notice me go upstairs. On my way past the studio, I saw that the door was ajar. I gave it a shove with my elbow and entered, closing it carefully behind me.

Enormous canvases I didn't recognize leaned along two walls. I stood them up and, fascinated, examined them. Gone were the varieties of lips and eyes and hair and hands. Now all the fragmented women had amalgamated into one, and this one woman, painted in an explosion of colors, formed the heart of the composition on each canvas. The lips were full and the nose wide. Because the skin was in every piece a different color, or a combination of colors—carmine and cyan, mauve and magenta, the blues and yellows of flame—I didn't for a long time recognize anyone I knew. Every face was painted over with wild splotches, but the body was unmistakable. The breasts were substantial, one nipple pointing toward the left, the other to the right. On one canvas the woman was dancing; on another, lounging on a couch—our couch—and eating from her lap a box of chocolates lined with a white doily. Her eyes, though shaped like the leaves of the mountain dogwood, recalled Egyptian tomb paintings. Even when her head was in profile, the eyes still faced me and seemed to follow me around the room. Another painting portrayed her bathing in our bathtub with the lion's claws, rainbow-colored candles surrounding her and her breasts afloat. In another she was half hidden by a white lilac tree and held a wilting bunch of blossoms coyly in front of her lower belly. Another rendition, only partially completed, much of it still penciled, showed this woman standing in front of a bureau, the one Mimi had brought in the school bus from GranPearl's house. The model's buttocks were two fleshy crests, and she was pulling out from the top drawer (I recognized Mimi's sock and panty drawer) strands of opalescent pearls as if the bureau were a bottomless chest of pirate's treasure. At the bottom of a pile of sketches was a woman wearing only a charcoaled-in, high-necked blouse, lying on her belly with her hands cupped under her chin and her legs spread slightly, toes pointing to an alternating lily and lion pattern in the Persian carpet.

In the background of every painting, as part of the decor in the room, was another painting. I knew each of these background paintings well— the nudes Mimi had painted before. My heart at a fast clip, I ran down the hall toward my room and stayed there; when I was called down to supper, I said I was sick to my stomach.

Although it was usual for Mimi to disappear during the day, now she began to be gone at night, too. Then the quiet of our house no longer comforted, but brought a strange hollowness, and boredom took me over, possessed me, poisoning me as if it were a drug.

My parents developed opposite schedules. He rose early, and she went to bed late. They left each other notes taped to the bathroom mirror. He paced from window to window and peered out into the darkness. Sometimes when I came home from school and she wasn't in the house with Graceanne, she would be talking on the telephone and would immediately hang up, or she would lower her voice to a whisper. Other times, I would walk upstairs and, if her studio door was open, catch her standing in the middle of the room, a blank canvas in front of her, and staring beyond it out the window. Once when I entered the room, my footsteps creaking up to her and my breath certainly loud enough to hear, I startled her, and she gasped and knocked over her palette. Her face went white, then filled with blood, and her fingernails dug into her fists. I ran out of the room and slammed the door behind me.

An hour or so later, she knocked on my door. "I'm sorry," she said. She offered no explanation, but after that the studio door was always closed.

The next morning Mimi took the VW and left. "Guess I'll go check out a new gallery in Coeur d'Alene," she said. That evening Dad seemed particularly distracted, rubbing his eyebrow with a forefinger and flipping pages at random. I was bored of listening to the rabbit's claws skittle over the bare wood, and so when he asked me if I would like to accompany him downtown to the bookstore, I said yes.

It was a foggy night for October, the sort of night that might bring us to the threshold of winter, the vapor crystallizing into bits of snow by dawn. The store was so cold I could see my breath, and Dad left his jacket on while he dug around in a drawer under the cash register. I put my hands in my pockets. He switched on only one light; the unstained pine shelves, even the cedar walls, looked dingy and depressing despite the posters he'd tacked up. He opened the storage room, walked in, and dragged a carton out into the main room. He cut into the box, pushed up his bright-blue bandanna, and began to stack books on a chair. I called from the front door, "Okay if I walk around a little? I'll stay close to Main Street."

I walked out into the night. This was still relatively new, this walking by myself after dark, and the sense of liberation propelled me as if it were adrenaline. The fog clung in little drops, clammy and cold on my neck. It hovered in the air in thick clumps and filled my throat, as if to suffocate me from within. I brushed my hair from my forehead, felt my hair curling wet and closer to my scalp.

I peered into the dark windows of Alice's Hair Art and Satellite Health and then meandered toward the yellow light in the Short Branch Saloon. Through the narrow slats of the bamboo shades, I saw the flannel-shirted back of a young man I thought looked familiar. He turned his face to the side, and I caught the profile of Karl, the logger who trucked wood down the mountain for us. I had a clear view, even through the smoke. He was so big that I couldn't at first see whom he was dancing with; in fact, for a moment I thought he was dancing by himself. Then he pivoted his partner, and I saw that his meaty hands were surrounding the small waist of a person obscured by his bulk. And that small dancer was wild. She wore a long-sleeved T-shirt and jeans, a feather earring bobbing from one lobe, and she gyrated, her breasts shimmying and bursting through the cotton shirt, like a woman in a cage. His red-plaid shirt was unbuttoned to mid-chest, and the T-shirt underneath was matted to his neck. Her face shone with sweat, a damp curl clung to her forehead, and perspiration had stained a big circle under each arm. She was barefoot; he wore boots. She seemed to be looking at a point I knew nobody else could see, beyond the hurricane lamps ringed with Coors and Pilsner ads, beyond the Formica-topped tables in the corners, beyond the graying acoustic tile on the ceiling, and would probably not have noticed if his heavy boot had landed on her naked toes. He lifted his hand from her middle to wipe the sweat from his forehead, and I thought I could see the white scar that I knew was slashed across his forehead.

Then he lowered his hand as if to wrap it back around her waist, seemed to think better of it, and cupped his palm to her cheek. She lifted her face into that big hand, rubbed her lips across it finger to thumb. He winked at a fellow at the bar, then gave a slow smile on one side of his wide mouth. It took me several minutes, the last few seconds of which my heart was fluttering against my ribs, to fathom that this woman, his partner, the dancer, tiny and untamed, was my mother.

As I hurried away, the look on her face stayed with me. I knew I had seen that expression before; I just wasn't certain where. I was quiet on the drive home and went immediately upstairs.

Dad napped on the living room floor; his snores echoed in the house, which was eerily quiet when Mimi wasn't playing her music or talking with the rabbit. I wandered from room to room, overturning piles of books, peeking in closets, sweeping my hand along dusty shelves. Then it struck me, where I had seen that look. I pulled the photo albums off the shelf in her room and impatiently flipped through pages. And then I came to an empty place, where a picture had been removed.

I slammed the album shut and on a hunch began digging in Mimi's dresser. In the bottom drawer under a pair of black nylons I'd never known her to wear was an unmarked envelope; inside was a photo. On the back was printed: "Making invitations to wedding #2." And there they were, looking like the perfect couple, smiling as if posing for a magazine, their arms locked around each other's back. They were both smeared with paint. He sported a streak of it under each eye like war paint. He looked proud, cocky almost, inebriated with the pleasure of a messy task. His fingers were extended toward the camera, V'd in a peace sign. But otherwise he was focused on her. Her hands were coated with so many colors that they looked mud-caked. Her black hair was streaked and speckled with red, yellow, blue, and green; it fanned out wildly from the crown of her head. One eye was smudged with purple, and flecks of gold and silver shone on her cheeks like sparks. And there was the expression I had seen less than an hour before at the Short Branch—a look I rarely saw. It was the look of joy. I searched in this happy couple for a sign of my father, but I found none. It was clearly Mimi and Dyl. I tiptoed back to my room as if I had committed some infraction, some injustice.

Curled on my side, I lay on the floor, my ear to the planks, my knees up against my chest, and watched the moon ink shadows on my closet door. The fog held the moonlight and gave everything it illuminated in my room a silver aura. The door closed quietly, and she stayed in the kitchen for a long time. Then I heard the water in the bathroom, and my father's sleepy step on the floor. I stole into the hall and came down a step or two to hear what he had to say. I rested my hand on the newel post as if preparing to spring back up to my room. I felt like an intruder, self-righteous, as I waited for something dramatic to happen. But all my father said was, "What time is it?"

"I don't know," she answered. "After midnight."

"How was Coeur d'Alene?" he asked groggily.

"Fine," she said, and then the sound of the tub running blocked out the rest. But I suspected that there wasn't much more. I heard my father lumber down the hall to the stairs and ran into my room, my heart pumping.

He was snoring again within seconds, just enough time for him to re-move his clothes and set his alarm. I waited for Mimi to come up. The room became oddly dark, the shadows no longer discernible. I must have drifted off because when I heard her soft step on the stairs, the fog had lifted, evaporated into just a vapor around the half-moon outside my window. She took the stairs two at a time, and I listened to her late-night litany to the rabbit. I pictured her clasping it to her chest while she rubbed her cheek against its long ears and whispered to it. At first I thought she was saying over and over "s-s-s-s-" like the calming sound she made when I would wake past midnight with a fever. But then I caught, or thought I caught, her words, "young skin, such sweet skin."

the course of history

At the onset of winter, I took up with Dallas. He slouched in the far back seat in the corner of the eighth-grade history class as if he were trying hard not to be noticed. I'd seen him tinkering with his truck parked in back of the gas station at the edge of town. We'd never been in the same class before, so I figured he must have failed a grade. He appeared older, too, more square around the jaw. His upper lip was shadowed with fuzzy dark hairs, which looked as if they had been shaved once or twice. He habitually wore black. His jacket was always inside out, and he never brought a book to class. Every day he bit his pencil eraser down to the metal ring and drove it into the desk, gouging it as if at random. His lids drooped over his eyes as if they were visors; his lashes were thick, and when he was on the edge of sleep, the lids would flutter open for a second before shutting tight. The teacher, Miss Whiteside, ignored him most of the time, except when he began to snore, and then she'd threaten to send him to the principal, and he'd just shrug. The surprising thing was that he smelled like Paco Rabanne, a cologne I used to hold under my nose when nobody was looking at the Spokane department store counter lined with all the stuff for men—not the men I knew but those Aunt DeeDee talked about, the sort who carried briefcases and called Tokyo or Paris on their WATS lines and asked svelte women to forgive them for being late and played racquetball and squash. In Dallas, I might have expected woodsmoke, or the sweat that collects in the folds of the thigh and the groin, but not something calculated to please. It made me smile, and at first he glared, then nodded.

He took his leather-covered forearm off the desk as if to show me his secret. He revealed what looked like a relief map, mountains carved in the old wood, the peaks pointy. I was stunned at how much they looked like the Sawtooths. The splintery look and the dust among the grooves added to the effect that it resembled something real. Then while I looked on he brought his pencil to his mouth and wet the metal end with his tongue, deliberately without smiling or a trace of irony. He let the saliva collect on the metal and slowly lowered it to the carved map of the desk and with precision pushed the metal into the desk until his knuckles were blanched; he pushed the pencil smoothly, snaked it around the carved mountains, then wet it again. And I knew right away what it was: It was a river, and I wondered which one. When I asked, he responded by cutting another nick into one of his mountain peaks. The next period I found myself doodling his name on my health class notes.

After school he waited for me in his blue Ford pickup spattered with mud and rusted out in random patches. Over the gun rack a baseball bat had been chained. He opened the door as I passed by. "Ride?" he asked.

With a glance at the crowd elbowing each other at the door to the bus, I climbed into the cab. It was adorned with images of Jesus in His various manifestations. A picture of the Lord was suspended with fish wire from the mirror. When the heavy door whooshed shut, the photo spun. A bronze statue of the Almighty Counselor on the cross stood erect on the dash; perhaps it was bolted there, though it may have been simply a magnet. A key chain hung on the gun rack; a circle the size of a silver dollar, embossed with Jesus the Shepherd, dangled from its loop. On the mud-streaked glass separating the cab from the bed was affixed a dime-store print of Jesus of the Bleeding Heart, the sort in which the eyes seem to follow you wherever you go. I was beginning to be sorry I had closed the door. But as we got closer to my house, and so far the topic of soul-saving had not been raised, I relaxed.

When I climbed out of the pickup, he said, "See ya," and I thought I saw him wink.

I felt relieved to see Mimi and Graceanne in the bay when I walked in; I hoped to slink upstairs and think my own thoughts without being noticed. I smiled hello and had turned toward the stairs when Graceanne launched into another of her stories. Suddenly her voice became someone else's. The timbre and inflection she adopted were breathtakingly different from her own, and I immediately recognized the voice. It belonged to Maybelle Purdy, the school bus driver, and I stayed to listen.

"The gal who flips hotcakes at the grill up to Priest River walked around for two weeks with a burn the size of a crab apple on her shoulder and kept telling all the folks who sat at the counter, all the coffee drinkers who hung out and visited just like it was some bar and she was paid to listen to them, she told 'em all that she was getting clumsy in her old age, but truth to tell, at least according to the gal who comes in on Thursday mornings regular, the one with the rash on her neck, probably from all that boozin' if you ask me (she's always red in the face or neck, unless she has one of those sunlamps and just pointed it on her neck kinda careless like), but she told me what she thought, and it kinda had a ring to it, ring o' truth, that is." Graceanne's performance was hypnotic. I moved toward her in the living room. "It was that no-good man of hers, hit her with her own skillet one day, probably sizzling, too, those hotcakes falling to the floor, no one knows for sure why, but probably for the reason that she was a woman. Couldn't change that. Not that he wanted her to."

When she was done, she smiled, almost shyly.

"Oh, tell us more," Mimi begged, and without missing a beat, Graceanne continued.

"That woman whose husband owns the mill?" She was using her own voice now, and I felt a tinge of disappointment. "Comes in and asks for a leg wax. She stays for a couple hours, catching me up on the doings about town." She paused to balance her cup on the sill. "That's how I heard about you."

I was concentrating so intently on the rhythm and cadence of her voice, I almost missed the meaning. I was afraid to look up, to look at either of them. She lowered her pitch and then the volume, and I had to strain to hear. The voice continued slowly, more carefully than I had ever heard it. "They say the married hippie woman who lives in a purple house dances with a young logger, a tall blond with a baby face and a scar on his forehead. He drives up from Deary, some say not so much to cut timber as to see her."

Mimi picked up her plate and left the room. The light was changing in the bay, and the sunset looked like a latter-day triptych: in one side window there were rosy tufts; in the other side window, orange streaks; and right in the middle, the gold light refracted into shafts, gilding all the leaves and the hills far away and all the things we couldn't see, housetops and chimneys, waxwings snapping up blackberries along the creek beds, whitetails nuzzling balsamroot in the meadows. I knew all were illuminated like a Rembrandt painting, giving the illusion of being ethereal and eternal, the light that he must have been born with, but that no particular, no extraordinary combination of genes, no mere accident could have produced.

Graceanne finished her pie, licked the crumbs from her plate. When she left, instead of picking up her cloth shoulder bag and walking quietly out the door, she carried her plate into the kitchen, dusted the crumbs off the sill, and, turning to me, said almost gently, "Tell her I'll be back tomorrow."

After supper I left the house, saying I was going to take a walk, and slammed the door before Mimi and Dad could react. I took off in the snow toward the gas station. I saw Dallas's black jacket from down the road and almost lost my nerve. He was talking with the mechanic who sometimes fixed our VW, but then he spotted me and strutted toward me. Although it was a wintery evening, I was already feeling the warm winds of independence whirl around me.

As soon as I hoisted myself into the truck, he jerked it into gear and pressed his boot to the floor. We took the curves down the lake road with the needle on the speedometer vibrating out of control. There was no heater, and I could see my breath in little puffs. The vinyl on the bench must have been waxed; I slid from one side of the cab to the other. Sometimes I'd fall into his shoulder, and sometimes into the ragged armrest on the passenger side.

He swerved on black ice onto a logging road, and I watched a vein in his neck twitch as the truck twisted up the mountain. We bounced and jarred from its ruts and gullies that felt like craters under the wheel, and I thought his head would hit the ceiling. Dallas seemed to think this jouncing was fun, but his hands gripped the trembling wheel, and his grin looked set. He stopped without pulling over to the side. He breathed heavily for a minute or two, as if he had been practicing for a marathon, looked straight ahead, and handed me the beer between his legs. I had tasted beer once or twice; I'd sneaked a few warm swallows from the cans Mimi left partly full when she watched Karl bring and cut the wood. My parents and Dyl and Jillian drank wine from big jugs but never offered me any. On Friday nights teenagers drank beer around the lake, but they never invited Paris or me. I could hear their high-pitched laughter echo across the water in the dark.

I took the beer from Dallas's hand with a nod. The beer remaining in the can was warm from his thighs and made me think, in spite of my resolve not to do it, of the source of that heat, and then almost immediately of the flush on Mimi's face, the sidelong glances the logger cast her as he bore down on the maul. I squirmed. Dallas turned his head.

"Cold?" he said.

I wasn't sure if he meant the beer or me, so I grunted, a safe sound when you're alone with an odd boy in a truck out in the boonies, even with only half a beer.

I sipped it, held it in my mouth.

"I seen you before," he said. I resisted an uncomfortable urge to correct his grammar.

"How'd you know that?"

"I used to watch you walking down this road, the other way, to your house. You were always kicking up gravel and making dust, or digging trenches in the snow."

I felt something like guilt: I couldn't say that I remembered him at all.

"I was a couple grades ahead of you," he continued. "I flunked. Then I just up and quit for a while. Worked with my father, swept the mill, logged some, that sort of thing." He paused to remove his glove, took a vicious bite out of the cuticle of his forefinger, minced it between his teeth, then spat out the skin. It landed on its way to the dashboard. I tried not to notice exactly where. He put his glove back on. "Then I woke up one morning and realized the fire hadn't been made, my toes were freezing their asses off"—I noted the unusual expression, the mixed metaphor—"and I knew that my father had dumped me."

After a moment I asked, "What did your mother do?"

"What mother?" he said, and smiled with his mouth only; his eyes looked vacant and then away. He took the beer, slanted the can toward his mouth, and let the last two drops fall on his tongue. Then he crunched the can with one hand, roughly, and tossed it out the window. He pulled me toward him and the gearshift rammed into my stomach.

"Ouch!" I said.

The only thing I knew about romantic kissing was from reading. But I'd gleaned the nitty-gritty how-to tidbits from the *True Confessions* magazines Aunt DeeDee and I had often pored over together, and that, much to Mimi's chagrin, she left in my room for me. From these magazines I'd learned not about the egg-and-sperm bit, but about the heart-thudding, earth-moving important stuff. Until then I had had no idea that you were supposed to open your mouth while engaged in what was apparently an art; I had had no clue that there was a right way and a wrong way to do this. And the idea that I might be judged on one more thing in my life was making my insides churn in dangerous ways, especially so far from a bathroom.

I parted my lips slightly, just as it said to do in the magazines, and as I did I felt his tongue slither between my teeth. I gasped and must have bit down, because he sprang back and said what must have been "shit" but sounded like "thit." He held his tongue between his fingers.

"I guess you'd better take me home," I said.

"What'd you do that for?" he asked, an edge of anger to his tone.

"I didn't mean it."

Then he came toward me again, and this time, in the wake of failure, I let down and let him into my mouth, and my life. His saliva tasted like Skoal, and where our mouths weren't touching at all points, it felt cold. His lips skimmed the limited exposed surface of my neck and left an icy, wet streak like a road on a map. Then when he tired of that, he approached my ear, taking the top part of it between his lips and then engulfing it with his entire mouth. For a second or two the warmth felt good and sweet, and then I knew it would be frigid and damp. I can't remember doing anything at all except moving my neck and shoulders around to maximize the warmth. It occurred to me that I should be making noises (the magazines always said "moans and groans of pleasure," and occasionally someone would exclaim "yes!" for reasons beyond me), but the noise he made was more like a grunt between pants. It wasn't in my vocabulary, and I didn't think I should return it, so I just matched him shallow breath for shallow breath.

His hands stayed behind my back a rather long time and then inched closer to my sides. Soon one hand moved to my front, though it took me a long time to notice it because I was wearing the jacket I wore when I split wood for the stove. When I looked down at my chest, I realized the hand was kneading the mounds of Polargard layered over my left breast. I grabbed his wrist and extracted his hand. I could even recall the page number of the magazine from which I'd picked up this particular move. He immediately clamped his mouth back on mine, and when I looked again, I saw that my upper right quadrant was the current target. This time when I grabbed the wrist, I met resistance, and suddenly his body fell on me, pushing me backwards and knocking my head against the window. Then I heard a yell and for a second thought it had come from me. I opened my eyes and saw him grabbing with both hands at his lower belly; his jaw was set and his face looked like a specter. Suddenly I was alarmed. "What's wrong?" I gasped.

"Gearshift," he said through clenched teeth, and although it was all I could do not to laugh, I suddenly felt unfamiliarity lift from the air. I moved toward him and kissed him. His tongue was chilly, tasted like beer, and I had to wipe my nose with my mitten. He bit off the end of one of the fingers on his glove and ran a fingertip along my lips.

"Nice," he said, and then said nothing as discernible as language until we reached my house, when he mumbled, "'Night." Or perhaps it was, again, just "nice."

The windows fogged, and I removed my mitten and wrote with my forefinger, "Dallas and Lake," enclosing it in a lopsided heart. As he drove away, I could see him lean over and wipe the window clean with his half-gloved hand.

After that, instead of riding the bus home after school, I joined Dallas in probing the network of logging roads radiating from the lake. He would let me off close to where the bus did, and I'd walk from there. By February Dallas had bitten off all the fingers of his gloves and was finding amazing places for them to explore on the ready map of my body.

sneaking out

All through the winter Karl's presence flashed at me behind my eyelids—the hand encircling the tiny waist, the yellow hair hiding the white scar. It was only when I was with Dallas that these images took a backseat to whatever was truly in my face.

At first I saw him surreptitiously, but I had learned only too well that a secret in Wilders Ferry was a contradiction in terms and would be short-lived. I'd nod to him in the back row of history class, take my habitual seat. There were usually a few empties between us, even on a day that wasn't prime for hunting. After school I'd linger at my locker and wait for everyone else to leave, then walk outside and head toward home until I spotted his truck on the shoulder of the road, waiting for me.

No matter who else knew, I was determined to keep this relationship a secret from my parents. I told myself I just couldn't imagine him sitting at supper with us, wondering where to put his elbows while Mimi licked her fingers and placed her plate on the floor, the click a signal for Georgia to hop out from under the table legs to lap at the remnants. But the real reason was that it felt exhilarating to deceive them.

When they expressed curiosity about my getting home late in the afternoons, Dallas and I began to sneak out of school at the lunch hour. He forged a series of notes for both of us. He would sign his notes "D. Glascock," which anyone who wanted to know, he assured me, would assume was his mother or father. I'd glance nervously at the messages he forged from Mimi, checking to make sure the grammar was correct. The notes claimed we had an appointment (he alternated between the doctor in Sandpoint and the dentist in Priest River), and even if he brought me back early, he would simply stay out of school until just before the closing bell, when he'd show up for the last ten minutes or so of class, I suppose just so he could roar off in his truck in front of a ready-made crowd.

I was hurrying out of a classroom to meet Dallas in the parking lot when I felt a familiar presence at my side. "Lake," Paris said. She sounded breathless, as if she had been running to catch up with me. I stopped and took stock of her, trying to see her as Dallas must see her. Her hair, still straight, straggled to her waist. She still had her baby fat. Over her wool socks were strapped suede sandals, Birkenstocks, like Dyl's and Mimi's.

"I wanted—my mother asked me to invite you to—" she paused, as if she knew the word she was about to say sounded silly, "—luncheon again. She said, 'Tell Lake we'll eat like duchesses.'" She kept her eyes on the scuffed linoleum, and her glasses slipped slightly down her nose. The frames matched Jillian's tortoiseshell hair clip.

"Paris, today I'm just too busy." I lowered my tone to a conspiratorial level, sounding remarkably like Aunt DeeDee. "You know. With Dallas."

She nearly interrupted to say, "It's okay about today. How about tomorrow?"

"I wish I could, Paris. But tomorrow I've got a test to study for at lunchtime." The color rose to her face, made perfect round O's on her cheeks.

"Call me?" she said, her voice hesitating. A locker slammed far down the hall, and I watched the O's deepen to scarlet and spread to the rest of her face and down her neck like a bloody shadow.

I was about to touch her shoulder, but I heard the horn blare from Dallas's truck and said, quickly, "I will," before running outside. When I climbed into the truck a few minutes later, Paris was watching from the curb.

Dallas snickered. "Isn't that your little Granola friend?"

I cast him my frostiest look. "Don't call her Granola. It's just that her family—"

"No sweat," he laughed. "I didn't mean nothing by it."

The next day at lunchtime the truck was just pulling away from the school when I saw Jillian's car turn into the parking lot. I ducked down.

"What're you? Crazy?" Dallas asked, reaching down to drag me back onto the seat.

I waved him away as if he were a mosquito. "It's too complicated to explain," I whispered, as if they could hear me. I waited for a few minutes for Jillian to have enough time to pick Paris up and drive away; then I sat up again. But as Dallas's truck pulled out from the back of the building, Jillian's car crossed in front. Paris was buckled into the passenger seat. I couldn't see her expression, but I thought I knew what it looked like. It was hardest that first time, watching her expression fall; it reminded me of Jillian's the afternoon she left the purple house the last time she had visited, when she had left early and Graceanne had stayed.

Dallas drove fast into the hills on the west side of the lake. The bleeding hearts pushed up through the lingering patches of snow. At the edge of the woods, he pulled off the road and killed the engine. He grabbed a wool blanket from under his feet, got out of the truck, and walked into the trees. I followed, and he kicked some rocks out of the way and spread the blanket.

"I have only twenty-three minutes," I said, sounding so much like Dad I could have kicked myself. But fortunately the "twenty-three minutes" part was muffled by the pressure of Dallas's mouth.

"It's spring. You don't need this anymore," he said, unzipping my jacket while I stood stiffly facing him. "C'mon, Babe," he smiled and tugged a little and we sank down on our knees on the blanket.

Something hard jabbed my shin. I squirmed, and he maneuvered my body downward so that we were lying face-to-face. He pulled me toward him and put his hands under my collar. I jumped a bit with the chill and then settled into the sensation, conscious of the feel of his palms, ungloved and naked on my skin for the first time; a callus scratched a path on my top vertebra. One hand rubbed in circles down my spine, and the other pushed down on my bottom as he thrust his pelvis into mine. I moved back.

"Relax," he whispered into my mouth, while I tensed at the vision of my mother somehow or other springing out of the next copse of trees, brandishing a paintbrush, while I assured her, "We're not really doing anything."

Dallas interrupted my incoherent fantasy by fiddling with the zipper on my Levi's. I drew in a breath. My blood was pumping into places I couldn't trace, somewhere between pleasure and fear.

"I really think we should be getting back," I said. "I just remembered I told Paris I'd meet her after lunch."

"Look," he said icily, "don't lie to me. I'm not your little hippie friend. I'll get you back as soon as you need to be back." And he rubbed his hands all over me, more slowly now, and under my clothes, and I found myself inching closer to him and before long pressing my pelvis toward his. He laid me on my back, rose to his knees, and straddled me. His body seemed to rise above me like one of the firs that surrounded us, and I thought of how, at the Short Branch, Karl had had to arch over to whisper in my mother's ear. Above me, as if in slow motion, Dallas wriggled his arms out of his sleeves, worked his T-shirt over his head, and threw it behind him. Then he pulled up my T-shirt and with two fingers on both hands, lifted my bra, and my breasts sprang free. My heart flew up into my throat, and half from embarrassment I reached up and grabbed around his back to cover my body with his and mashed him against me. His breath came in shallow spurts. He rolled onto his back and pulled me on top of him and slipped his hand under the waistband of my tight jeans, and I gasped. But instead of removing his hand, or moving away, I waited. Waited for something I could just begin to feel, and now, with the touch of him on skin no one had longed to touch before, I began to want.

I closed my eyes, and pushed out all thoughts but my skin. He paused to fiddle with the zipper on his jeans, and my eyes flickered open, and just then a white spider scurried across Dallas's bare shoulder, and Dallas jerked up and I screamed. He brushed it off, then reached for me again, but this time I pushed him away. I sat up, rearranged my bra, put on my T-shirt, and handed him his shirt.

"Gotta get back."

"When?" he asked, as he straightened the spread and I glanced in the mirror and finger-combed my hair.

"Now. I really have to—"

"No. I mean, when can we do it?"

I was about to ask what "it" meant, then felt a jolt of recognition.

I did not know what was the socially correct answer, even after having read all those magazines. It had never occurred to me that "it" was where we were heading. I suppose I thought myself immune from those things. I was different in other ways; why not in this?

"I don't know," I said.

"Well, think about it."

All the way back, of course, I fought the thought of it. I tried to empty my brain of the one vision I should have known I'd have in full force sooner or later—the look of it, the smell of it, the fleeting feel of it. And when Dallas pulled up behind Wilders Ferry Central School with its peeling brown and yellow paint and its shrill buzzing bells and its graffiti-scratched lockers, packed with the progeny of mill workers and shopkeepers, the time when anything within those walls, even Paris and the guilt she instilled in me, had been important or powerful already seemed far away.

"Tell me when," he said, grabbing my sleeve as I opened the door to the truck.

"Not outside in the woods," I said firmly.

"You didn't answer my question."

"It didn't sound like a question to me." I slammed the door. But his response made me want to see him again soon, and to hurry; Dallas was smarter than I gave him credit for.

All weekend I stayed in my room. The house was unusually still, so quiet that it was hard to sleep. I didn't even try to imagine where Mimi was, whom she was with. I flopped on my bed, thumbed through old books, stared out the tinted window. I thought of nothing, simply trying to recapture the sensation of flesh on flesh.

Monday, as soon as I walked into the building, I knew something was wrong. I could almost smell it. I saw Paris out of the corner of my eye. I took a deep breath and followed her to the end of the hall, calling her name, though not loudly enough to attract attention.

She walked purposefully ahead, not glancing to either side, and I realized she was pretending not to hear. She was about to turn into the library when I caught up with her and reached for her shoulder. She stiffened. I tried to sound casual. "Hey. What's up? Sorry I didn't call this weekend." I couldn't even think of a good excuse.

She just bit her lower lip and shrugged, and looking at her wool socks and sandals, said, "I don't appreciate you doing that to me."

Suddenly the tug of responsibility I felt toward her turned to anger. I ran my tongue along my teeth, searching for speech. "Doing what to you?" Then I had the giddy sense of feeling nothing. How free, I thought, not to feel at all.

"I know you know, Lake. I know you know." Her chest heaved, and I noticed how much weight she had gained. She covered her belly with her books. "I don't know why I ever believed you." She waited for me to apologize—at least to respond. I just looked at her. Her eyes filled; her body shook from her blond head down. The first-period bell rang. Suddenly she darted down the corridor.

I pictured myself running after her, weaving through clumps of other kids in the hall. But I was rooted to the floor. She was about to disappear when I called, almost too softly for her to hear, "Paris! Wait!"

She stopped, pivoted, and screamed back, the words resounding down the corridor and halting the conversations of every passerby as if buckshot had discharged into the metal of the lockers. "Your mother lost her virginity in a hearse!" Then she fled down the hall, her golden braid flapping against her back.

scars

Sometimes, even today, I see them together, my mother and Karl, the young logger.

———————

He has worked in the woods since he was seven, carrying the lunch pail for his father and trying his hand on the grip and throttle of the chain saw. After his mother leaves the two of them for a man and a job in Seattle, they bring bread and butter and Kool-Aid, and eat from the Styrofoam plates that hamburger comes on at the grocery store.

When a cable snaps and half a ton of timber rolls downhill, crushing his father and leaving his carcass in a compressed heap on the slope and turning his scar-riddled skin blue, Karl takes his place in the crew. It is more than genetic.

Karl has collected scars as if they were organic to his anatomy, like the growth plates articulating one bone to another, meniscus to meniscus, concave to convex, and Mimi reads them as if she were reading the rings of an evergreen. She is greedy for them, as she is to be a part of all of his life. All of those years she has missed being with him cause anxiety to flutter inside her ribs.

My mother uses her mouth and hands to see Karl's scars. Not simply to see them clearly, but to understand them, internalize them.

She starts and ends at the top. She takes her mouth from his, where it has been for nearly an hour, and moves it down his cheek, then neck, leaving a wet streak on his collarbone, like the bottom of a dry riverbed just beginning to fill with mountain runoff. When she gets to his shoulders, and he moves his arm to accommodate her, the deltoids remind her of a horse she wanted to ride once, and of something else, she can't afford to take the time to figure out what. She thinks it has something to do with wings.

She rests her cheek on his chest, just right of the sternum, and contemplates the blanched ribbon that crosses his biceps. She runs her forefinger along it; it narrows toward the back of his arm.

"How'd you get this scar?" she asks. It takes him a while to answer. While she waits, she is content to listen to his blood.

"Thinking of you," he says at last, a little tentatively, as if this were a question. But he sees that this answer pleases her, is indeed the right one, the only one.

It is his first time cable logging; he's the landing man, the guy who stays on the road to unhook the chokers and saw off limbs. As he watches the logs ascend the hill, dangling fifty feet above him from the chokers as if they were nooses, he squints into the sun. Something—a piece of bark or a bit of dirt—lodges in his eye, and it waters. Through the liquid film he sees my mother. She is wearing an evening gown; it shimmers with sequins, trembles behind the tears. She has white gloves that come up to her elbow. Her hair is piled on top of her head with diamond-studded combs, and she lets it down with her gloved hands. It falls the way it used to when she was a flower child, over her shoulders and to her waist, then continues to drop to the pine needles on the ground. She lifts the gloved hand to her mouth and runs it along her lips. Then she floats toward him just above the earth, her long curls flowing behind like a wedding train.

And suddenly a snag, the pointed end of a dead lodgepole,

drops down as if from the sky. He turns to run, but the snag hits the edge of the road. He throws his arm up to block his eyes from the blinding sun, his face from the falling limb, and the end whips around, tearing through his arm. He keeps on working, visions of my mother a narcotic against the pain.

Mimi squeezes her eyes shut, partly to wince against his pain and partly to see more clearly. She inches down his rib cage. Words she recalls from making hospital rounds with her father come into her head, and she whispers them: "pectoralis," "serratus," "abdominal oblique," "rectus abdominus." They hiss thick from her mouth as she slides down, past the pelvis, her lips marking a path down the thigh.

"How'd you get this one?" she asks, her eyes on the level of a diagonal line, a slash across the shin.

And knowing he has hit on the answer that pleases her, he says again, not at all hesitantly, "Thinking of you."

He's bent over to saw off a vertical limb and holds the saw sideways. The exhaust is roaring, and sawdust sprays up; the chips sting his face. He turns his head to the left to protect his eyes, and he sees her lying on her back on a stump. She arches backwards over the stump as if she were a gymnast. Her hair is the same color as the bark. She is wearing his undershirt. As she bends bowlike into a half-circle, the T-shirt steals up her thighs and pauses at the point where her torso begins, just barely covering the curly triangle between her strong thighs. The tops of her toes and the tips of her fingers graze the ground, and he takes in the pine needles clinging to the arches of her small feet.

The saw blade strikes his chaps and stops. The silence takes him by surprise, like a kick in the groin, steals his breath, and gives him time to look down, his eyes drawn to his leg like steel to a magnet, and he sees the tear in the leather and the blood that is already filling it and spilling down his leg like the creek down the mountain in spring.

She inches down to his feet and finds the scar that circles his ankle like a manacle. She runs the heel of her hand along it, and when she is done examining its shape and counting the number of whites—she finds eggshell and vanilla and pale, specter white— she fingers its puckered edge to study the changes in texture from dead flesh to living.

And she asks again, "How'd you get this one?"

He grins this time before he says it.

He's up on the landing, kneeling in the brush and sawdust to fill the saw with gas. He hears the deep growl of the crane straining under its load. He looks up the mountainside at the crane and instead sees her on a horse, a young horse, a roan. She is grabbing his rust-colored mane with both fists and pressing her elbows tight against his withers. The roan's flanks and her thighs glisten with heat. The horse turns, flicks its tail; she leans forward and as she braces for the jump, her small buttocks rise from the horse's sweating back. The horse leaps and keeps going, flies up into the clouds. Karl looks up to follow them and sees the cable go slack, then hears a change in pitch. The engine screams and the cable whistles as it rips unbridled through the air. He drops to the ground and rolls away, but the steel lashes his ankle.

She scoots down, tucking her knees under her and crouching at the foot of the bed to examine his toes. A thin line nearly bisects his big toe. He is cutting limbs off with a chain saw, standing on top of a felled fir. The saw vibrates up his fingers, down his wrist, up his veined forearms and around the crook in his elbow, into his chest and shoulders, while it slices limbs from the tree. He turns clockwise, patient, methodical, getting into the rhythm. Each limb seems thicker than the one before, and he catches his breath before he turns a few degrees more. He stops to wipe the sweat from under his eyes and lets himself look across the valley at the mountains and the glittering water. He sees my mother in the shadows, across the notch in the landscape. She walks into the light, dives naked from the peak into the lake and spirals down; little bubbles spring free from her mouth and float ahead of her to the surface. He thinks he can see her smiling at the purple depths and knows the water feels chilly to her teeth. He waits for her to rise to face him, standing way up on the other side of the hills on this tree. Her hair will be wet, the curls slicked down, and her body will be goosefleshed and need warming.

And then he tries to hurry. This is a mistake because for a moment he loses his rhythm, and the tip of the chain saw grabs the limb and kicks the blade forward. It slices through the steel toe of his boot, splaying it open an inch wide.

She takes this all in with the fervor and faith of a monk, and asks no questions, demands no confirmation other than the intimate peace this indisputable knowledge gives her.

She travels up his body fast, as if she were emerging from the bottom of the lake. She arches back and leads with her chest, her breasts on his skin turning to gooseflesh and making him shiver. When she reaches his head, they are both breathing shallowly. With the back of her hand, she brushes aside the yellow hair that falls over his forehead and notices a horizontal line that would pass in an older man for a wrinkle. When she has her nose almost up against it, she sees the little ridges. She thinks of a horizon with the smallest of hills.

"How'd you get this one?" she repeats her litany.

This time he merely moves his mouth with the shape of the words, "Thinking of you." And he smiles a slow smile that illuminates the space between them as if the light in the room were filtered through the rose windows of Chartres.

He's shooting pool at the Short Branch. His opponent is blurred from the beer he has downed. He's been there since twilight, balancing mugs on the rail of the table. He recalls only a skinny moustache, something light-catching around the neck, perhaps a gold chain. Karl sinks the eight ball into the side pocket and picks up the ten-dollar bill on the side of the table. The guy swears and kicks a barstool. Winning and holding this money makes Karl think of Mimi. His gaze dips behind the Coors signs to the hallway that leads to the men's room, and there she is. This time she is wearing only blue jeans; they are rolled at the bottom and stained with paint. He's color-blind and can't tell what color but thinks it's probably green. She emerges from the shadows of the hall with her hands cupped around her breasts, and he sees how small her hands are. She is wet, as if she has just come out of the lake. The maverick curls that aren't flattened to her head curve up and drip water onto the backs of her hands. She lifts her hands slightly away from the nipples, then moves them toward him, fingers parting slowly, fanning out, and his eyes follow their slow path. And the other guy charges him like a bull, and his upper teeth make their mark.

And then she searches his body helter-skelter for the tiny

wounds that build up in the flesh, from working inside: the slivers in the palm and forearm, the dust in the eye. Only when she has found every one does she look for the scars that are invisible, and ask him about his mother.

lunch

Whenever I saw Dallas, the question of when and where occupied our lips in most of the moments they weren't otherwise engaged. In school I tried to keep my distance. In some ways it was easy. His corner place in history class was frequently empty; there were no new valleys or canyons or familiar-looking mountain ranges cut into his desk. But when his large and dark presence was indisputably there, across the empty row in class, or ahead of me strutting down the hall in his tight jeans, the faded circle outline of Skoal embossed on his back pocket, or especially in the truck, I couldn't resist the pull of whatever was new and dangerous inside of me.

These stirrings got me through the year. For one thing they gave me a new sense of self-righteousness, particularly when I felt most guilty about Paris. Though every now and then something that reminded me of her—*The Princess and the Goblins,* which she had given me for my birthday; a melody on the radio that we used to sing together while we were swinging from the gymnastics bar Dyl had rigged up in her yard— would make my heart soften toward her.

But, more important, Dallas distracted me from the rising anger I felt toward Mimi. One afternoon, as I sprinted upstairs to hide in my room and mull over the newest turn my gropings with Dallas had taken, I literally ran into her.

"I have a question for you," she said. I exaggerated a sigh. "Why don't you see Paris anymore?" I tried to squeeze by her, but she stuck her arm out, making a symbolic barrier. "Dyl told me she's been crying on her bed."

"He would," I said just barely under my breath. She leaned toward me, her eyes homing in on me like a hawk's. "I'd appreciate it if you responded when I speak to you. There's virtue in politeness, you know."

"A lot you know about either one," I spat out, knocked her hand away, and sprang upstairs. After that I did my best to avoid her. This was surprisingly easy, and if I had been more cognizant of my surroundings I might have noticed that she was also avoiding me.

Every few weeks I'd see Karl's truck parked in town, and I'd find myself looking for him around every corner, knowing that Mimi might be close by. I walked around town more, peering into the shop windows and especially into the bar, searching. The idea that they could sneak up on my emotions again at any time almost as if to materialize from the air, like the sudden release of a flock of frenzied birds that picked at my eyes and ears, left me in a state of perpetual and growing tension, and my heart felt tight as a bowstring. I almost wanted to see them, even catch them in whatever act they were guilty of, just to feed the harpies that hungrily attacked from within.

When Mimi was home in the evening and asked me if I needed her to do anything for me, I'd answer, "What do you think? I'm two?" When she'd come toward me as if to hug me, I'd lunge away and run upstairs, spitting out to the air between us, "Can't you ever give me space?" After a while she stopped asking.

More and more the house would be empty, and Mimi would tell Dad in the morning that she had packed him a sandwich because she had an appointment with some art dealer in Spokane or a gallery owner in Sandpoint. She would return long after I got home from school, and when she did she would get out of the car slowly, put down her things, play music on her tape recorder (more often Heart or Tina Turner than Puccini these days) at a much lower volume than usual, and pace with a lighter step, almost the well-disciplined grace of a dancer.

One day just a few weeks before the end of school, Dallas found me between classes and pulled me over to a locker. Usually neither of us wanted this much visibility, and I kept seeing snatches of the other kids looking over their shoulders at us only marginally shielded by the locker door.

"I need to talk with you," he said. His voice had an urgency I had come to associate with the "it" question, so I was leery.

"What?"

"I'm moving."

I tried to imagine my life without him, without the smell of his leather jacket and the gas fumes, without the cold, wet taste of him, and it was amazingly easy. Then I tried to envision life without feeling the razor edge of wickedness, returning to simple differentness instead of calculated rebellion—and my heart stepped up and sounded hollow. That would be more difficult, and I felt a sorrow grip me, something new.

"So?" he was saying, and he moved his face down within an inch of my own. "When?" he whispered right at my mouth, and his gaze swept over my face like a searchlight.

Without thinking, I moved forward to kiss him, and he pulled back. I turned my back to him, got my books out of my locker, and as I walked away I called back, "Lunch," my blood pounding like the pulse of a rabbit in a trap.

As we approached the purple house, I clutched the seat. I was riddled with anxiety, more over discovering something than being discovered myself. I looked around, half expecting to see Karl's truck, but I noticed instead the color of the barely opened blooms clustered on the hawthorn tree, a purplish pink, a hue just next on the spectrum to that of the house. It struck me that Mimi more than just had an eye for color; she could see what the puzzle would look like even when all the pieces weren't yet in place. I took a deep breath and let it out slowly, so Dallas couldn't hear.

"Park your truck around the corner," I directed, trying to sound in control.

He pulled on the wheel and winked.

We entered through the mud porch. I listened at the door and again just inside, and relaxed. He put his hat on the breadboard, and I made a mental note to remember to take it off there, not to leave any evidence. He turned to me and raised his eyebrows, waiting for me to say or do something.

"Well?" I asked nervously.

"Well," he said, taking my hand and leading me into the house. "Do hippies sleep on real beds?" If he hadn't squeezed my hand I might have socked him in the stomach.

"Why are you whispering?" I asked.

"Because you are."

I led him up the stairs, and I was certain that in the quiet he could hear my heart thump. I dug my nails into his palm.

We were nearly at the top of the staircase when we heard the music. I froze. "Cool it. Just a car. From the road," Dallas said, but his voice was low. He took a step ahead and turned his ear to the back of the upper floor. I calmed down a little. It probably was just a passing car with its radio blaring. It was, after all, a sound that would often rise into the upstairs rooms, and I waited for it to pass by. But when I had waited long enough for fifty cars to pass, the music was still there, the pitch and volume the same, and my heart dropped to my belly. I was about to turn and flee, imagining Mimi and her young logger doing unimaginable things on the paint-splashed floor of her studio. But Dallas put his finger to his lips, and when I tried to pull his arm toward the staircase, he shook his head and resisted. The music sounded like wind chimes, beautiful notes but tuneless and relentless, on instruments I didn't recognize. The pungent scent of incense was already clinging to our clothes. And then reality lifted its velvet curtain, and I followed Dallas and the sounds and smells beyond it, as if in a trance. We tiptoed past the studio. Its door was ajar, and a shaft of sunlight entered the hall through it. Dallas peeked in and motioned me forward, and when I walked in, I saw it was empty. Then I heard a sound that I associated with summer, the small splashes of the lake when I am immersed in it and no one is looking and I am playing in it as if it were my only friend. And I felt like I was floating toward its mesmerizing and strangely familiar sound, the lapping water, down to the end of the hall. The bathroom door was open only an inch or two, but even several feet away I could tell the shades had been drawn, and in the dark space between the edge of the door and the molding in the hall, I saw the flicker of candlelight. The music was muffled by the rushing fall of water into itself.

Dallas let go of my hand and motioned me to follow him back downstairs, back to safety and security, though I knew these places no longer existed, or if they did, they were closing rapidly around me. As he walked away, I stepped closer, close enough to look. Framed in the opening of the door no bigger than my hand I saw Mimi's bony back and curly head upright in the deep old tub, one arm draped over its curled edge, the fingers dangling, and all the colored candles in small glass jars around the periphery of the lion's feet claws. Mimi's tape recorder was on the floor in the corner. Her other hand was raised to squeeze a sponge at the nape of the wide neck in front of her, the water from the sponge flowing down the broad back like a sheet of liquid glass. Something, I remember thinking, about the hair seems out of place. And then they laughed, and a deep voice said, "I'll be right back," and I turned and ran down the hall, waiting at the top of the stairs, trying to force my breathing into silence.

The music changed, the volume increased, and the blaring of the Shirelles followed us down the stairs and out the door, with the ooohs of "Will You Still Love Me Tomorrow?"

We said nothing on the way back. And it wasn't until we were almost at the school building that I let myself remember that voice so as to hear it again. It sounded so familiar that I thought I might have fabricated it myself, in my fantasies, but it crept into my reality layer by layer like water through porous rock, and down to the level where I knew it was the voice of no logger. It had resounded like the cascading of great rivers, and I heard it the rest of the day and all the hours of the night and in some ways the rest of my life. And I knew that the hair was not blond at all, but straight and black, black as the bark of the honey locusts after a rainstorm.

the opening

For the next few weeks I avoided Dallas. Even the thought of articulating what we had seen made my heart flutter erratically. And an amorphous guilt, more poignant than any tryst would have produced, left me feeling listless. It didn't take me long to realize he was avoiding me, too; it was something tacit between us. From the window on the last day of school I watched him pull out of the parking lot, and as his truck screeched away I thought I saw him nod in my direction. It didn't occur to me until I returned to Wilders Ferry for the last time that in all the days we spent together he never spoke my name. Life without him left me with an emptiness, and I spent the summer feeling like a ghost, pretending I was invisible as I rushed past Mimi and Graceanne to pass the afternoon in my room. Occasionally I thought about walking past the Satellite with the vague hope that Jillian or even Paris would spot me and invite me in, but mostly I remained behind my closed doors.

One August evening I walked downstairs as *La Traviata* vibrated through the house. Violetta was taking her usual sweet time to die, and I found myself at the window, telling myself that I wasn't waiting for Mimi. The sky was already streaked with carmine and violet, and I could picture Dad checking his watch. When Mimi stayed away all day, Dad had taken to filling the house with her music; when she was with us, he would turn down the volume. I wanted to get on with the evening, lie on my bed and sort out my life.

As soon as I saw the headlights of the VW, I ducked down, not willing to give her the satisfaction of seeing me wait, or of interpreting my behavior as eager for her company.

Mimi entered the house and threw her backpack across the room with a dramatic flourish. "I did it!" she exclaimed. "I did it!"

I glared at her, covering my fear of any confession, no matter how tempered with hyperbole or fantasy.

"Oh, Lake. You're going to be so proud of your mama." Dad came into the room. He moved his hand as if to rest it on her shoulder, and then lowered it to his side. "I have a show. In Sandpoint. All me. All my work. This fall. I mean, wow, I thought it would never happen. And the owner has connections in the East, and hinted that maybe, just maybe, we could go on to New York." She hugged herself and twirled around.

My most pervasive feeling was surprise: not only had I never heard her sound excited about New York, but I had never entertained the question of her genuine talent. I didn't know what to say.

"This is going to be the second-happiest night of my life," she said and reached toward me, but I ducked out of range, busied myself with setting the table, and kept myself from asking her about the first.

"We'll welcome you home with roses," Dad said, and she smiled, a dreamy smile. Then she seemed to stare through the walls of the house at something we couldn't see and, I was convinced, didn't want to.

For a while the distractions of Mimi's show seemed to lift some of the weights we carried so separately. And in some ways it did feel like old times. While Dyl was sequestered with Mimi in her studio, helping her frame and mat, Jillian and Paris joined Dad and me in the kitchen. Once in a while I caught Paris staring at me and then jerking her head away, and I detected more than a little coolness in Jillian's voice, but as we busied ourselves with baking for the reception, we all seemed to relax. I watched as Jillian cut sheet after sheet of cookies into crescent moons and taught Paris how to shape bite-size cream cheese crusts for miniature pecan pies. Soon the freezer that had held homemade jam and ricotta cheese containers of huckleberries was stuffed with the sort of precious-looking little edible things that might not have looked entirely out of place at Wedding Number One.

Every few days Mimi trekked to Sandpoint to check on lighting and hanging arrangements, to measure and paint the walls. Much to my dismay, Dyl and Dad made plans to haul the larger-than-life paintings to the show in the painted school bus. She had 174 cards printed with a photo of one of the paintings, and she hand-lettered on the back of each an invitation to the opening. I recognized only a few of the names and wondered if she had found some in the phone book. A card to my grandparents was not among those I saw. Aunt DeeDee, the first and only to respond, sent her regrets rather formally, on a powder-blue note card. She was sorry, she said, but I. Magnin, where she had just been hired as a "scent specialist," was sending her to a training session that weekend at Big Sur. Mimi sniffed when she read it.

One evening my father was grating zucchini for bread, and as Mimi breezed in on her way upstairs, he said, "Why don't you get Graceanne to do some of this? Is she so busy gossiping all day she can't lend a hand?" I felt the tension hover around us. No one had mentioned her name in days, and had I let myself think about it, I would have noticed just how strange her absence had been.

Mimi's face clouded over. "I told her we could do it ourselves," she said, and walked out of the room and up the stairs, taking them one at a time.

Mimi seemed increasingly antsy. She tensed when she heard a knock at the door, even though it was almost always Dyl or Jillian on some opening-centered errand. And as soon as she walked into the house after one of her trips to Sandpoint, she would say, even before she put down her backpack, "Did anyone call?" When I would shake my head, she'd glance out the nearest window, and it was difficult to read her expression. But I sensed an intrusive presence, a ghostlike shadow.

The Saturday of the opening, I awoke before dawn to the sound of my parents bickering. I spent the rest of the long day wandering around the lake, a book unopened in my hand, imagining myself as a central figure, the critic for the *Spokesman Review* or even the *New York Times,* or the real star of a real show, in a real opening, one in a city. I'd pull up in a white stretch limo at a glass-and-steel building that shot the sunset back into the faces of the masses on the street. The chauffeur would offer his arm to help me out, and while I was smiling generously at the crowd gathered at the door, in ermine coats and black ties, he would reach in for Aunt DeeDee, and our handsome escorts would appear from one place or another.

By the time I came home my parents were already getting dressed. I was afraid they would be annoyed that I had disappeared, but they hardly seemed to have noticed my absence. As I passed their bedroom door, Dad waved to me in a distracted sort of way. He was wearing an unbuttoned, pleated white shirt, a tux jacket with tails, and boxer shorts. He said, "I think we'll need both cars, don't you? Is Graceanne coming with us?"

From the other side of the room, Mimi said, "Yes, two cars. Dyl's already putting gas in his." There was a silence.

"So? What about Graceanne?"

Mimi shrugged. Then she walked into the closet and as far as I could tell just stood there. Her words were muffled. "She may not be able to make it. She'll see it on her own time. You know how she is."

I watched them from the half-open door, watched them fiddle with things in the room and put them down, listened to them not talk. After a while Dad said, "Why not?" His voice had an undercurrent of anger, a tone that surprised me. I had expected he would be relieved when he figured out Graceanne would probably not show.

"I don't know everything about her, you know." Her words had an edge, but a weariness, too. "If she can't come, she can't come. She'll see the show another time. No big deal. Anyway, I'll understand. That's what friends are for."

He clipped on his bow tie and straightened it in the mirror as she stood behind him and studied his reflection.

"Maybe I should rip up the cummerbund and make a silk bandanna to match my duds."

I expected Mimi to laugh, at least to smile, but she was absorbed in looking at his hair; her gaze was almost critical, as if she were seeing the length and shape of it for the first time.

I went to my room to get dressed. She came in a few minutes later, in the black leotard and tights she'd had since (according to Aunt DeeDee) GranPearl used to take her to weekly ballet lessons in junior high school and an orange-and-red long-fringed scarf, which I recognized as Jillian's, wrapped around her waist like a skirt. From each earlobe dropped a silver bell-shaped flower, also Jillian's. She asked if she could borrow some beads strung on leather and made from Idaho polished rocks, which she had given me for a birthday present and which I had never worn. Dad followed her and laid them over her head and around her neck ceremoniously. When she sat on my bed to put on her sandals, I said, "Don't. Just this once." She began to raise her hand in protest, but then went to her closet and, after kneeling in it for a while, emerged with a pair of black ballet shoes, worn at the toe, and slipped them on.

Dad walked into the room and glanced at them. "Nice touch," he said, approvingly. I sighed, as audibly as I could.

Dyl and Mimi went ahead in the VW. Paris and I rode with Dad and Jillian, who sang all the way there. Jillian's lilting soprano carried my father's tuneless stabs at music, and they made a strange, almost pleasant harmony. Paris inched away from me so she wouldn't have to touch me, and I just looked out the window at the yellow triangles of tamarack that dotted the forests all the way to Sandpoint.

The Art Star Gallery was wedged between a bar and a stationery store, the kind that sells lots of candy bars and greeting cards of children with horizontal oval eyes, and Idaho souvenirs—candles in the shape of potatoes, inlaid wooden boxes with sliding tops, and T-shirts printed with IDAHO IS WHAT AMERICA WAS. There was so much schlock in that display that it detracted from the window in the building next to it, which was empty except for a small square sign resting on a plate stand with MIRIAM ROSE, ONE WOMAN'S VISION in Jillian's blood-red calligraphy.

As we entered, a glass bell on the door tinkled.

Dyl was already unpacking his dulcimer. He sat down on a folding chair and tuned up. Mimi had asked Jillian to play the flute, but she had declined. Dyl looked funny in his rented tux, especially with his felt hat, which the gallery owner, I heard later, had tried to take for him at the door. But he seemed oddly in his element. Looking back on it, I understand my surprise at how comfortable the adults in my Wilders Ferry life were in this setting, fitting into this mode of public receiving and entertaining; they had all been born to it. While I . . . I had merely been born to them. A being once removed.

The room was unadorned except for a table of all the food we had been preparing and bottles of champagne lined up next to stacks of plastic cups, and Mimi's paintings. Against the stark white background and in the paling daylight, they looked riotous with color. They raved and flailed out from the walls and screamed for attention. The saturated primary colors grabbed my eyes and sent my breath shooting up my chest. Mimi whirled around the room, opening her arms as if to embrace each canvas. "What do you think?" she said to no one of us in particular.

"See," Dad said, putting the centerpiece, which was already looking wilted, on a chair. "No reason to be nervous. This is great."

Mimi stopped her dancing and said, "I wonder if anyone will come."

But come they did, many more than I had imagined. And they all looked more like my parents than anyone else I had ever seen. Earrings dangled, and Birkenstocks scuffled. Even the two or three men in ties wore them with jeans and unironed shirts. The bell tinkled perhaps a hundred times that evening, and each time it did, Mimi glanced at the door. When the bell wasn't sounding, her laugh was loud and ubiquitous. Her cheeks were flushed from both the champagne and the attention. She accompanied groups of people to a corner of a painting and sucked in every word while they praised and analyzed, or asked questions as if expecting her to respond as a learned professor. A couple of times guests came up to me and remarked, "You must be proud of your mama," and I said something marginally polite in response.

But I had to admit, she looked almost beautiful. Her skin had a luster, and she swept about the room as if she were imbued with a power from within. She was incandescent with it. Mimi was immersed in people and had just reached for her third or fourth glass of champagne when I saw Graceanne pull up and park, then peer through the window at the crowd. Her body, backlit by the streetlamp, looked like an apparition through the plate glass. As I waited for the sound of the bell, the fast-moving form of a dancer's body making its way toward the door jostled my elbow.

"Mimi, wait!" someone called, and the body stopped. I watched Mimi stand sideways to the person, lead away from him with her shoulder, steal glances at the window, and finally pull away, take a few steps, and stand still at the window, her back to the mass of her guests. Graceanne was gone. Mimi's shoulders let down, a slump that curved toward the floor. The rest of the evening Mimi moved more slowly, with a heavier step, her smile in and out like the September sun. Several times she asked the gallery owner what time it was.

As if sensitive to the lassitude in her rhythms, the guests began to depart in a steady stream, and only a handful of well-wishers remained when the bell sounded one more time.

At the threshold Graceanne paused; she seemed to take up most of the space. She took a few steps into the gallery and stopped to straighten her skirt, smooth it over her kneecaps. Then she signed the guest book, taking her time with it and pressing down hard with the pen, almost as if she were imprinting her name and the full details of her residence through layers of paper.

She walked toward the center of the room as if she didn't notice what was around her. This deliberate not-noticing made the blood rise to my face in anticipation of the moment when she would take it in. Her hand rose to fasten the button at the top of the neck, as if a reflex action to shield herself from the eyes of strangers, who were searching for their coats and setting down their plastic cups and napkins.

She looked up and faced the enormous canvases on all the walls around her. She turned four times, square to each wall, one by one. And then she turned again, and again, a circumscribed version of Mimi's dance around the periphery of the room. It must have been like entering the funhouse in the room of mirrors, seeing herself outsized and distorted on every wall. Then, she staggered. For a moment I thought she had been struck, paralyzed with the sense that she was so exposed, so literally taken over by these flaming-color translations of Mimi's inner images—images that connected her to Mimi more intimately and permanently than any other evidence ever would.

She put her hand into the pocket of her skirt, and I realized she was hiding from sight the snake ring with the garnet eye, the single exposed feature that would be indisputably recognizable.

Mimi ran toward Graceanne and threw her arms around her. Graceanne held still as a statue, and Mimi said, "Where've you been?" Her pitch was a little too high.

Graceanne shrugged and pulled away.

"C'mon. This is your night, too."

Graceanne just stared at Mimi; she looked like a shadow over her.

"Like hell it is," she said, almost a hiss. And it was as if the curtains had been drawn back on a stage, the house lights dimmed. The remaining guests all seemed to turn in unison toward the two women. I held my breath.

Mimi giggled and put her arm up to Graceanne's neck as if to guide that neck and that face down to her so she could talk more privately; for a moment they looked like ballroom dancers. But Graceanne stiffened her shoulders and didn't budge. The red in Mimi's cheeks changed shades; the color spread down, nearly to her collarbone.

"Shall we get some air?" Mimi's voice was breathy, strained, and as she lowered her tone, the room hushed completely. I wanted to make noise—shout, scream, dash the empty bottles to the floor, anything to mask her panic. I looked around desperately for the musicians, but I was frozen in place. So, it seemed, was everyone else. Then Dyl took a step toward Mimi and Graceanne, but Jillian held fast to his wrist.

"I wanna know why you did this to me."

"Graceanne. Please." I caught the strain in her voice, coming from deep in her throat, and thought I saw her look at me, pleading, but I angled away and pretended to be absorbed in Paris, who had fallen asleep in the corner, blanketed in Jillian's shawl, as if she were years younger than an eighth grader.

"What's the matter with you? You deaf? They're all looking at me. They're talking about my body. *Mine.* Not yours or anybody else's." Graceanne's clenched fist made her skirt pocket bulge. "You never told me it would be like this."

"Graceanne." As if disembodied, Mimi's hands rose to her face, and she stared at her own fingers, stiff and quaking before her eyes. "I'm sorry," she whispered.

Graceanne walked around her, moving slowly, like an underwater swimmer, like a lioness toward certain prey, toward the canvas on the far wall, the painting of a woman with skin the colors of flame, a woman lounging on a couch and eating chocolates from her lap, and in the same fluid motion Graceanne hurled her drink at the canvas, splashing her likeness in the center of the belly. I couldn't help thinking of that water falling like the sheet of liquid glass down her back in the lion claw tub. No one looked more astonished than Graceanne herself, and she covered her mouth with her hand and walked out of the room proudly, her neck still unbending.

Dyl wrenched free from Jillian's grasp, grabbed Mimi's elbow, escorted her into the back room, and shut the door. The rest of the guests muttered their good-byes and left in a mass that filled the doorway.

Jillian said, "It's time to go, girls" and herded Paris, who was oblivious and rubbing her eyes, and me out the door. I was still too stunned to protest. The last image I recall of the Art Star Gallery is my father squatting by the far wall on his knees and blotting with paper towels the champagne, which made Graceanne's red thigh shine like fresh blood.

place of comfort

We said nothing on the way home. Jillian didn't even play her tape deck. Paris slept in a cocoon of her mother's shawl, and I have always imagined that Jillian later carried her into their house that way, undisturbed. As we drove by the kiln from the mill, it spat out orange smoke, and flame illuminated the sky. When we pulled up to the purple house, Jillian offered to wait until my parents got home. For a moment I was tempted by politeness. I looked at her face, but her eyes were fixed on the uncurtained window behind me. So I said, "No." I couldn't stand the awkwardness, but also a peculiar coldness fanned through me; it seemed clear to me that my parents would never come home, and if that was the case, then there was no reason I had to contend with Jillian's emotions as well as my own.

She walked me to the door, leaving the motor on and Paris sleeping. "I'm sure your father will be here before long. Call me if he doesn't get home in half an hour." I nodded.

There was something extraordinary about the tenor of her voice, as if the night for her had brought out something else, different from what it brought for the rest of us. Perhaps it was the surreal quality of the evening, or my own drowsiness, or my unshaped fear of what would happen next, but just before she turned to go, as we stood on the porch in the purply dark in front of the purply dark house, dark on dark, I had a vision: the delicate threads she used to sew and weave and embroider, arrange and rearrange with meticulous care; the thousands of strands she had chosen, glided her finger along, held between her lips, ordered into design, into service and beauty. Something in her voice made me see all these threads, see her as if she were wielding scissors (sharpened enough to slit your skin if you just skittered them lightly along the sensitive tip of your thumb), and so heavy that it took both hands and every muscle in her forearms straining to sever all the strands. The voice was the snipping of threads—relentless, inexorable. In the days that followed, as much as I was obsessed with the problems behind my own doors, the problems with Mimi and Graceanne, and Dad and Dyl, the clip of the scissors echoed in my head.

When I turned on the front room lights, Georgia scurried about in her dollhouse, throwing out paper shavings and carrot parings onto the floor. Ignoring her, I ran up the stairs. I sat on the floor of my room, looking out into the midnight sky, devoid of cloud-light, stars, or moon, just thick and viscous. My elliptical window and the universe beyond might as well have been a black hole; I felt that dislodged from all I had come to depend on. I dozed a while, the fall chill creeping up at me from the floorboards, and my eyelids fluttered open to a blanket being tucked around my shoulders.

I don't know how much time passed before I opened my eyes again; the oval had turned gray, either the promising gray of early light or the lifeless gray of rain. And as I listened for the sounds—the swallows or the raindrops—to see if I should be getting up, I heard something else. Almost a siren. A wail, the voice not quite a man's, not quite a woman's, not even quite human. And then weeping, but muted, as if it were reaching my room through gauzy layers.

I tiptoed down the hall, leaned down to put my ear to the heat vent, and followed the sound downstairs. I walked slowly, trying to avoid the creaking places on the steps, and as I descended, the noise became louder, but not clearer. At the living room door I stopped. Nothing there. Georgia was still asleep in her dining room. I shivered. No one had bothered to light the woodstove, perhaps because Mimi always had faith, no matter how unfounded, that the elusive sun would warm the house by afternoon.

I walked through the living room and pressed my ear to the cold wall that separated it from the kitchen. Sobbing—huge, uncontrollable sobs. I felt my heart swell for a few moments, witnessing her raw suffering, and I was on the verge of running into her arms and sitting on her small lap and holding her, or letting her hold me.

I took a step onto the threshold of the kitchen, and then I saw Mimi and Dyl, sitting next to each other by the unlit woodstove, holding each other, rocking back and forth slightly, as if the movement would lessen the pain. The gulping sobs rose from somewhere between their bodies. And I knew this invisible place between them was the essence of comfort, terrain that to me was pristine and intimidating, a place I had never been.

On the way back to my room, I crossed to my parents' room. The door was ajar, and I peeked in. My father was sleeping on his side, near the edge of the bed and facing the wall, his hand cradling his face and his narrow feet sticking out of the sheets. The other side of the bed was unwrinkled, and on top of the pillow, still waiting for my mother to claim it, was the rose in tissue paper that he had bought her to welcome her home from the second-happiest night of her life.

I walked slowly down the hall, the two scenes I had just witnessed already grafted onto my psyche—Mimi and Dyl, my father alone—and wondered if they didn't fit together, jigsawed into being for some reason. It has taken me years to see the simplicity in this—Dyl was, after all, her oldest friend. But then, the question that would ride the cells in my veins long after I had dismissed it whispered itself into my inner ear and made me grip the banister to steady myself on the stairs: what's wrong with this picture?

Back in my room, I enveloped myself in the blanket one of them had brought me and looked out the open mouth of my window. Outside, the dawn and the rain were both colorless.

vigil

The next day, Sunday, I slept late, awoke to a quiet house, dressed slowly, stayed in my room for most of the afternoon. Nothing happened, yet the tension in the house made me think that the air had been siphoned out of it, that it was sealed off, if only ephemerally, from the chaos beyond its walls. Everything was happening outside it, and as soon as I left it would explode off the planet, the topography itself broken into bits and floating in the air as in that scene in *The Wizard of Oz* where the Wicked Witch of the West is pedaling furiously and houses and barns and uprooted trees are streaming by.

My parents left notes: "At Left Bank" and "Out for a walk." Mimi's paint box and sketchbook stood at the back door, as if she had thought of taking them and at the last minute changed her mind. I made myself a sandwich. The bread was stale and my slices uneven; the no-preservative peanut butter stuck to my mouth.

Dad called midafternoon. "Any word from your mother?"

"Just a note."

"Tell her to call me as soon as she comes home."

But he arrived home before she did. For about an hour he read the paper and interrupted my own blank thoughts to read me particularly entertaining front-page headlines: "Ladies Gather for Meeting," "Thornycroft Trip to Palm Springs Above Par," "Vandals Take Move Signs." And on the back page: "Reagan Asks Increased Military Aid to El Salvador." Each headline fell into the air and stayed there; neither of us reacted. Then he put the paper into the recycle pile on the mud porch and paced, peering out each window one at a time, clockwise around the house. His sock-covered footsteps padded above me as he walked from window to window upstairs, too. When the shadows lengthened, he called Jillian and Dyl's, and let the phone ring for all the time it took to slice the leftover baked potatoes into strips for frying. We scrambled some eggs in the same skillet and ate them sitting on the floor in the living room by the bay, trying to convince ourselves that we were engrossed in a picnic and not a vigil.

Every time the floor creaked or the house made the sort of noises old houses make, of which nobody even tries to guess the source, I found myself half expecting Graceanne. Possibly I may have expected Mimi to be only a footstep or two behind. But I wanted Graceanne to come in, to reenter our house, and our lives, to help herself to our food and our space and talk to us in her gravelly voice, to break the spell that was sucking the air from the rooms, to dispel the sense of complicity that, even without Mimi, would surely smother us. We were drowning; this much I knew.

Dad and I spent the rest of the long evening curled close, side by side at the base of the woodstove, his arm around my shoulders. I let him do this because I felt sorry for him, but there was a comfort in it, too. We both knew that some arbitrary combination of events had brought a dangerous realignment to the order of our lives.

Suddenly he stood up and walked upstairs. He returned with what appeared to be an oversized greeting card painted thickly with a swirly design. "She did every one herself," he said.

"Did what?"

"Designed them. Painted them. With a spinner she and Dyl rigged up from an old phonograph. She'd seen it at Expo '64 in New York City, the year she went to Vassar." I could see the photo Mimi kept under her black nylons. I took the card from his hand and opened it. Hand-penned in brown ink were the words "Come celebrate the wind and the earth and the land and the lake, and our love, which like them, will last and last. Miriam and Kirk." I suppressed a laugh.

"I wanted to add a quote or two from e. e. cummings, but Mimi had had enough of famous poets from college, so . . . well, we didn't."

I smiled. He took back the invitation and looked at it as he continued. "We—all of us, not just Mimi and Dyl—had to scramble around for places to dry them. They were all over the place. Even on the mattress we slept on on the floor"—here he paused for a smile at happier times— "and on the flat tops of the front yard junipers. Cutting those junipers always made me think of the flattop haircuts my father insisted I get until the year I left for college."

"Go on." It seemed to be getting increasingly difficult to keep my father focused; yet it soothed me somehow, listening to him talk in this nostalgic vein.

"Only a handful of people came, of course. Dyl and Jillian were the attendants. The officiator was a man called Whale, looked a bit like Friar Tuck. No one seemed to know his last name—or maybe *that* was his last name. His father was an itinerant minister in Missouri around the turn of the century, a second cousin once removed from Jesse James, and I suppose that connection made it romantic. At least for Mimi. He was the only one who wore shoes. We blasted the music from a Sony on eight-track tapes, 'The Age of Aquarius' to walk in, 'Sergeant Pepper's Lonely Hearts Club Band' for the recessional, which is what Jillian kept calling it." His tone seemed to get more removed at the sound of her name. "Dyl rented a motorcycle for us, for afterwards. Boy, did that baby ever spew out pinecones."

His voice trailed off, and he seemed suddenly lost in his oddly Mimi-like reverie. Then he said, "I remember Mimi's hair most of all. It was wavy and bouncy—all the way to her waist— and she had a daisy behind her ear. I don't remember how it got there." I searched his face. It occurred to me that I knew how it got there, could almost see Dyl plucking it, carrying it toward her head, touching his palm to her face, brushing away a strand of hair in the process.

When we finally saw her walking up the driveway, the sky was a bruised blue; there would be no stars. She moved with small steps, pausing, hugging herself with her arms, or shivering against the chilly breeze, I don't know which.

She was still yards from the house when Dad walked to the door and opened it for her. The storm door glass fogged up from the stove heat inside, and we watched her slow approach as if through a fog.

"Where were you all this time?"

She headed straight to the kitchen, filled the teakettle and put it on the stove. We followed her like a couple of bloodhounds. "Are you going to answer my question?" It was the first hint of anger I had ever heard from his voice; it had a crude edge, like a penknife against steel.

She waved her hand as if to dismiss him for the moment while she contemplated the ceramic canister she kept tea in. He grabbed it from her hand and knocked it off the counter. It broke into fragments on the floor. I gripped the molding around the threshold and listened to myself breathe. She stepped over the chips and shards as if walking over a minefield and turned off the stove. "I've been with Dyl," she said.

"Dyl?" He looked surprised. On his face relief flashed for a split second, and I wondered if all this time his greatest fear was that she had followed Graceanne to some unreachable remove on the other side of the universe. But once that fear was gone, another, more poisonous one immediately took its place. It was the closest to naked jealousy I had seen in our house.

"I called his place. No answer," he said. She didn't respond. "Unless, of course, you took the phone off the hook."

She glanced at me, and he said, "Lake, why don't you go into the other room?"

"Are you asking me or telling me? If you're asking, then I don't want to."

"Lake—" he started, his pitch rising dangerously.

But Mimi interrupted, her voice hollow and tired. "Jillian's gone."

Dad froze, then moved toward the broom closet as if he were walking through water, got out the dustpan, and bent to sweep up the jagged fragments, some of which had skittered over the slick tiles around the woodstove.

She put her hand on his arm. "Don't," she said. "They're how I feel."

white wine and yellow roses

know now that illusion can do wondrous things. When I saw Mimi and Dyl in each other's arms, my thoughts were far from Jillian. Now, every time I see them, I see her too, like a cloud streaking over their image. And sometimes in that vaporous superimposition, I understand them, the way she must have seen them—revolutionary, adulterous. I believe there was no sex between them, just the same fires that compelled them to fight in the sixties for what they knew was right, and that they carried with them when they fled, separately, to Idaho. Running from the backfires of the revolution, the sputtering of the counterculture, the ascending ash heap of the Movement, no phoenix rising above it. Content to hold each other. Something impenetrable, a fortress against suffering and impotence. What I had seen was Dyl comforting his closest friend. That was all I knew how to see. Did Jillian, the one among us untouched by revolution, possibly untouched at all, see in her husband and his friend, in that embrace, a place beyond sexuality that she knew she could never enter?

Her Grandmother Skinner wanted her to study music at the Sorbonne. She gave her the open-holed flute in the velvet-lined box after tea one Sunday afternoon. On Sundays a maid in a scalloped apron served them with the silver tea service and the fluted bud vase with a yellow rosebud. Grandmother Skinner wore cologne that smelled like violets and had her yellow-gray hair tinted the color of steel. After Jillian came to live on Park Avenue with Grandmother Skinner, she would drift through the house, through labyrinths of china and alligator cases of flatware with all the serving pieces initialed in a convoluted script, and drawers of linens— table linens and pillow slips and dust ruffles, all lace, hand-crocheted in France. Grandmother Skinner would open glass cases with gold keys she kept inside her white glove, show her rows of figurines with painted faces, all musicians. At the end of the row was the elegant little flautist, looking somehow more fragile and more costly than the oboist or the French-horn player or even the pianist delicately seated at the shiny grand. Grandmother Skinner would stroke her thinning hair with her forefinger and say, "I had these hand-painted, and this one is from a photograph I gave the artist . . ." and then stroke Jillian's head with the same cold finger gloved in white. She sent her to college with eleven pairs of white gloves, all slightly different, some with lace around the wrist, one with a red velvet ribbon threaded through. When she wasn't accepted to the Sorbonne, the old lady wept.

Jillian met Dylan in Washington Square. She'd driven into the city with a few other Sarah Lawrence girls, but she hung back to watch. People threaded their hair with feathers, draped love beads around their necks. Some had slashes of war paint under their eyes. Shirts were open to the navel. Dylan wore a felt hat and came up to her eyebrows. He carried a ukulele on a string around his neck like an amulet. The sweet smell of marijuana clung to her hair, and she lifted the end and swept it under her nose. He saw her doing this, and she let him watch.

The first time they slept together, she sprayed herself with powder scented with lilies of the valley. He'd come right up from the rally and said, "I have to take a shower," and she said, "I've never seen anyone sweat as much as you," and he said, "A girl like you shouldn't have to," and stopped right there, though she could smell his strong male smell and his beard was rough on her cheek.

That night he ran his hand down her full-length slip. It was real silk, and the touch of it was more than he could take; her skin was just an extension. These hands that had held boards with placards and clay grenades and bloody sheep skulls. Her breasts strained against the ivory sheen on the material, and still he hesitated.

"Dylan," she said. His shoulders stiffened. Then he turned his head, and she saw the tear streaks and walked over quietly, so as not to intrude, to take his hat from his fist and hold his hand.

"I love you so much!" he cried. "I can't stand this world." And he had her then; she had never before seen a man cry, and she thought he was crying for her.

Dylan had seen pictures of Idaho in a magazine at the Strand. He'd said it would be the perfect place for a commune. He wrote letters to friends from the Movement, but the only response he got was from Miriam. They'd met in Washington, D.C., at the march on the Pentagon, and she held his draft card by the corner as he set it aflame. Afterward, in the shadow of the Lincoln Memorial, they shared breakfast—saltines and an Almond Joy.

Jillian and Dylan drove into Idaho in a wet chill, legs cramped over duffel bags and her grandmother's flatware. The early June snow was slushy on Lookout Pass, and they spent their first night just beyond the Montana border, at the Stardust Motel in Wallace, where the time changed from Mountain to Pacific.

Miriam and her boyfriend, Kirk, had told them they'd join them by the end of a fortnight, but Miriam's parents persuaded her—when her father came on the phone, he had tears in his voice—to stop living together out of wedlock (that's the phrase they used) and have a wedding, in St. Louis in the fall. When Robert Kennedy was shot, they made plans to join the Mobilization Committee in Chicago for the Democratic Convention. After that, they felt beaten down by it all—the barbed wire around the site, the clubbings and clouds of tear gas, the Jeeps and tanks in the streets, the police in Lincoln Park yelling, "Kill, kill, kill!" By the time they got to Idaho, Miriam and Kirk had changed their minds about living with Jillian and Dyl in the commune, and it soured them all a bit.

One day, at the end of their first Idaho winter, Jillian, walking home from town, spotted Dylan and Miriam in front of her house. Miriam was wearing ballet tights. She'd cut a hole in the front just under the elastic for her belly, and she'd lifted up the T-shirt—it was white, one of Kirk's—and Dylan was rubbing the swelling in circles with his open hand. Jillian wasn't close enough to see if her eyes were closed. Miriam stayed still, holding the shirt out of his way.

They made Paris on May 8, the night I was born. My parents hired a midwife, but Dylan really delivered me. "C'mon, Baby," he kept saying over and over. "C'mon, Baby." Jillian averted her gaze when the baby squiggled out. Dyl cut the cord, and Kirk took the baby, her flattened nose swollen and the gray foamy stuff splotching her skin. Miriam looked like an animal, her thighs trembling, her teeth bared like a mare on the last lap toward the ribbon, sweat glistening on her upper lip and in crescents under her eyes; grunts came from her mouth. At Dylan's tears, Jillian turned away.

They got home just before dawn. It was light enough so that they didn't have to turn on the lights, and as soon as they walked in he whirled her around and kissed her. She let go of her shawl, and it rippled to the braided rug. The night was cool, and so was the taste of him. Dylan took off her clothes in the gray light, and she watched his ribs expand and contract while he barely looked at her.

She knew the Satellite Health store wouldn't allow them to make a living. That must have been part of its appeal, the fact that not many people would go there; it was quiet and dark. She liked the unfinished floors and the boxes of herbal teas, the barrels of grains—barley flakes and bulgur wheat, and brown rice, and the wild rice Dylan bought in St. Maries.

After the Weathermen he'd lived with were bombed in the Village, the dreams started. The body parts floating among bits of debris. Dylan would wake up in a sweat. It was unpredictable, no pattern. She stopped sleeping; she got in the habit of lying awake waiting to be called by Dylan or Paris. That way she didn't dream either. When she'd wake up for Paris, her daughter would quiet as soon as Jillian started toward her in the dark. The baby knew the smell, and it made her anticipate the touch of her mother's breast to her cheek.

When Jillian gave birth to Paris, she wanted her out as she had wanted nothing else, wanted the other life forever extracted and her body to be her own again. But afterward, in her room alone, she had the sense that there had been something stolen from her.

Paris taught herself to read. Her first word was "sweet." When she smelled the white lilacs at the back of the house and when she touched the back of Jillian's hand, she pronounced it "swee." And she was musical; she hummed in the cradle, tunes of her own imagining, reverberating, set free from the double helixes of her genetic matter. Later, she liked to brush Jillian's hair with her silver brush, the initials engraved, an oval mirror to match. When she was older she brushed Jillian's hair two hundred times each night, counting out loud. Then her chubby hands would lift the burnished hairs one by one from her mother's shoulders.

Sometimes with Miriam and her toddler, in the mornings, they'd drive around the lake to the woods. But Jillian liked it best when she and Paris were alone. She'd put her triangle next to Paris on the seat; her flute in the diaper bag. Jillian played her flute, the notes coming from invisible places inside her, and she danced into them and out again, while Paris's small eyes followed her. When Jillian paused, Paris would make little noises, to tell her she wanted more.

The men at the mill or in town would watch them walk by; she could feel their eyes like lasers at her back. But with Paris swathed in her white crocheted bunting, or riding in the wicker buggy that her father and his new wife had sent from London, the men could see a Jillian that no longer existed. They couldn't see that she felt marred, that a line like a scar bisected her belly, that she was dry and tight inside, and her thighs seemed permanently opened and stiff. Dylan wanted more children, but she said no. She thought of many excuses, but she knew that she could never love anyone else as much as this.

When she and Dylan began to argue, he always apologized, looking like one of her uncle's hunting dogs after a day of too much work. And it was then she knew she had begun to love Paris too much, taking her into her bed, waiting for him to leave in the morning so they could be alone with the sun in the bay with that Idaho light that bounced off the white, white snows in the dirtless air.

The night before she met the man she called Robin, the moon took on the color of the grain, and she knew something was in the air. He was the first and only customer the next day. He wore new wool slacks, a clean white shirt, a leather belt with a hammered copper buckle. He was in no hurry, never said anything, just looked around, picking up things and holding them, as if he were looking for something to do. He walked over to her with a bar of patchouli oil soap in his palm, put it on the counter while he looked right into her face, and smiled. He didn't talk at all, just laid the money in her hand, not on the counter. He wore a ring with a star sapphire; she remembered how she'd met a boy at a cotillion, and how the sapphire in his ring had caught the candlelight when he served her punch, pink punch, "Pink to match your dress," he'd said, and that was all he'd said to her the entire evening. He was the son of a friend of her mother's, and after that when his mother would visit, Jillian would walk into the music room and close the door, but he would stay there, on the other side, and listen. She could see his shadow under the crack in the door. He wore white buck shoes, and his name was Robin. She named the customer after him.

This man returned a month later. It was right before closing, and Dylan had gone to a meeting in Moscow. She had already put up the CLOSED sign when she heard a tap at the window, a gentle tap, and then she saw that smile. She opened the door and let him in.

"Thank you," he said. His voice was soft, had a whisper to it. "I'm on my way home. It's another fifty miles, and I need something to tide me over. I'll hurry." But he stayed for almost an hour. Finally, he reached for a Halvah and held it, then decided on a Tiger's Milk Bar. On his way out the door, he paused for an instant by her weavings, and she thought she caught the back of his hand brushing against a fold in the cloth. After he left, she picked up the Halvah he had held and felt the shape of it the same way he had.

When Robin invited her on the picnic, the first thing she did was rub her finger along her wedding band. It was cool to the touch even though it was late summer. Then she told him about Paris. He glanced down at the Raggedy Anne on the floor. "I like children, too," he smiled. She felt something lift from her that she hadn't known was inside; it floated away like breath.

She brought the quilt Grandmother had given her to take to college, the one with the double wedding ring pattern that she'd spread on the floor of the tent Dylan and she had lived in during their first weeks in Idaho. She laid her flute on the top of the picnic basket.

He took them to the woods in a white car with gray upholstery that smelled new, and she played her flute shyly, keeping her eyes focused on Paris as she danced about, weaving in and out of the tamaracks. Only after she put the flute away in its case and saw that Paris had curled up on the needles and fallen asleep in a patch of sun did she look at Robin.

He made her make the first moves. His eyes made her stand, walk closer and closer to him, as he fluffed up the quilt like a big white sail and dug his hand under it along the edges to remove the pine cones and fatter twigs, brushed them to the side, and lay down first, waiting to see where she would position herself. She stood there for only a second or two, his pull was that great, and then lay on the quilt, diagonally like him, but careful not to touch, not just yet. Then she cradled her head on her arms and faced away from him, tried not to listen to her heart pound, so aware of the nakedness of her arms, her elbow crooked as if she were readying her flute for music, and her heart making noise like just before a recital when the hall is filling up with furs and pearls and expectations, but the musician is backstage, a tattered velvet curtain away from the first note and that sense of falling. And she listened and heard her breath, and his breath, and by then recognized the sounds of the landscape, but heard nothing outside the quilt, not even Paris, though she tried to listen for her and was certain she would sleep. The quilt square drew a line around this new, circumscribed world, and it was hot, though she knew the forest shade was cool, and the invisible line blocked out all sound beyond it and all visibility, and the only air in the universe was in that space, and they were to breathe it all. For the time it takes to move the lip over a grace note, she realized that he had done nothing except lie still.

She inched close enough to feel the heat of his body on her forearm. And she thought: this is the moment, this is the pivotal point of my life. And then she turned her head and looked into his face, and saw him doing nothing, just waiting, as if he were about to implode, a face impassive, emotionless, just waiting for her. And then she moved her hand from under her chin, held it a moment suspended in midair, opened the fingers and let the tips drift down to his face, and she made invisible stripes down from his forehead to his jaw and felt the rough afternoon stubble. She thought she saw his mouth move slightly, the corner stretch infinitesimally. And then she moved again, aligned her body all the way down, and touched him.

He grinned, so sudden it frightened her, and grabbed a fistful of her hair. It pulled back the skin from her temples and stung. He covered her mouth and dug in with the heel of his hand, and her teeth cut into her lips. Then the words began. They spewed out like vomit. Her head split with them while he ran his other hand up and down her body and then stopped the words, and for those seconds she stupidly thought he would stop and let her go, go back to the way she was and should always have been. But then she felt his knuckles grind between her thighs to open them, and the words that she had never heard spoken returned forever, and the terror sent a rushing noise to her ears, like a giant conch shooting air inside her head and blocking out everything else.

Afterward there was something like silence, and then she felt a swish like a pine needle on her arm, looked up, and saw Paris. If Paris had seen anything, or heard anything, Jillian never knew, and could never bear to know.

She stayed home more after the time in the woods. Dylan was happy at first; he thought she was trying harder. One night after she put Paris to bed, he turned out the lights and opened the drapes and let the moonlight in. She stared at the shadows from the sumac outside the bedroom window, concentrating on the shapes of the sculptured branches. He came toward her, encircled her in his arms, and lifted her blouse from her back. But she held her arms at her sides and stared at the gloom in the open door to the living room. He circled his hand on the indentation of her spine, then pressed his palm hard into the small of her back. I am a statue, she thought. A marble cast. He must have felt the cold of the marble. Before long he lifted his hand from her skin and left her standing alone in the center of the room. It was the first time she remembered he hadn't asked her if he could. Even a week before she might have wept.

At home, when Paris came into the room, she would sit by Jillian's side but not touch her, or lie on the floor and stare at her aslant and wait for her to say something. Jillian searched the air in her throat for something they used to talk about, and came up with nothing. The house looked not just dirty but unclean—no matter how she mopped and scoured, scrubbed on her knees, her fingers wrinkling, the skin splitting in lines that looked like patternless webs from the buckets of water she ran over all its surfaces. She began to notice the cracks in the ceiling, and then to examine them. She closed herself in the laundry room, and still she saw them. She saw in them the sinews in a forearm, the scar down the side of a chin, the hard flesh around Dylan's thigh, places she knew belonged to men. One afternoon she watched a spider weave in the lattice of the bedroom window. The liquid silk flowed from her spinnerets and hardened into thread. She thought she might be a red-legged widow, so much poison collected in her fangs. Every night she spun something new. She could leave her work so easily.

This is the time when she began to lock doors. All the doors, not just the front and back. If she was in a room, she'd lock it until she was ready to leave. She'd lock out the spiders, every one of them, the orb weavers and the comb-footed, the triangle spiders and the tangled-webs. They lived with them as an army lives with its conquests. She fell asleep staring at cobwebs in the corners of the ceilings. And in the daytime, she ran her rag to the sides of them and around their peripheries, refusing to sweep them away. She just watched to see what they'd do. When Dyl came in at night, he would open the door and the chill would enter with him and surround her like an aura.

Later, after Paris started school, she would come home right after the last bell, not even stay after to talk to a teacher or stop at the drugstore for sodas and fries. Just come home and be with her. Sometimes they'd read and sometimes they'd look out the window, and since Paris never asked her what was wrong, Jillian never had to lie.

She didn't tell anyone about the hearse until Paris was so hurt, so rejected by her only friend. Jillian wasn't surprised when Paris told her what I had done, was doing to her. And when Jillian told her about the hearse, she knew the story had been waiting to come out for a long time, waiting to be used.

"Miriam seduced him," she told Paris, "the way she seduced us all. She was magic. Luck followed her around as close to her head as a halo." It was Miriam's idea for the hearse. They got one in Poughkeepsie, at the height of the Tet Offensive, just after she returned from semester break. She wanted to buy the hearse, but they hardly had the money to rent it. They drove it out to an overlook on the Hudson, where the ice crashed from the trees into the water. Miriam took her own candles into that vaultlike tomb on wheels and pulled the black drapes. Wax dripped on the upholstery. She sprawled on the leather seat, removed her own clothes first, told him to watch from the opposite side. "Goddam pigs," she said. "Goddam everyone." Miriam told Dylan all about the wax, but not about the seduction, not the way the cold leather felt on her naked thighs, the carpet between her toes, how ashen Kirk must have looked at having to meet his manhood in this place of death. She had pasted glitter to her cheeks, and it flashed in the candlelight; she took her long hair from down her back and brought it forward to let it fall over her breasts. All this before she let him touch her. Jillian told this story to Paris, not the one Dyl told her, and not the one that she knew really happened, but somewhere in between.

They made me in Chicago, after Kirk gripped Miriam's arm and fled with her away from the Conrad Hilton, where in the klieg lights the crowd chanted, "The whole world is watching! The whole world is watching!" away from the policemen with guns and the shattering of glass and the thudding of wood on flesh.

Jillian's flight from Wilders Ferry was late in coming. She knew she should have given her leave-taking to Paris long ago, an unwrapped present that she might never understand. And she should have given it to Dylan, too. She was choking both of them. A morning glory.

It wasn't just the scene at the makeshift little gallery that triggered it. She couldn't stand the undifferentiated pain, the magnitude of the exposure—Miriam's and Kirk's, then Dylan's, even Graceanne's. Nor her own, weaving through theirs. She knew she was passing it on, had passed it on already. She watched their backs as they went into the room where nobody else was. Their shoulders were curved down toward the ground, like frowns. Their heads were almost touching. What she saw in that moment at the gallery was something she had always known, but that finally released her: She knew Miriam would take care of him; she would keep her promises in ways Jillian herself could never learn.

By the time Jillian had walked me to my door, Paris was already an infant again, someone she could bundle in white and keep warm and fold a blanket over her eyes to protect them. And abandoning me at the threshold of my house was perhaps just practice for what she needed to do. The sad thing was that it didn't surprise her, that she could do this.

She couldn't bear to pack. For one rash moment as she found herself pulling wool socks on Paris's feet against the summer night chill, then tiptoeing toward the moonlight outside her window, she decided to take her with her. She saw herself carrying her, bearing her weight easily, keeping her swaddled in that afghan. If the child cried out, she would close her mouth with kisses. Letting herself see this made her let it go, release it like a balloon into the blue. A dot on the dome of the universe.

When she walked away, she took only her flute, still in its velvet-lined case, the flute she had last touched in the woods, at the edge of the quilt that more than anything, even her only child, made her life what it had to be. And she left her revolutionary the one thing that might have made her peace, the sole thing that would ignite his anger and consume it, the only thing that was ever truly hers to give: She left him their daughter, Paris, named after all that was undone in their lives. She left him the only part of her worth keeping, and knew he would never understand. It would be part of her punishment.

She envisioned, decades down the road, on impulse calling Miriam from a hotel in Paris and getting her sister on the phone. Miriam's sister would say, "You're too late. They're all dead." She imagined hanging up and ordering from room service a glass of white wine and a yellow rose. She wanted to believe that the message was a lie. But somehow what the sister said rang true. To Jillian they had been dead all along.

best friends

We drifted awkwardly through the confusing, grief-infused days that followed. When my father asked his wife how she had filled the day she had begun before dawn and extended through half the evening with Dyl, not interrupting their time together for even a phone call to her husband and daughter, she answered sadly, as if she knew she had failed, even after nearly twenty hours had failed, "We tried to answer the question 'Why?'" Then she walked upstairs, gripping the banister as if it were a crutch, and sank into a corner of her studio.

"What in hell is wrong with her?" Dad asked periodically. "I don't think she even liked Jillian." I think now it was a matter of theft. Jillian had stolen something from her that night.

Complicity hung in the air. Jillian's flight had usurped not only Mimi's glory but also the power of the new drama the show had brought to Mimi's life. Mimi's focus was out of kilter; she asked and offered nothing at all about Graceanne, whether from faith, or knowledge, or guilt, or forgetfulness, or all four.

In the early morning, after I saw them in our kitchen, Mimi and Dyl had returned to his house and searched frantically for a note, so that

Paris would not wake up and find it before they did. But no words were found from Jillian, only the articulation of something infinitely more lasting and damning to us all. As she passed the loom, perhaps on her way out the front door, she had severed and unraveled every strand, and the yarn had fallen in a heap, the gold threads she laced into every design, elongated spirals on the floor.

There are shards of Paris's pain that I can still feel sting me from under my skin. Abandoned. Bereft. I would spend years defining and redefining the shape of those words. I would examine them from all their angles and all their curves.

Mimi invited Paris to stay with us, but she refused. She began the slow process of starving herself to death. I always associate November, when other people are feasting on the earth's bounty, with the food Paris refused to eat. Mimi would visit her every day, bring her a cornucopia of bananas and dusky grapes, apples shined and walnuts shelled. She buried them in crusts and cream, sliced them with lemon and brown sugar, made clown designs and daisies with them on plates with fluted rims, held them close to Paris's nose as if she were Georgia and had to become familiar with them so they wouldn't frighten her so. Whenever I came into the kitchen and saw Mimi peeling and slicing and arranging, I'd ask, "What's that for?" and she'd unfailingly answer, "Paris."

Every day Mimi asked me to come with her to visit Dyl and Paris, and every day I said, "Tomorrow." I didn't bother to fabricate an excuse.

Every night Dyl put Paris to bed, asked a neighbor to watch her while she slept, and came to visit Mimi. His eyes were permanently veined with blood; his skin tinged with gray. His voice would break with the simplest questions. Sometimes, when he was merely walking from the entryway to the living room, he would hold his arm to his face as if he were blocking a blow, and stand there shuddering until Mimi led him to a place to sit down.

My father would pat Dyl's arm or press his hand into Dyl's shoulder, as if he were a foreigner to the land of grief. And when Dyl didn't snap back or resume normal conversation, my father would hover helplessly for a moment or two, then pick up a book and wander into another room. He began to go to the bookstore at night more often.

Mimi purged the house of all of Jillian's images and gifts, all the memories, and in their absence they became sacred. I see these more than anything else, all that she left, in the purple house. The cherrywood–framed photo of the four of them dressed in black and white for the Moscow Mardi Gras Ball, the men on their knees in front of the women, every snapshot of Dyl and Paris and Jillian because Jillian was in every one of them, and Mimi couldn't very well cut out the part of the paper showing Jillian's body and make of their albums a paper doll cutout book. The pillow covers Jillian embroidered, the poster she designed for the show. All vanished from the purple house.

One night the sky was inky before the doorbell rang. Dad was at the store, and Mimi and I took turns looking out the window. We waited for him as an old woman with cancer of the marrow waits for death. By the time the bell did ring it was too dark to see him coming. When I opened the door, he stood at the threshold and didn't move. His arms stayed limp at his hips. His skin looked so thin and pasty I could almost see the outlines of his skull underneath it, and his hair straggled to his shoulders. He stared through us.

"Come here," Mimi said, taking hold of his wrist and leading him toward the kitchen. "Take off your shirt." He did as he was told, and the muscles in his face twitched a bit as if he were grateful to be led around and given direction. He fumbled with the buttons.

"Here," she said, taking the bottom one in her own fingers, and meeting him in the middle. He removed it and stood there holding it balled up in the front and looking bewildered. She took it from him and hung it on the back hook on the mud porch. He stood still, looking like a little boy in his white T-shirt and jeans.

She turned on the tap at the sink and tested the temperature of the water with her forearm, just like a mother testing a bottle. She walked over to get him, letting the water run, an indulgence she never allowed herself. "Wasting the gorgeous rivers of Idaho?" she'd said many times when I'd let it run while doing dishes. "Over my dead body." Now it cascaded into the sink and filled the pipes, gone, or maybe sacrificed, forever. She came toward him, led him to the sink.

"Let me help you," she said, as if he were doing anything at all. "Lean down." And she reached up to touch him on the top of his head; she had to stand on tiptoe. He leaned down into the sink, and she wet his hair and poured her shampoo into the palm of her hand, and then she smoothed it over his scalp, circled over his bald spot with her forefinger, soaped his head and neck, and blew the lather from her fingertips before she rinsed his head. She threw a wedding towel, monogrammed with

"MRD" by some guest who had assumed Mimi would change her name to Davis, over his head, and he stood up.

"Sit by the stove," she said. She waited a few seconds, then pressed her hand on his shoulder, sat him down, and knelt behind him. She rubbed his hair dry with the towel, dipped down to dry his ears and his neck, then his face, and took a comb and ran it through his hair until it was neat. She brought out a quilt from the closet and draped it over his shoulders, then held a mirror in front of his face. He winced and looked away, opened his palm in front of it so he wouldn't see. Then she got a book and read to him until after midnight.

Paris stayed home from school for nearly a month, and then Dyl would drive her there, but she'd walk home in a few hours, sometimes before Dyl arrived at the Satellite for work. I did my best to avoid her, which was easy mostly because her attendance was so erratic. When I did see her in the building, she looked like a zombie. She exuded a sense of death, almost the smell of it, and the kids in the corridors gave her room, parted like the Red Sea when she came through.

One night when he knocked, I answered the door. I pulled it open only wide enough for him to pass into the hall, and I turned to get Mimi. But he said, "Wait. I came to see you."

I looked at the floor, at the dust balls gathering in the corner.

"Can we sit down?"

I walked into the living room, knowing he would follow. I had never talked to him alone before. He was always a part of a group, or the smaller group of him and Mimi. He'd always been pleasant, playful, and I would probably have liked him a great deal had he not looked so obviously Granola. But I found the prospect of talking with him alone unnerving, and I looked around like a frightened fawn for a sign of someone else in the house. I knew what was coming.

"Lake. I came to ask you to talk to Paris."

I drew back, expecting him to cry and plead, to stomp and shake my shoulders, to threaten and cajole, and I readied myself for retreat. But he sat still, calm. For some time I looked anywhere but at his face; my gaze ricocheted around the room, fixing on the cobweb floating in the corner of the ceiling, and when I mustered the courage to look at him, he smiled a little. I hadn't seen a smile in the house in weeks. I took a deep breath and nearly smiled back, but somehow I just couldn't say yes.

"I'm going to take her away, to live with my parents in Chicago. Then we can figure out what to do. I've put some ads in papers for Jillian . . ." Here he drifted away, then bit his lip and continued. "I gave the Chicago address. We'll be there by Christmas." His jaw thrust forward. "Funny, isn't it? Everything we wanted to leave behind is there." I didn't know what to say. "Maybe she hated Idaho," he said. "Anyway. You are her best friend"; for an instant I thought he meant Jillian's. The outermost layer of frost encasing my heart almost warmed at the thought of being a best friend. But a second later, the promise of heat vanished. Parents know so little about their children. I wasn't any more Paris's best friend than she was mine. Neither of us had any friends. We had that much in common.

"I won't ask you to promise anything."

When he left, he paused in the doorway again. "Paris told me once that she thought you were the smartest person she ever met. I remember feeling jealous." I handed him his cap. "She's all I've got left, you know." Closing the door, I wondered where that left Mimi.

I went to see Paris a few days later. My parents were going over to help Dyl pack boxes, and without saying anything I just joined them in the car. Paris had stopped making the pretense of going to school at all, and stayed in her room. I walked right up to her door. She hadn't turned on the lights, though the white ruffled curtains Jillian had made her were closed, and the room was dark. I stood in the doorway to give my eyes time to adjust.

"Paris? Are you awake?" I whispered at the shadow lying on the bed, hoping she wouldn't hear me or would choose not to respond and I could go home and away from other people's burdens.

"Why did you come?" she asked. "Did my father make you?"

It was a question I wasn't prepared for. I nodded, though she probably couldn't see the gesture in the dark. I walked toward her bed to switch on the light.

"Don't. I can't stand the light. That's why I wasn't doing well at school, you know; it was too light in there. And even on sunny days, they were always turning on the overhead lights, and they made that awful, loud buzzing sound, and my ears would hurt."

I'd rarely heard her say so much in one breath. I sat down on the bed, and she moved over and stared at the ceiling.

"We're leaving."

"I know."

We sat for some time like that. I sat rigid, afraid to move for fear I would touch her, as if she were in a casket. I knew her hands were white and cold. Her eyes were open, and she stared at a single spot on the ceiling, one that to me looked exactly like all the rest. In the background from downstairs, I heard the sounds of boxes being dragged across the floor and muffled voices, newspaper crinkled for packing.

I don't know how long I stayed by her. Neither of us said anything. My cranium felt hollowed out, all thought drained from it. Then I heard Mimi call my name.

"I have to go," I said.

Paris said nothing.

I tiptoed to the door, touched the knob, a glass knob, one Jillian had brought from her house in New York, when Paris called to me. I paused. I didn't want her to thank me. I'd done nothing, and would have done less if it hadn't been for her father; the thought of receiving her gratitude dug like a thorn into my spine. "What?" I asked, the frozen edge in my voice shocking even me.

"Lake, did they tell you? She left because of me."

My hand encircled the knob and rotated it, and with the speed of flight I ran out the door.

from the road

When Mimi paced the downstairs rooms, pausing for a few moments from all the business of readying our house for solace to stare out a window, I would ask her what she was doing, and she would say, "Just listening to the ice snap the branches," or "Taking in the sound of the snow." I wondered whether she was indeed straining to hear a sign of Graceanne, the unmistakably soft opening of the door, and whether Graceanne had rid herself of us forever.

When she wasn't listening to winter noises, Mimi plodded on with the purpose of easing Dyl and Paris out into the world beyond Idaho. Back to Chicago, where the lake was gray with grime and white with ice caps and the streets between buildings formed wind tunnels to sweep the grit into your eyes. Back to the place where in 1968 the Establishment had beaten hundreds of students while the nation watched. Back to the events that had spawned me.

On moving day the sky was cloudless in every direction, the blue icy and piercing, the color of camas blossoms. I watched the sky not change as Mimi and Dad brought out a lifetime of possessions one by one and crammed the U-Haul full. The adults stood staring in silence at the packed truck; then Dyl slammed the door. It thudded shut with the finality of a prison cell. Mimi helped Paris into the passenger seat.

"She's so young," Mimi said to no one in particular.

"She's only a year younger than me," I said, walking toward the truck.

"I didn't mean that."

Then there was nothing else to do. As Mimi and Dad and Dyl hugged good-bye, I bent down and picked a piece of granite from the road, a chunk with pink stripes and translucent scallops, but smooth on one side, curved like the runners on a baby's cradle; it fit the shape of my palm. It was frosty from the winter air, and I held it a while to warm it. I stepped onto the running board of the truck and faced Paris, her gaze fixed straight ahead, just as it had been that night I had sat with her on her bed in the dark. Her face in profile, expressionless, without the dimples or the chubby cheeks, looked like the outline of a skull.

"Here," I said, holding my closed fist in front of her face and then opening my hand when I caught her eye. "Take it with you. I warmed it for you."

She shook her head, but I reached into the cab and grabbed her hand and closed her fingers around it. Her lower lip and the liquid that collected in her eyes trembled, but she said nothing.

Dyl got into the driver's seat and adjusted the mirror. "Come visit soon," he said, kicking the truck into gear.

"I promise," Mimi called as he rolled up the window. As they pulled away, Mimi walked, then ran after them, waving until the truck took the fork to Coeur d'Alene and the freeway.

We drove home in silence. I sat in the back behind the driver's seat. My father, who usually had an eye for creatures as small as owls and magpies and hummingbirds and would often drive onto the shoulder in his excitement at discovering them, somehow missed the large figure that was walking on the side of the road that led to our house. The stately body, the wide shoulders, the generous hips, the black hair cut blunt at the neck, moved down the road with the grace of a filly. In one hand she held what from farther away looked like a spot of red the size and shape of a wing tip. As we came closer, I saw that it was a package wrapped in shiny paper. As the car was about to pass her, I held my breath, hoping Mimi wouldn't see her, as if not seeing her would make any difference in what was to come. The way she held her head, her unwavering gait told me where she was going, if I warned Mimi or not. I knew Graceanne had returned to us.

Suddenly Mimi yelled, "Stop!" and Dad stomped on the brake. The car swerved toward the right, kicking up gravel and dust.

"Jesus Christ," he hissed.

Mimi opened the car door, stumbling a little on her way out. "Sorry, Kirk," she said, and paused to put her hand on his arm. "See you at home." Then she carefully shut the door.

I purposely didn't look behind me at the two figures, and staring straight ahead, I saw my father's knuckles turn ashen as he gripped the wheel.

disappearance

For the next weeks we tiptoed around, barely talking to each other. Jillian's disappearance, Dyl and Paris's departure, the return of Graceanne made us oddly tender. And when I began to feel inside me the first eruptions of disease, I told myself, and I believe my parents told themselves, that these were merely the physical manifestations of the strain in our lives. Now, I think they must have felt guilty, and that's why they didn't take my complaints seriously until it was almost too late.

It began with a raw throat, which my father, absorbed in *National Geographic,* diagnosed as a virus. When I woke up the next day, I was shivering. Mimi felt my forehead. "You'll live," she said and tried to kiss my head, but I turned away.

I spent the day listless in a corner, as if the angles of the walls could protect me from the hot and cold inside me. It wasn't a very high fever, as Dad kept pointing out when Mimi would insist that he put his palm to my forehead, but it was my constant companion, like a devil on my shoulder, or something transplanted there, threatening to take over my body.

By night, my throat swelled shut. I could feel nothing else, and the air was too thick to breathe. I fell like a heap on the cushions by the bay window in the living room and lay there until one of my parents—I couldn't tell which because I was so clouded over with pain—picked me up and carried me upstairs.

I stayed in bed, waking only during those transition times—when evening hovered like a pale stripe across the sky or just before morning broke away from the gray of dawn; I never saw night or day, just a glimpse here and there of those times in between. When Mimi woke me up to take my temperature and press a cold rag to my face, I caught muffled words, the tones subdued, whether from the fever or from her lowering her voice, I don't know. I heard my name, but I was already gone, removed from the tension between my parents and from the organic world of day and night, seasons, mobility, and sustenance, the primary passage to my brain blocked like a mountain pass in January. Even turning my head to the side was work. There was no difference between sleep and nonsleep; my body hung between, weighted down and swinging on the tip of a pendulum.

Voices swam around me at hours I didn't recognize as discrete times of day. Words floated around my brain as if there were a moat between them and my perception of them. I had to force myself to think the word "neck," so I could define it, focus on it enough to spark the correct synapse. I was a disembodied person adrift. I quietly removed myself from the bed, the room, the house, the town, the adults who watched, and waited to have myself returned to me.

After a while I could discern night from day, sleep from waking, but I continued to perceive the world through a febrile gauze. I walked around the house slowly, gathering all my energy just to go back to bed. Before fatigue took me, I grasped at the familiar, grounded myself more in space and time, trying to concentrate on the objects within my four walls: the carved footboard of my bed; the ceramic bell Mimi had placed in my hand so long ago; the conch my grandfather had sent me through Aunt DeeDee. Then I concentrated with all my force on the migrating source of pain: one day a hot swelling in my ankle; a few days later in my knee; by nightfall, bullets of fire lodged in the tip of my elbow. I didn't want to admit to these changes, so haplessly beyond control, or allow them to remain part of my daily life, which I tried to believe would be restored to me. But they surfaced and lingered, like scars flaring scarlet.

I had been out of school for about two weeks when I sensed Mimi's presence next to me. She was holding my hand and trying to straighten my fingers. I stared at my useless hands palms up, as if they were holding something imagined.

"Lake, it's time to go to the doctor."

The next day she took me to Sandpoint, to Dr. Colburn, who had delivered 90 percent of the people in Wilders Ferry under twenty-two years of age. Climbing onto his examining table left me breathless. While he listened to my chest and probed my facial openings, he talked to Mimi about the overspending by the school district and railed against the evils of socialized medicine. Even a month earlier I might have flinched with every word, held my breath waiting for Mimi to say something embarrassing. I would have had to have grown up blind and deaf not to know that Mimi espoused the opposing positions on these particular issues. But now I simply didn't have the strength to care, and Mimi was strangely quiet. I vaguely wondered how he could hear and see what was going on inside my body while he was keeping up his end of the conversation.

Finally, he shrugged. "Can't find a thing. Looks like she had a little bug. Gone now. What's left is probably growing pains." He patted the top of my head and held the door open for us to leave.

When I came home, I went directly upstairs. The rest of the day and into the evening silence enveloped me—indeed, it enveloped the entire house—like a fog. The only sound was the brushing of rabbit paws on bare wood, Georgia's usually barely audible scratching now magnified. That night I heard voices, snatches of discussion, nightmarish dialogue as if my life were a play and I hadn't been told I had been given a part. The whispering outside my closed door seemed to seep in with the yellow light from the hall. In my half-sleep I caught scattered speech, pauses where the responses could be, extended silences, and in some oblique way I knew I was hearing half of a conversation over the telephone.

"Are you sure? . . . We have hospitals in the Northwest, too. . . . I could go to Spokane. I could drive her every day. It isn't that . . . I'm sure they have the—Seattle's only three hundred miles away. Will you make the appointment? Fine. No. Don't pick us up. I'll rent a car. Just do it my way for once. Okay." When I turned into my pillow and felt the tears rise to my eyes, I thought I heard myself crying in the other room.

The next morning I awoke to sunshine and my father's voice. "Lake, your mother—we think you need to go to a specialist." I waited, facing my dresser mirror and gazing right through my reflection so that I didn't see it at all.

He cleared his throat. "There's a doctor in St. Louis, a friend of your mother's father—"

"There are doctors in Spokane," I said.

As if that grated on a raw nerve, he bit his lower lip. I sat on the bed as far away from him as possible.

"How long?" I repeated. Our voices were fading and crescendoing in no discernible pattern, and the room seemed to have vanished, leaving us suspended in unfamiliar and unenclosed space.

"Not long. Just until we find out what's wrong." He waved at the air, at his own words, as if they were a circle of dying flies.

"Aren't you coming with me?"

He smoothed the wrinkles his body was making on my bed. "Mimi is."

"Why not you?"

"I have to work at the store. And you won't need me, Lake. You'll have your grandparents—"

"The grandparents I'm not supposed to like?"

After a pause, he said, "They'll take good care of you. And as soon as you're well, I'll be there to bring you back. We *both* will."

"Do you promise?"

"I promise with all my heart."

Promises, assumptions, truth—all were elusive. I was learning that there was no depending on any of them. "When do I leave?" I asked.

He stroked my head, and I pushed his hand away. I thought I saw tears in his eyes, and I didn't want them to be there. "Tomorrow," he said, standing up. I remember wondering bitterly if his mind was already back with his books. "Early."

At dawn the next morning, as I disappeared from Wilders Ferry, a twist in the road obscured the lake from view; my gaze rose and stopped. Just before it reached the slate-tinted sky, it fixed on a barren strip among the evergreens—a new site of clear-cutting on the mountaintop.

The rest of the way to the Spokane airport, I dozed in the backseat, an afghan tucked around my shoulders and my pillow on the armrest, covering the rip in the upholstery. For a while I believe Mimi sang to me in her tuneless way, melodies from her collection of 45's. She gave me "Mr. Blue" and "Tell Laura I Love Her" over and over while she took those back-road curves. Neither of my parents talked on the drive. From the seat I imagined the hills, the winter wheat piercing the melting snow. My head rocked over the pillow, and I had to use my arm to brace myself. She was pushing the speed limit. When we got out of the car at the airport, I refused to make eye contact with my father and kept my arms rigid when he hugged me good-bye.

At the gate Mimi left me like a bundle on a chair and walked to the plate glass. I watched her study the 727. Even behind her I felt the movement of her hard gaze from the cockpit down to the wingtip, to the tail, outlining the silver monster-body again and again.

"It's show time," she said finally, when all the other passengers had entered the ramp and the uniformed assistant nodded pointedly in our direction.

In a rented car, Mimi drove from the St. Louis airport toward downtown, the brick and concrete of my first major city whizzing by my feverish eyes. When she finally slowed down, I raised my head to see the late-afternoon sun flash back a blazing reflection at us from a massive complex of buildings straight ahead. The sign said BARNES MEDICAL CENTER. I was aware of a vague disappointment that my grandparents had not come to meet us; my guess now is that Mimi needed to do something for me herself.

Inside the medical center Dr. Goldstein introduced himself as the son of a colleague of Vinny Rose. "I promised your grandfather I would take good care of you. You know how stubborn he can be," he winked, as if I could have known that. I spent the afternoon feeling exhausted and humiliated in turns. At the end of the day Dr. Goldstein studied a screen behind me. I knew the answers were on that screen, the inner workings of my life reduced to electronic projections of wavy lines the color of my reluctant blood; I just didn't want to know what those answers were.

After I got dressed, and Mimi and the doctor finally emerged from his office, they were whispering. They avoided looking at me. "You may need a wheelchair," he said, avoiding my eyes and touching her shoulder lightly. I thought he meant a wheelchair for her, she looked so white, as white as his jacket, and was shaking slightly as she nodded good-bye. She didn't even say thank you.

As she silently turned her back on him, I stood to walk down the hall, but she ran to me and placed her hand firmly on my shoulder. She seemed to be trying to keep her voice from trembling as she said, "We've got to slow down, Sweetheart." She had never called me "Sweetheart" before, and I almost wished she meant someone else, someone invisible.

On the drive to the suburbs, she merged into the highway lanes slowly, as if she never wanted to get to the house she had been brought up in. I felt the car dip and shift and speed and stop. When she glanced at me in the rearview mirror, I moved my lips as if I were talking to a deaf person—"I hate you! I hate you!"

I fell asleep in the car, but I believe she drove and drove, exiting and reentering, the highways looping under her, the harsh road lights blurring her vision, and went to her parents' house only because she could no longer think what else to do.

That night, my first in my grandparents' house, I slept fitfully. Even only semiconscious I was aware of how fast my heart was working, like the wild, quickening speed of something much smaller and less substantial—a swan, or a sparrow. And my dreams echoed with the amplified sound from a score of stethoscopes—a blowing, like a cyclone just beginning.

the swollen heart

I woke up sometime in the middle of that night, drowsy and disoriented, to the first touch I can recall of my grandmother's hand. Her cool fingers held mine gently, so that I was hardly aware that they weren't mere extensions of my own, and she didn't move at all when my eyes flickered open to the dark room. Behind her I saw a squat, shadowy figure, and as my eyes adjusted to the dark, I could have sworn that on the shadow behind her was the face of the dragon on the back of the school bus my parents had driven to Idaho. I was about to give myself back to sleep when I heard her whisper something, her first words to me. Fuzzy images of screens with jagged lines and distorted faces in surreal close-up circled in my head, and I struggled to understand her. I believe she said, "Welcome home."

In the morning I saw that I was in a bed in the living room of 11 White Oak Lane. The bed was wedged into a room full of furniture alongside a picture window that looked out on a lawn as smooth as a carpet, and straight ahead was a triangle of three thick-trunked trees, their still-bare branches sharp as etchings against the gray sky. Among the trees the ground had been made ready for spring plantings. A flagstone walk wound toward the street, and I sat up in my bed to trace it down the long slope of the yard to its terminus.

"Don't!" Mimi's voice startled me. She was suddenly at my side and placed a firm hand on my shoulder, pressing me toward the bed.

I wriggled away. She stared at an invisible point on the pillow behind my head. The pillowcase was trimmed in eyelet; the sheets were printed with yellow butterflies.

She sat down on the bed and reached for my hand. I snatched it away.

"Lake," she said, her voice quavering a little, "you have to take care of yourself. You have rheumatic fever."

For a minute I thought she'd said "romantic fever."

Then Mimi continued. "An enlarged heart, a murmur. It means you have to rest."

I said nothing. The place, the voice, these words were all perceived by someone else. My heart felt fine. Nothing was wrong with me. I waited for the nightmare to leave me alone. Then I looked down at my white hands, the fingers curved only so much as a mother would notice, and panic gripped me. I sat up, threw off the sheets, and swiveled my legs over the side of the bed. She came toward me, arms open as if to embrace me, but I knew she wanted to entrap me. I squirmed, but she encircled me, her fingers against my spine.

"No," she whispered into my ear. "You have to stay in bed. You'll be able to return to school before long. Less than a month if everything goes well. Then I'll take you home."

"Dad said *he'd* come," I said, lying back but looking away from her, out the window. She described the course of my life in a forced voice as if she were explaining the logistics of a picnic in a state park. I was instructed carefully not to sit up, not to get excited, not to move unnecessarily, not to cry. It seemed to me that I would not for a second be able to forget that something was wrong with me. Indeed, the inklings of a deeper illness than I could admit were beginning to swell from inside, press like my enlarged heart into my lungs. I was beginning to feel the symptoms of a new form of exile, one I had never even imagined.

I looked around the room as if for escape, and my gaze landed on a framed photograph. It was an enlarged snapshot of my grandmother, her two daughters, and a baby: three generations of women, Mimi looking uncomfortable holding a squirming baby in a white-and-blue sailor suit. The face is nondescript, like its father's. What's wrong with this picture? I thought as the sight jarred my brain. I turned pointedly away.

I saw my grandparents only in flashes, entering the room to bring me a tray with sandwiches and juice or a pill with water, or to ask how I was, as if they were staying out of Mimi's way.

That night, as Mimi stood to turn off the light they'd placed on the coffee table by my bed, she said, "Tell me the truth. Isn't there anything you want me to do?"

I wanted to demand that she explain why she had lied to me, why she had never told me that I had met my grandparents before. But something insidious made me say, "Leave. Just leave." I glared at the framed photograph until she left. From the other room I heard a muted sound like the mewing of a wounded kitten. I buried my head in my pillow.

The next morning I heard her whispering to her mother in the hall. I could see my grandmother's skirt at the edge of the doorway. "I really need to get back. Kirk needs help at the Left Bank." I bit my lip; Mimi had rarely helped my father at the store. "Besides, this is the opportunity you've been waiting for—to get to know your grandchild." I couldn't tell if she was being sarcastic.

Mimi walked slowly into the living room, pausing for an instant at the threshold. When she leaned over as if to kiss me good-bye, I put my hand over my face and closed my eyes. "We'll call you every day—and see you soon. I promise," she said. There was a catch in her voice. I kept my eyelids shut tight as I heard her leave the room and a sound I would soon recognize as an electric garage door open and close. When I opened them, I gazed past the spot where Mimi had sat with me the afternoon before and through the window out at the suburban drive, and imagined the road to Wilders Ferry. All the way down the road I saw, as if at an unfathomable distance, a happy child, dinging a ceramic bell and dancing with her mother under the tamaracks.

In a few minutes my grandparents appeared at my bedside, and I saw them clearly for the first time. I tried to think about those precious first gifts they had sent me—the conch and the Barbie doll, and later, the silver locket, about their messages through Aunt DeeDee and the postcard from Florida—and tried not to be angry with them for never having come to see me. GranPearl looked handsome in her teal-blue suit with a gold stickpin. I was surprised at how silver her hair was. In the only photos I had seen of her, in Aunt DeeDee's albums, her hair was still dark; the shade reminded me of Mimi's. GranVinny stood slightly smaller. He wore an olive-green scrub shirt with ST. MARY'S HOSPITAL stenciled on it. His skin was tough and ruddy, and his gray eyebrows were drawn together in a thick line over his generous nose. He cupped his hand over his hearing aids and with his eyes followed her lips when she talked. Their eyes shone with tears.

GranPearl arranged the sheets under my chin and bent to kiss me. I hadn't allowed Mimi to kiss me in years, and the touch of GranPearl's dry lips on my cheek felt odd. "We'll be back after you rest," she said. Then they left me alone, and as I watched the light leave the sky, I searched their big, empty front yard for a sign of something familiar. If only I had been able to feel the full force of my abandonment, I might have been able to alter the course of my life and save those I loved most from some of the pain I caused them. But for the moment I held back my tears, though my heart felt swollen indeed.

Later that afternoon GranPearl appeared with a large mixing bowl (one she said she used to make filling for blintzes and ravioli) full of water, a bar of lilac-scented soap, and a piece of flannel that looked as if it had been torn from a nightgown. Her suit was covered with a full-length white apron; she wore gold beads and matching earrings, a slash of red lipstick across her wide lips. Her hair was coiffed and sprayed into place.

"Time for your birdbath," she said.

"No thanks," I said, and prepared to ask for a book.

She acted as if I had said nothing. As she lifted me up and removed my pajama top, she talked to me, slowly. After a while I forgot about the chill of the water, the indignity of the nakedness, the intrusion on my solitude, my powerlessness as she moved my arms and legs and shifted me on first one side and then the other; and, surrounded in the sweet and comforting scent of lilacs, I listened to her cadence and her words, the stories that had been kept from me all my life. She talked incessantly, welding one anecdote to the next, but without sequence, so that the narratives pieced together like a crazy quilt of colorful and fine-textured details. How GranVinny was carried to a rowboat as an infant in an ivory cut-lace tablecloth stained in the center with red candle drippings. How his enterprising seventeen-year-old mother took flight from poverty and rowed away from Sicily, first using sheets from her hope chest to pay a man to take her to the docks in his wagon from Campobello. How GranPearl's younger sister was so beautiful that their mother stashed pennies in the belly of a pepper mill to buy her elegant clothes, which she hid in three trunks in the attic. How GranVinny, a dashing young doctor who lived in tents on the plains of Africa during World War II, was promoted to lieutenant colonel. How when Aunt DeeDee was a baby she would sit on GranPearl's shoulders and comb her mother's hair with her chubby fingers. How GranVinny's mother taught GranPearl to roll out sheets of ravioli dough the consistency of linen. How her grandfather was a rabbinical scholar, whose calling it was to interpret the Talmud for the community, which paid him a salary to sit at cafés and study, or preside over discussions. I waited for her to give me stories about Mimi, but she never did.

After that first birdbath I watched my grandfather outside. He nodded to me as he clipped the junipers and bent over the earth to turn the soil in his hand. When he finished his work outside, he walked into the room, bent over me, tugged at the hospital corners GranPearl had so carefully constructed, and, grunting only a little, swooped me up in his arms.

"Now, a tour," he said. It was the first time I heard his voice. His words were murky, as if he had a sore on his tongue and it hurt when it touched the back of his teeth. And the volume was too loud, especially so near to my ear. Edging away from the noise of his words, I pressed into his shoulder, and, he, thinking I had hugged him, squeezed back. It took days for me to realize that his speech was distorted because so few of his own sounds registered in his ears.

"Good idea, Vinny," GranPearl said, her voice even louder than his. She removed her apron, folded it carefully, and left the room. In a few seconds she reappeared in the hall, a skillet in her hand, wearing a nearly identical apron, this one in indigo. "Introduce her to her surroundings. Just don't strain yourself."

For a second he lurched under my weight, but then I was aloft, and almost laughed. He carried me like an oversized, limp infant around the first story, introducing me to the kitchen, the powder room, the sun porch, the family room, and the downstairs guest bedroom. Years later I wondered briefly why they didn't put me in the guest bedroom, and the only answer I could come up with was that he wanted to be able to see me when he was outside. He didn't say a word, just brought my body up close against points of interest and nodded selectively. At the kitchen, across from the refrigerator, a door was closed tight. He stood at it and raised his eyebrows and smiled enough so that a dimple appeared in his left cheek. I could only guess at the significance of that door; I let myself imagine that behind it was a treasure chest, or some exotic bird in a gilt cage. His muscles bulged, but his steps were steady, and I could hear the stepped-up beating of his heart as he took me along every wall, close, so that I could see the paintings. One was an Arab woman with a veiled face, a basket in her hand, against a backdrop of maize-colored hills. The others were almost exclusively landscapes, no people in them at all: mountains slanting into lakes; fields of wheat, July-high and a dusty gold; forest-green firs pointing up like miniature triangles in the distance. Although the terrain looked like Idaho, I couldn't place any of the scenes. There was a dreamy quality to them: they were luminous, impressionistic, delicate, so different from the interiors with the gargantuan tropical blossoms on the wallpaper. If he hadn't moved tables and pedestals and chairs and shelves to ensure that I was close enough to see the signature, even running his fingers over the letters, I would never have guessed that Mimi was the painter.

I was astounded that he didn't bump into furniture as he wove in and out of the rooms; their house was packed with it. In the rectangular living room, beside my bed, were overstuffed chairs abutted in a semicircle around each of the two couches (or "sofas," as GranPearl called them). A kidney-shaped coffee table held piles of photo albums and a beaten-copper vase with silk flowers. A baby grand piano, its ivory chipped and yellowing, took up a quarter of a room. Shelves were tucked into nearly every corner, and three glass-door hutches held knickknacks.

When the tour was over, he put me on a brocade loveseat and took a record album out of the stereo cabinet, dusted the disk with a chamois, and placed it on the turntable. He turned up the volume and looked at me as if to ask me if I could hear it. I gestured for him to turn it down. It was a familiar melody—Puccini. "*La Boheme,* the bohemian," GranVinny shouted over the music, handing me the album. On the cover two lovers touched across a bare table with spindly legs in a shadowy room. Their clasped hands were backlit by the enlarged flame of the stump of a candle. While I listened, he ratcheted up the bed with a crank, so I wouldn't have to strain my heart by sitting up. Before he left the room, he picked up the album and pointed to the picture of the lovers. "I named your mother 'Mimi' after her," he said. He dimpled. "Don't tell your grandmother. She thinks we gave our little bohemian a Jewish name." He winked, put me on the bed, and left.

Every day, he took me for another walk in the house, and several times a day he carried me to and from the bathroom. Sometimes he carried me outside to chart the progress of the small shoots pushing through his new flower beds, but my gaze was always drawn to the stone tower that rose from the west end of the house. Near the peak it had a small window; the shades were always drawn. I suppose I was too heavy for him to carry me up to what must have been the third floor.

Every day GranPearl gave me my birdbath and served me my meals on a tray. In the course of these daily rituals, I learned that my grandparents were the offspring of immigrants who had of necessity—a pogrom and the promise of plenty—left behind the few things they had managed to accumulate. They changed their names, learned English, began the important work of collecting things—bulky things, things that would be difficult to dispose of after they passed into their new life: cherry chests with brass handles, marble pedestals, heavy silver goblets and platters, even the cut crystal thick and substantial. Nothing fragile, nothing to remind them of the fragility of place and life in one place, as if the very bulk would give them a sense of permanence. When GranPearl met GranVinny, their families, the Rosenblooms and the Rosattis, lived next door to each other on Cass Avenue, in a neighborhood of dark brick duplexes recently abandoned by the people who had populated St. Louis for years before the Europeans came to seek whatever they came to seek.

When they became engaged, they did it secretly and didn't tell their parents for an entire year. After their wedding, they changed their name to Rose, in a protofeminist compromise that must have signified for them only one of the multitude of changes in their new life together. They promised the Rosattis to raise all the children Catholic, which they never got around to doing, and then they moved out to the suburbs and began the serious business of full acculturation. I wondered why I had never heard any of these details, neither from Mimi nor from DeeDee.

I saw Dr. Goldstein every few days; as a favor to GranVinny, he came to the house on his way home from the office. He listened to my heart and drew blood and took my pulse. When he left I fell back on my pillow in exhaustion.

Every few days I received a present in the mail from Aunt DeeDee—one for each letter of my name. She called frequently, at odd hours, to tell me she was coming to visit as soon as she "could arrange her life." Every morning my parents called, always before eight o'clock Idaho time, when the rates were cheapest; and often when the phone rang before ten o'clock, I'd shut my eyes or make snoring noises. When GranPearl saw I was asleep, she'd take the call on the extension upstairs so I couldn't hear. Other times I would simply tell GranPearl that I just felt too tired to talk.

Sometimes Dad would call me from the bookstore in the middle of the day, and GranVinny would bring me the phone and put it on a little table by my bed. My heart would skip a beat. The first question I'd ask was, "How long do I have to be here?" He'd always answer, "Just a while longer, honey. Your mother talks to Dr. Goldstein every day," and then he'd change the subject. When he asked me how I was, I'd say, "Fine," and he'd say, "Great," and then neither of us would say anything. Every time we hung up, a steel knot seemed to roll around inside of me as I conjured up images of them without me. And sometimes, in spite of my efforts, a fleeting vision of Mimi stayed with me the rest of the day. Sometimes I saw her gyrating behind the slats with a blond man with a scar slashed across his forehead; but more often I saw her in the lion claw tub with a raven-haired woman.

When GranVinny noticed I was especially blue, he would play the piano for me. Or he'd put on a succession of his records, one Italian opera at a time, turn up the volume so loud that the soapstone figurines on the stereo vibrated, and sit beside me. He would hold my hand and tell me in a booming voice about his childhood in East St. Louis, always mentioning with an impish smile how, to pay for his piano lessons, he ran bootleg whiskey across the state line for his father.

Many hours I simply spent passive as a puppet, gazing through the picture window next to my bed. Sometimes GranPearl played me her scratchy Al Jolson records, and once in a while she'd belt out a chorus of "Mammy" from the kitchen. But I marked time by watching GranVinny work his front lawn. He spent enormous blocks of time outdoors, muddying his knees in the damp soil, or shaping and patting it as if it were clay, exacting and obsessive, like Mimi when she painted. He'd stay outside until GranPearl called him for lunch or supper, or sometimes even breakfast. He would crouch, or stand, his head bent slightly to cast his full attention, as if he were a stern principal and they were his pupils, on the rows of plants, the shoots and blooms and the invisible garden when all the human eye could see was loose earth, a hose, or a spade in his hand. I often assumed he had forgotten I was there, but once or twice a day, he would do something outrageous. He'd suddenly stand up from hunkering over his seeds and, looking stern, take a finger full of mud and smear his face with streaks and arcs, pose there like the painting of the Indian chieftain used to illustrate Dad's *Last of the Mohicans,* then spring back to the ground as if it hadn't happened at all. Or he'd uproot an errant growth with his ungloved hand and, holding it in his fist, brandish it as if it were a trophy of war and grin like the naughty boy GranPearl always called him. Then he'd glance my way to see if I was still paying attention.

He seemed to prefer this sort of communication, with me inside and him outside the glass. When we were together in the house, he seemed jumpy. Every half an hour to the minute he would ask me how I felt while placing two fingers over my pulse, and then he'd ask GranPearl questions about me as if I weren't there. What was my pulse the half hour before, how much had I eaten, was I sleeping? Then he would pace around the room while she answered them in the loud voice he had become used to hearing as the voice of the world. At first I tried to talk to him, but my voice was too weak, and he would look alarmed when I seemed breathless from having to repeat something so he could hear. He'd instantly reach for my wrist and squeeze my hand, then boom GranPearl's name, expecting her to hear him and come running, no matter where she was.

Every day, though I often tried not to, I asked one of them the same question, and the answer was always the same—"Soon, dear, soon." Although every morning I looked forward to their opening the heavy drapes that kept me from seeing the green shoots rise into tulip buds and the tender crocuses open purple and white, the picture window may as well have been bars; the cheery sheets, manacles and chains. And when I thought about my mother and the anger crept in, I hooded my eyes and made a show of doing nothing.

chocolate shoes

It wasn't until the latter half of April that Dr. Goldstein cautiously declared my heart on the mend. "Just a few more weeks of rest," he said into his black bag. I focused my gaze on the drapes, counted almost twice the number of weeks Mimi had told me I'd have to remain in exile. That same day, Aunt DeeDee, having "arranged her life," came to visit. She walked directly to my bed, arched over me, and kissed me on first one cheek and then the other, and again, over and over.

"Oh, my poor, poor baby," she wept into my face. "It hurts me to see you this way." Her mascara ran down my cheeks. She sat down on the chair by my head and held my hand.

"How long will you stay?" I asked, glancing at the suitcases GranVinny was piling in the hall to take upstairs.

"How long do you want me to?" she smiled.

I could hardly speak the answer. I squeezed her hand and shut my eyes tight as if I wanted to preserve this dream forever. She reached behind her and gave me a package; it was small and flat and wrapped with blue foil and tied with a silver ribbon. Under the foil was a cellophane-covered box of chocolate Dutch shoes in miniature, each identical to the others in the row.

"Shoes," she said. "Aren't they adorable? I got them from a man who answered my last ad who said he likes sweets. He's a candy distributor, and this is from his international line."

The next afternoon GranPearl brought me the phone, and I was surprised to hear Mimi's voice.

"What's new on White Oak Lane?" I could tell she was trying to sound upbeat.

"Nothing," I said.

"How are you feeling?"

"Fine."

She sighed, then tried again. "How are Vinny and Pearl?" I didn't even answer this time, just counted the furry petals on the African violets on the windowsill.

"Well, Sweetheart, rest well so you can come home to us soon. I—"

The word "home" unleashed a slough of images: the words "Lake the Flake" written with fingers in the condensation on the bus windows; Jillian's threads limp and unraveled, her loom abandoned; Graceanne's thigh painted shiny red.

"Aunt DeeDee's here now," I interrupted. A split-second pause. "She gave me some chocolate shoes."

"You can't have chocolate. Didn't your grandmother tell you? You can't have fat or salt. Let me talk to—"

GranPearl took the phone and listened for a few seconds. "Of course, she can," GranPearl said, her voice low and deep. "Dr. Goldstein said nothing about—Miriam, please calm down." Aunt DeeDee sat down next to the bed and slit open the package. A little chocolate shoe popped out and bounced down my side on the sheet. Aunt DeeDee picked it up. "DeeDee," GranPearl sighed, handing her the phone, "she wants to talk to you."

After a few minutes Aunt DeeDee said, "Come on, Mimi. Since when did you get to be such a stick-in-the-mud?"

When Aunt DeeDee hung up, her face was pale. She studied her nail polish. The room was still, suffocating. Then GranPearl said, her voice controlled and refined, "I think it will be all right for Lake to have one."

For a moment, silence. Then DeeDee handed me the chocolate shoe. My throat tightened, and for a second I thought I couldn't breathe. A feverish chill whooshed through me. It swirled in my chest and rose to my face, and my arms sank into the sheets like lead. Then I felt the cool chocolate against my lips and took a bite that felt like a steel bullet all the way down my throat.

When GranPearl left the room, Aunt DeeDee leaned toward me. There was an odd look to her, an intensity, and when she leaned toward me I thought I saw a twitch in her jaw. "She's still upset at her, you know." I threw a questioning look her way. She picked up the dish towel GranPearl had left. "She's worked so hard all these years for her, and she always gives her trouble. She's giving it to her still."

By now I had gathered that it was Mimi she was talking about. I squirmed to the side and stared through the window. She bent down to put her lips to my ear; her breath was warm and moist.

"Mama was never the same after Mimi told her about, well, you know." Perhaps I was tired of being the one not to know things. Or perhaps I was just protecting myself from the emotions of yet another revelation, but I nodded, as if I did indeed know what she was talking about.

My recognition seemed to be the cue for her to relax. "Of course," she whispered, "at least the pregnancy didn't show at the wedding. That black eye from the Chicago riots was enough to do us all in." She shook her head, clicked her tongue against her teeth, as I had seen GranPearl do.

DeeDee continued to talk, but I didn't hear a single syllable. I was straining to recall the photos of the wedding in the woods, and when they came back to me I was mesmerized by them. Although the pictures didn't hint at it, I was there with them. I was no larger than a fleck of mica by the lake, not yet a convexity under the bride's sacklike frock. But she already knew about me—a tinge here, a queasy wave there, a tightness back of the nipple that she who knew about these things could distinguish from adolescent yearning, romantic impetuousness, the sharp scent of freedom that this particular ceremony proclaimed. That night after everyone had gone to sleep, I peeked out the drapes at the starless sky and wept at their deception: how happy I had imagined them then.

By the next morning, my obsession with wondering when I would be sent home faded with the rest of my feelings, and I was distracted by Aunt DeeDee, who after the first week, extended her visit for another. And another after that. She moved the television so that, wedged between the stereo and a loveseat and balanced on an end table, it faced my bed. "In the morning we'll do the game shows, and after lunch we'll have our stories," she said. I missed hearing my grandparents' stories and music, the details of their lives, but I loved impressing my aunt with knowing the answers on the quiz shows.

"In Hollywood you'd be a shoo-in, Sweetkins," she said, "and I could be your manager. As soon as you get well, that is." She had grandiose plans for our winnings. "For starters, we'll buy a home in Beverly Hills, nothing fancy, just a swimming pool, no tennis court. Then we'll purchase franchises—"

I shot her a skeptical glance. "Kinda tacky, don't you think?"

"We're not talkin' fast food, Honeykins; we're talkin' health clubs. There's a chain of them that's the coming thing in Frisco."

"Stories," it turned out, was her euphemism for the soaps. She seemed delighted to be the one to initiate me into the wicked pleasures of television, the lazy, passive activity of not thinking, and while she stared wide-eyed at the screen and wept in all the appropriate places, I offered my analysis about the characters' intertwining lives. The first day I was self-conscious, but by the second I was scribbling notes on prescription pads that GranVinny had piled in corners throughout the house, under drug advertisements for Enovid and Tagamet and Reglan. Eventually these scraps of paper allowed us to develop a system for predicting who would do what with whom, and soon we were taking bets. There was something of the familiar about these stories: the people wore fancy clothes and either didn't seem to work at all or were at their professional peaks, but although in many ways they wore the masks of the upscale culture I associated with Aunt DeeDee, under their skin these were the people I knew in Wilders Ferry. And as a bookie about their lives, I was a winner.

As soon as the fatigue became less draining, I began to sit with the three of them at the table for dinner. I rather enjoyed talking with my mouth full—a necessity, or dinner lasted for several hours because we'd have to chew every bit of food before we opened our mouths wide to scream loud enough for GranVinny to hear. He always sat at the head of the table, far away from all of us; that was his place, deaf or not. In the center of the table GranPearl always placed a vase of flowers from the market, even if they obscured our lips, and, I secretly thought, blocked some of the sound so that we had to work harder; it was GranPearl's way of showing him that we were all willing to prove our love.

After dinner Aunt DeeDee sat by my bed. We'd read magazines or pore over the *Riverfront Times,* circling and erasing ads with a pencil. She liked to compare the available men in the Midwest to those in the West.

As my breath came easier and I was able to sit upright for increasing lengths of time, I began to wonder whether I really wanted to return. I spent my fifteenth birthday ensconced among satin pillows in GranPearl's rocking chair while she and GranVinny and Aunt DeeDee took turns bringing me whatever they thought might please me. It was only when the phone rang that my stomach tightened and I squinched my eyes shut.

The morning before Aunt DeeDee was supposed to leave, my three caretakers went to Shaw's Botanical Garden to look at the cactus exhibit. I felt so well I begged them to let me stay alone. I spent the morning dozing, enjoying an intoxicating sense of freedom I hadn't felt since I had disappeared from Wilders Ferry. I was startled awake by the telephone. At Mimi's "hello," my spirits flew away like a flock of captured birds let go.

"Where's Dad?" I asked.

"He went to the store, and I decided to check up on you. Lately, every time I've called, your grandmother says you've been sleeping." I could feel my cheeks getting hot. No one had told me in several days that she had asked to talk to me.

"I was probably just busy with Aunt DeeDee." I tried to sound aloof and played with the lace on the pillowslip.

"I thought she had left." I shrugged, didn't respond. "Lake? Are you okay? How long is she staying?" The tension in her voice gave me a perverse pleasure.

"Forever," I replied, and saying it I felt a sweet surge of power. Silence. "She moved back home." Still she did not respond. "You know. Because of earthquakes." I was struck by images of my tiny aunt stuck in a doorjamb, arms and legs stretched out at angles, legs spread, like that da Vinci drawing of the man spread-eagled in the circle, and I giggled.

"Lake," she said with alarm. "Is that what she told you? Are you all right?"

"And GranPearl says there's no rush to get back to Idaho. She knows how busy you are." I was on a roll, jabbing at all my mother's buttons, some of which I could only guess at.

That evening GranPearl came into the living room and said, "Your mother called just before dinner. She and Kirk have made arrangements to come get you. I told her I'd tell you." My grandmother kissed me, then fussed with the pillows on the sofa. "Dr. Goldstein will check you tomorrow before your parents get here. He says you may need some help learning to walk again." I looked up at her, expecting a sign of joy, or relief, but her mouth was drawn in a tight line.

After she left the room, I watched the polluted sky through the trees. Suddenly I turned and saw GranVinny. His jowls sagged, and he looked at me sadly, as if there were already two thousand miles between us. At first I didn't recognize his voice; it was muted, as if he didn't expect me to hear it. "On their wedding they stayed up 'til dawn. And I watched them. Oh, it's not what you think." He dimpled slightly. "My Mimi was never one for convention, always had to do everything her way. Instead of doing what they were expected to do on their wedding night, they painted a school bus. And a 1951 bus at that. They paid me back for it with the money my cousins stuck in the groom's pocket. At least they waited until your grandmother went to bed, I'll give them that much. I watched them make that old school bus into . . . into something magical. That forest." He looked down at me as if he had just remembered that I was there. "Lake, so many times I've imagined you in that forest. She thought of everything. Even a dragon. Right before dawn, she dipped his yellow brush into the red bucket and right over the sun she painted a peace sign."

He turned as if he had heard my grandmother call him from the other room. Then he caught my unsettled expression and continued, "I helped them pack the heavy stuff. We put a table saw and a barrel of nails in the back. They bought them with the money they got from returning some of that fancy china and silver Pearl's family had given them. They left an area in the front of the bus clear for living space, except for a small refrigerator and a Coleman stove. And then there was that dining table"— he looked a little sheepish—"that they used as a honeymoon bed." He rubbed his open palms together as if he could wipe off remnants of the past. "Then they drove to Idaho." He put his hand over his eyes, and when he lifted it I could see that his eyes were wet. Something in the litany-like quality of this description reminded me of home, of my mother. I set my jaw so it wouldn't quiver.

The next day, after listening to my chest for nearly half an hour, Dr. Goldstein proclaimed me well enough to walk. Standing alone I felt dizzy, oddly tall and flimsy, like a beanstalk in a windstorm. Taking my first staggering steps along the tulip blossoms now lining the flagstones on the lawn and staring up at the mysterious tower, I wondered if among the things I had yet to find out about my family was the fact that I had learned to walk for the first time in this very place. And I felt somehow older, different, if not ready to return, then at least at the brink of something new; for the first time since the night of the art opening, I had an inkling that I could indeed heal, and not just physically. Both my parents were coming to reclaim me, just as they'd promised.

keeping the promise

This is how I have imagined it:

———————————

The trip to Denver, where they have to change planes, is a little rough; the landing, they agree, is like a carnival ride they both dislike. And the flight to St. Louis is delayed, so for a while they tour the lobby in tandem. Both of them have developed a shyness around strangers that each of them would deny. They stop briefly at a counter to buy Dramamine. Dad wants an excuse to sleep all the way. Mimi's heavy backpack bites into her shoulder, and she will neither let Dad hold it nor leave it untended by one of the vinyl-covered seats. He wanders from store to store around the terminal, lingering behind for a last look at the book stands, buying a Butterfinger as an excuse, unwrapping it slowly.

Walking toward the ramp, Mimi sees the plane outside the plate glass. She recognizes it as the masterwork of McDonnell Douglas, engineered and assembled, welded and examined in St. Louis, a mighty scion of bulky others that Mimi has seen in field trips led by my grandmother to the St. Louis airport, then called Lambert Field, when she was in first or second or third grade and GranPearl was always the room mother. She tells all this to Dad, but he is straining to look over the undulating motion in the corridor, searching the walls for a water fountain so he can take his pill and wash down the sweet of the Butterfinger, which is coursing through his flesh like a roller coaster, his abstinence from sugar has been so radical.

They sit toward the front of the aircraft, and my father is asleep before the doors are locked for takeoff. Mimi is contemplating moving toward the window, but just before the doors thud closed a young man in tight jeans and a black short-sleeved T-shirt stumbles into the cabin, shoves a backpack into the compartment above my father's head, mutters, "Excuse me," and pushes between my parents and the bulkhead, taking the window seat next to Mimi. She thinks she recognizes him from the Spokane flight, or, she muses, perhaps from some other flight from another airport. She smiles at this thought and catches his eye, but he holds his smile in check and looks only at her reflection in the window. She takes him all in. His arms are veined and muscled as if he has been drawn by an artist still enamored by his models. He is innocent, this young man, from a lentil farm in the Palouse country of Idaho, not far from Wilders Ferry, and leaves his arm on the seat when she carefully, so as not to alarm him, rests her forearm against his. My father is nodding, his chin dropping onto his shoulder, and she bundles up her sweater to prop his head.

She is lonely, feeling the core of loneliness she carries inside her spread, slowly take over. She thinks the feeling starts somewhere in her rib cage; when she feels this way she always presses her fingertips to the center of her chest and tries to touch the place where the feeling is born. Her comfort with bodies, her intimacy with the mysteries of the flesh, serves her well in fighting this invisible spreading. But she believes if only she could find the place it is born inside her, she could abort it.

When the right engine explodes, the fireball swallows the rear of the plane, and it flashes like a comet across the Midwest skies, she and the boy are thinking about each other and looking out the window at the plump, cottony clouds not at all like the layered vapors of the Northwest. The plane trembles and dives, drawing back the skin on her face, then levels off. My father stirs, openmouthed; Mimi pats his hand and immediately returns her arm to the upholstered rest she and the boy share. His fist is clenched, and she lightly encloses it with her hand as the plane's course lurches into clumsy circles. Mimi and the boy recall the fringe-winged speckled hawks beyond our road. Bits of hot metal shoot like shrapnel through the tail. The boy's eyes, Mimi sees, are terrified, and the spokes of green in the sky-blue irises seem to spin like roulette wheels. Mimi's eyes fill, and she touches his face as she looks beyond it out the window at a runway like a stripe in a cornfield. The flight falls toward the solitary runway, overhead compartments flapping open and cosmetic bags and alligator briefcases careening into the aisles. She lets my father snore on, just as she has protected him from so much knowledge of the dark and egregious for so long. He does not awaken until the last second, until the pilot screams, "Brace!Brace!Brace!" just before knowledge becomes horror. In the moment of the plunge, she moves toward that boy's arm slowly, the hairs on their forearms entangling and their muscles tensing while my father sleeps out the last of his innocence. The right wingtip slams into the tarmac, and the plane catapults out of control.

Her heart continues to plunge straight down, even though the plane is skidding sideways; but her loneliness lightens, gives ground, as the forward section of the plane is ripped from the nose and tail. The three of them are trapped in the mars-black belly of the plane, the heat already penetrating their skin, the smoke promising flame.

⸻

And what at last unseated the terrible loneliness as my mother only of necessity let go—of the boy first, then of the man, and last of her breath? In sleep, I shake with nameless hungers I know are hers. The nightmare is this—that it's not death that plucks her loneliness from her. Nothing so simple and permanent. The nightmare is that it's me.

the stone tower

There were no bodies. No flesh to lament or mourn or beat our breasts over, or throw ourselves upon, or dive into the grave after. No waxy countenances wiped clean of complexity to trigger the natural synapses of sorrow. Nothing, not even ash.

That first afternoon, after we heard the news of the crash, I lay, numb, on my bed. I tried to imagine that my head was propped against the maple frame my father had fashioned as one of his first woodworking projects. At the base of the headboard, he'd carved my name in a script surprisingly graceful for a man; when I followed each letter with my eyes, all the letters curved and looped in a continuous movement, like a ballet, and I imagine his hand was propelled with a precision he'd been able to achieve in nothing else. I knew if I could so much as touch the gouges in the wood, I might be able to feel, though feeling might be unbearable.

I was watching the room darken, the ghosts in my life shimmering on the ceiling, when I heard Aunt DeeDee's voice through the wall. The ghosts exploded and vanished like silent fireworks.

Something about the way she called my name, the voice so sad and yet suddenly similar to my mother's, made me dizzy. I felt as if my life were teetering on a jag of a cliff. A small shove and I would careen. Clinging to my own equilibrium, I said nothing.

She repeated my name, more intensely. I lay as still as a doe at the scent of her hunter. When she came upon me silent in the dark, she screamed, "Lake!" It was the first time I had ever heard my name articulated in fear. She crushed me to her and wept. And while her thick, spiky hair rubbed against my chin and cheek, I waited to feel.

"I'll take good care of you," she said into my neck. "The best."

The luminous disk framed in the picture window had a muddy orange cast, and I thought I could see storms swirling on the surface. When she left the house with GranVinny to drive to the airport, my body let down; the gravity of sleep had begun to pull me in when I heard from the next room another sound, unrecognizable at first, perhaps because it was so out of context: the slap of flesh on flesh. I bolted up, felt the quickening of my fragile heart. Another slap, then another. Slap, slap, a steady rhythm. I stole out of bed; it still felt odd, being able to decide to rise and walk, the carpet tickling my bare feet. I followed the sound into the guest room. In the gloom a woman pitched back and forth on a rocker; her left hand made a fist, clutched her breast; as the runners of the chair reached their point of return, her right hand rose to the rhythm of the rocking, and the flat palm slapped a cheek. Only then, at the sight of my grandmother, did I cry.

For much of the next week, while Aunt DeeDee arranged over the phone for a memorial service and for all the possessions to be sold or shipped to St. Louis, my grandmother rocked in the empty room. The first day after the accident, my grandfather locked himself in his basement study; the house echoed with his bellowing. When he emerged, in the middle of the night, I crept out of bed and saw him turn on the light in the powder room, wash his face, then rummage in the medicine cabinet for the things my grandmother liked: her lotions and powders and perfumes. He placed them on a silver tray and carried them into her room. The second day, he tried to tie her hand with his monogrammed handkerchief to the arm of the rocker, but as the soft material encircled her wrist, she screeched like an owl, and he bolted from the room.

I walked around awkwardly, pretending I was back in the purple house, mentally surveying the things we'd left in Wilders Ferry—from the wall-size orange-and-purple-slashed paintings to the small rabbit nibbling on the ficus. I felt unable to make distinctions. Every item held the same importance, and the enormity of that notion paralyzed me. It was as if I were watching a movie of my own life, a grainy black and white in which the actors were blurred and the dialogue faint and garbled. Perhaps Karl would take care of Georgia, I thought. I pictured her trembling in terror in the corner of her dollhouse, or scratching at her wood shavings while she waited for him to claim her.

In the hall closet I found my suitcase and opened it. A few T-shirts were in it still. I took them out one by one as if to recognize myself, the life that I would never have again in them. And then, wound up in a pair of jeans I must have already outgrown, I felt something hard and round. I unwrapped it carefully and for a moment just stared at it. It was Mimi's ceramic bell. I dropped it as if it would scald me, and lunged into the bathroom. The face in my mirror might have belonged to a dead person, so drained it was, and more confused than lonely, absolutely passive, as if the luckless person it belonged to were still waiting helplessly for the thud after the fall.

Dr. Goldstein advised me gently not to go to the memorial service; it would be too much a strain on my heart, he said, so I stayed in the living room in my bed, as if I were still sick, while they prepared for the service. When they came in to say good-bye, I closed my eyes and pretended to be asleep. At the sound of the garage door, I rose like a somnambulist. I tiptoed out of the room, turned down the labyrinthine hall, and, for the first time, climbed the stairs, my heart slamming against my ribs in fear of what might happen to me.

After the second floor the staircase spiraled into what must have been the stone tower. I tried to stop myself from panting, but my breaths were fast and shallow. At the top was a single door. When I opened it, a square of light struck me, and I knew immediately that this room had been my mother's. It was rounded, and I thought of a lighthouse, a place to observe something grand and mysterious like the sea. An oblong window was cut into the curved wall. From the window I looked down over a garden of daisies that from this perspective had clearly been planted in the shape of a six-pointed star. A four-poster bed with an ivory lace canopy took up most of the room. I turned the glass knob of the louvered closet doors. Behind them were a sink, a small towel rack, and a closet. The closet was crowded with piles of books, empty hangers, and childhood paintings, many of them framed—fish and cats and clowns and little black-haired girls swinging, all executed in surprisingly clear, broad brushstrokes in the purest of the primary colors. I could see my grandmother having this spacious closet built for all her daughter's dresses and skirts and frilly blouses, and my mother using only one drawer of her dresser, for jeans and T-shirts. Under the framed paintings was a shoe box of letters tied shut with a brown shoelace. I untied the bow but couldn't bring myself to read the letters. I lay back on my mother's lace coverlet and stared up at the canopy until I fell asleep. The room was nearly dark when I woke up to a sound from the floor below. I walked into the hall and listened.

A muted dissonance drew me down the stairs, and halfway down I recognized the tones of the baby grand. The rhythm was uncannily familiar, but the notes all wrong, an atonal sound-shadow of Chopin. I stood at the banister and watched. His body covered the keyboard, all the keys up and down the scale, his hands hesitating for only a second perhaps when he sensed my presence. He pounded the piano so that it shook; the bench vibrated, and I feared for its legs, which were older than my parents would have been. His wrists arched and dipped, fingers flew like butterflies. His veins bulged as he dug into the black and whites. I was afraid to look into his face; I knew what I would see.

My grandfather's face was still handsome then. In the piano light its Sicilian sheen softened the heavy features, and it reminded me for a second of Graceanne's. On the music stand above the keyboard, instead of a score, he studied the photo of the three generations of his women. His mouth was compressed thin and trembling; his eyes were shut, and tears marked wet squiggles down his face. I think I must have known even then that if I stayed at 11 White Oak Lane my heart would break along with his.

That night I helped my aunt undress my grandmother and put her to bed. When I returned to the living room, my bed had disappeared. Without a word I walked upstairs slowly. In the tower room the canopy bed was turned down; the night-light was on.

A week or so later when I came out from my mother's room into the hall, GranVinny was polishing the banister with one of his handkerchiefs. It was touching to see him do housework, taking over so quickly, so fully, his wife's role of the last half century. His hand circled the gleaming wood as if he were performing an incantation. I walked toward him and paused just behind him; I was afraid to touch him for fear of startling him. But he sensed my presence and turned toward me, brought me to him and held on to me, his fingers pressing into my back. Then he pulled away and nodded at me to follow.

Feeling like a distorted mirror image of the princess who followed an invisible string up the tower to her secret grandmother, I followed him down from the tower to the first floor and then down again, for the first time, to the basement. Immediately I recognized this shadowy space as his domain, a refuge from the heat and light. He had lined the walls with shelves and stacked all his treasures neatly upon them, labels in his generous script glued to the shelves. He pointed to the fishing tackle box he took with him to fish every Sunday in a lake a friend of his made and stocked for him. The sight of the gray metal tackle box made me stop dead. My breath tried to fill my lungs, and stuck. There it was: Mimi's paint box. For several seconds I thought it was the one that had actually belonged to her. Alarmed at the way I looked, he opened the box and showed me his flies, the plastic insects with red and orange fangs and wings. On the shelf with the tackle box, he'd piled stacks of papers and notebooks.

In the days before it was determined what would become of me, my grandfather appeared and disappeared like a ghost. He tended my grandmother as if he were a nurse, in the same way she had tended me during my illness. He would read to her in his too loud voice, gardening magazines and cookbooks, and then when he would emerge from the guest room, he would say nothing more. He seemed to float from room to room, soundlessly, as if he wanted everyone to participate in his deafness, hear exactly what he heard—nothing. He wore his socks or slippers around the house, kept his shoes by the back door and put them on only when he went outside to garden. He refused to wear his hearing aids, and his ears looked oversized and naked. And now when he belched or yawned or sighed, he performed these functions without sound, and he said no words at all. His eyes were always red-rimmed and bloodshot, and sometimes his hands shook, and his face looked damp, but I never heard him cry again. When I was pretending to read a book, or even just staring out the window, he would come up behind me, and simply stand there; I rarely even heard him breathe. He would search my face as if he were looking for something. He was like my own father: when I was with him, I never felt I had to talk, and I always had reassurance that he would say very little himself. GranVinny would always be there, even when I least expected it, so that I came to expect him everywhere, and his presence shadowed everything I did, and I began to rely on it. Sound became our enemy. My pain had fled into hiding and secreted itself under layers of skin and hard muscle and those infinite convolutions of emotion that breed inside us. I wanted to meet my own grief, to dig it out of my heart and face it, but it seemed to be buried inside me like a finch trapped in my rib cage.

the silent archivist

After the stream of sympathizers and the covered casseroles diminished, and Aunt DeeDee had cried what seemed to me must be all her tears, she occupied herself with the business of moving back to St. Louis, and I spent long afternoons at home alone with my silent grandparents. The more all of them showed their grief, the more awkward I felt about letting any emotion surface. Aunt DeeDee got a job as a perfume buyer at Neiman Marcus, GranVinny tended GranPearl, and I waited, numb, wondering when I would begin to mourn.

One morning I woke up to find a pile of books at the foot of my bed: three black ledgers of yellowing pages, the covers labeled with adhesive tape with dates from December 14, 1942, to June 1944. My grandfather's handwriting looped over every page. The books appeared to chronicle his war years. I skimmed through the pages, and my eye caught a phrase, "lion and lily pattern in the carpet." Mimi's canvas flashed into my mind, and I shivered. I stayed up until dawn that night reading and rereading, and when I finally slept, the nimbus around the nearly full moon outside the stone tower trembled in my vision. When I woke up the early-summer sunlight was already blinding, and the diaries were gone. I waited for GranVinny to say something about them, but he never did.

But after that, every day, he would disappear down the basement stairs and emerge with a family book—a scrapbook, or a photo album. At the end of each day, whether I had examined it or not, he'd take it downstairs again. I came to think of him as the silent archivist, tendering his treasures as if they were rubies and emeralds, protecting them from exposure and theft, and keeping all the gems in the family.

One afternoon after bringing GranPearl her lunch, GranVinny napped on the rug; his hands were folded on his chest as if he were mocking death, and a loneliness took me by surprise. The loneliness gripped me, and I felt my heart flutter dangerously. I prowled around the house, opening a book here, lifting a vase there, touching the cool porcelain and marble, the filigree frames and mahogany armoires, as if to ground myself in reality. And I now believe I was searching for something, more of the pieces to the puzzle that was my parents, more moments of raw discovery to make me feel.

I wandered upstairs to Mimi's—now my—room. Looking at all the dolls and knickknacks, I was struck by how few personal belongings from her life in St. Louis she had brought to Wilders Ferry. Since I'd moved into the tower room, I had been reluctant to touch Mimi's things, as if I wouldn't be able to bear what I would feel. But now I skimmed my fingertips along the smooth glass and over the lock of the bookcase packed with hardcovers. I ran back downstairs to get one of GranPearl's hairpins, pushed it into the keyhole, but the pin just bent. Then I tried a toothpick, and it broke off. I spent the better part of the next hour on the bed, asking myself where I would hide a small key if I were Mimi. I tried her jewelry boxes, mostly filled with buttons with sixties slogans such as MAKE LOVE NOT WAR and TO GO TOGETHER IS GROOVY—TO COME TOGETHER DIVINE. I lifted the lids of china pin boxes and swept my hand over the top shelf that held her dolls. I strained to decipher the code, and as soon as I thought of the answer I knew it was the right one. It was in an envelope taped under her bed; the envelope was bulging with curls that looked like the color of hers; the black of the hair obscured the silver of the key.

I opened the case and thumbed through her books. They were stacked two deep. Some were art books, but many of them were poetry. I removed *Kaddish*, by Allen Ginsberg, and saw behind it the orange binding of a small book covered in painted linen. It was a diary; the entries spanned two years. Mimi's doodles took up most of every page. The early entries read more like notes, largely about boys whose names I had never heard and homework assignments. But the last few passages, which sprawled over only a few pages, were clearly departures.

What I could glean from her words and illustrations—and what I have embellished as I recall it now—was that one morning a week or so before Mimi turned sixteen, she had awakened struck with the futility of cutting her hair, of wrapping it in those porcupine-spined and wire mesh rollers, of piercing each one with a plastic pin that pricked the scalp, of coaxing, then spraying it into shape, and so that day she did nothing with it. She intended just to let it hang, but it had a mind of its own, and refused. The curls flipped this way and that, flapped over her ears, cut into her eyes, and sprouted from her neck.

The boy in front of her in trig noticed it first. "You look like a witch," he said.

"Do I?" she replied bravely and, digging the metal end of her pencil into her wooden desk, carved his initials.

For a week or two GranPearl was patient, and then she started putting on the pressure. She made Mimi an appointment at Maxine's, a stylish salon wedged in between Saks Fifth Avenue and Montaldo's and patronized by the menthol cigarette–smoking wives of doctors and lawyers and businessmen. The morning of her appointment, Mimi took the family Cadillac but came back four hours later with the same hair, the curls still curving everywhichway and looking, to her mother, significantly longer than when she had left.

Then GranPearl decided to cut it herself. She lay in wait for Mimi like a cat poised to pounce on a mouse. She'd grab the scissors as soon as she called Mimi down for lunch or just before she left on a date. Not quite able to hide them behind her back, she was driven to concealing them at her side. At dinner she would stare at the ever lengthening strands obsessively as if she were waiting for them to do something outrageous on their own, while Mimi, oblivious, envisioned a painting swirling with color and thick with paint in the vortex of which she and a paramour, perhaps the boy in front of her in trig, rendered with flowing strokes and shimmering light, would kiss. And then the mishap would come, and my otherwise sane and loving grandmother would begin to shake from her Achilles heel, and the quake would rise in her and pour out her mouth in a shout—"Get your hair out of the zucchini!" And that was how Mimi and her mother had passed dinners and suppers and brunches and snack times, with the tension hovering around them close to their ears, like the humidity outside, always ready to squeeze against the skin.

When I returned the diary to its hiding place, I placed the books in the same order, put the key in the same envelope, but I slipped a lock of the hair between my pillowslip and the pillow. I murmured to myself, more than once, so that I could hear them in my own voice, my aunt's words from her first visit to Wilders Ferry, "Mimi overreacted."

A few days later, on a Saturday, as I walked by the stereo, I noticed a gash in the wood of the record cabinet and slid it open. I read the worn spines—an entire row of Italian opera, spanning centuries of passion, four disks to each slender box. The first I picked up was *Rigoletto*; I balanced the box on the top of the cabinet while I removed a white jacket. Right away I could feel something was wrong. Out fell a five-sided fragment of the disk, then another. My heart leapt with something like guilt. What had I done? How could I have broken his precious record? I grabbed the next jacket and pressed it in the middle with my thumb; it bowed. I shook it and then reached in. A sharp edge scratched my finger. I drew out a fragment. Then another. And another. I reached back into the cabinet methodically, determined to find a record that was still intact.

I saved *La Boheme* for last. Before I opened the box, I studied its illustration—the couple in the garret, their clasped hands—and imagined that those hands belonged to my mother, the bohemian. Then I shook the box; the broken pieces knocked against the cardboard. Anger held the tears tight to my eyes. My hand trembled. I lifted the lid and spilled the fragments onto the piano bench and began to piece them back together, one at a time, like a jigsaw puzzle. A gasp startled me, and as I pivoted to see my aunt, I scratched the jagged end of a fragment against the mahogany and left a wound in the bench.

I followed Aunt DeeDee into the kitchen. GranVinny sat alone at the table, in front of a bowl of tomato soup and a plate of hard-boiled eggs. Aunt DeeDee blurted out, "What did you do to all the records?" He stopped slurping his soup, held his spoon in the air, and his eyes darted from one to the other of us, must have seen something dangerous in our expressions.

She stood next to him and lowered the hand clutching his spoon.

Registering alarm, he let go of the spoon and started to rise from his seat when she shouted into his face, "Records, Papa! Lake wants to know why you broke them all." She whirled her finger in little recordlike revolutions. He shook his head back and forth so he couldn't see her, then carried his plate, napkin, glass, and silverware to the sink and walked slowly down to the basement. Chest heaving, DeeDee spun out of the room.

I felt a new panic rise in me. She's wrong about me, I thought. I didn't want to know why he broke them; I knew already.

When I walked back into the living room a few hours later, the cabinet was closed and the piano bench freshly polished.

It was then that I began to wait for the weekday afternoons, for GranVinny to nap and for time to discover more about my mother's life. A week or so later, I opened the door to a walk-in closet. I pulled a string for the light, but nothing happened, so I felt my way in the dark all the way to the back. It smelled like a curious combination of cedar and mothballs. Stacks of tissue paper and spools of ribbon occupied one of the back corners, and leaning on the opposite wall were a large sketchbook and clean canvases of varying sizes. I flipped through them all and then ran my hand along the textured surfaces. I was about to leave when I felt a piece of paper, smooth and thin. When I drew it out of the stack, the upper corner crumbled. I walked with it to the closet door to examine it in the daylight.

It was a charcoal sketch, only slightly smudged in the lower left corner, and the paper was yellowed the color of GranVinny's war diaries. With only a few curving lines, the face suggested a generous nose, sensuous mouth, arched eyebrows. Thick hair curled behind the shoulders and fanned out to mid-back, like an earthly aura.

The figure stood with one hand on her hip, the elbow forming a graceful triangle, in a pose that was wholly natural, unprovocative. She wore pants that hugged the ankle; from the waist up, she wore nothing. Her breasts were different sizes, the left slightly more pendulous than the right, and the charcoal had been rubbed with a fingertip along the curving lines to suggest fullness.

It had to be Mimi.

Something I only barely recognized as anger boiled inside me, and one hand pulled the sketch from the other, nearly ripping the fragile page. And when I moved my thumb, I noticed the signature. "Rose," it said, in the rounded, backhand manuscript I had been reading for weeks, and under it obscure letters, difficult to discern. Stepping out of the closet to lift the page toward the light, I strained to read it: "1944." Two years before my mother was born.

One morning GranVinny left with the car to buy some lotion to rub on GranPearl's hands, and I found myself on my own. Restless, and feeling more alone with GranPearl, helpless, in the house, I walked downstairs past the neat cases of things he stored on shelves and in cardboard cartons. The basement was like a labyrinth and seemed to extend much farther than the house above it. I turned a sudden corner, and an odd contraption under a well window caught my eye. It looked like some sort of greenhouse in miniature, light-green plastic with a hole for a grow lamp. A humidifier was plugged in and whirring on the floor. I pushed away the plastic and saw a rudimentary shelf stacked with shoe boxes. In some a scrawny plant was rooted in the soil. Each shoe box was labeled with two Latin words, which I took to be genus and species. Underneath, in GranVinny's handwriting, was the vernacular. They had stunning names, rich and mellifluous, words that, when I said them aloud, sounded oddly familiar—mountain lady's slipper, ragged robin, silky lupine, Northern suncup, owl's clover, scarlet gilia, pearly everlasting, narrow-petaled stonecrop, yellow bell. I uttered them over and over, just to hear the sounds, whispered them in rhythm with my heart, and then I heard the electric garage door, and suddenly felt as if I had been eavesdropping on the most private of conversations. I replaced the plastic, smoothed out its wrinkles, and before GranVinny's car pulled into the garage, I was upstairs and reading on Mimi's bed.

That evening, when Aunt DeeDee sat with GranPearl, reading magazines to her and showing her the pictures as if she were a child, GranVinny and I sat on the sofa watching TV with the sound off. My body let down, and I let the images on the screen, and the hum of the refrigerator in the next room, take me somewhere else, and found myself talking. I spoke straight ahead, in a normal voice. He couldn't hear me, but he sensed I was speaking and turned his gaze from the television to watch my face. I found myself spilling out words.

"GranVinny, it just hurts so much, I can't stand to watch you with your little handkerchief dusting all the woodwork the way GranPearl used to do, and I'm so, so sorry that I found out your secret with my mother, I feel like a spy, and I don't deserve you. And it hurts, and then I hear her rocking in the other room, the runners squeaking, the slaps on her cheeks, and I think about my mother, and I—I just can't, GranVinny. You just don't know how it feels."

His face reflected my expressions, and he reached for my hand and wrapped his arm around me, and his eyes filled with tears. Suddenly I heard a noise, jerked my head around to see my aunt, her eyes puffy. "Don't let me interrupt," she said coldly, and left the room.

Later that night I had just clicked off the light on the nightstand and was lying with my eyes open, adjusting to the dark while gray and black shadows distilled around the shapes of my mother's childhood treasures: a china lady in a hoopskirt, a stuffed elephant with a bow around the neck, a bride doll. My eyes were closing when I heard the squeak of the door and focused on the silhouette against the yellow light in the hall of my aunt in the doorway. "Good night, Aunt DeeDee," I said, feeling heavy with sleep.

"You don't have to call me Aunt DeeDee, Sugarcomb."

I nodded and muttered, "Good night, DeeDee."

And for a moment there was silence, and then I felt her move closer to me. My eyes were closed now, and I didn't want to take the trouble to open them, but I could feel her heat and hear her breathing, and then she lowered herself to my ear and whispered, "Call me Mom."

the loft

A few weeks into July, Aunt DeeDee came home late from work and announced that she and I were moving to the city, to what she called a "loft." She put her hand on my shoulder, and I withdrew, the way I used to when Mimi tried to touch me not all that long before. Aunt DeeDee's eyes widened. She added quickly that it had been GranVinny's idea. He was concerned, she said in a shaky voice, that White Oak Lane had become unbearably gloomy for me, and he wanted me to heal quickly. I wondered how much he had actually heard of what I had said a few weeks before. Since that night he had seemed to withdraw from us, to spend more time sequestered with GranPearl, talking to her in his loud, grainy voice, as if he were trying to reach that distant, elusive space his wife occupied.

The evening we moved out, he insisted on cooking us supper, but opened a can of Spam onto a paper plate for himself. "You must have developed an addiction in the army," Aunt DeeDee tried to joke, but even though I knew he couldn't hear it, it made me wince. I doubted if she had bothered to read his diaries.

When we left the house, he was still methodically eating his Spam off a paper plate. When we kissed him good-bye, he stared straight ahead.

I think Aunt DeeDee chose the Soulard area because an article in one of her magazines described it as "up and coming . . . the next Soho." Soulard, the oldest neighborhood in the city, was in all the important ways the farthest from Wilders Ferry I had ever hoped to be. The brownstones fronted directly onto brick sidewalks, and iron fences separated square gardens from the foot traffic. Awnings from corner restaurants and bars extended nearly to the street, and blackboards standing on easels listed daily specials. The trim on a few of the houses was painted pink or blue, no doubt reminding my aunt of San Francisco. I was grateful our loft was black; I didn't know how I would have reacted to living in a purple house again.

The building was graced with a shiny bronze plaque, SOULARD RESTORATION GROUP, screwed into the brick. I followed the brick-floored breezeway, which separated our building from the next and was barely as wide as my body and the suitcase I carried, to an empty birdbath surrounded by a tiny courtyard in the back. The cosmopolitan feel to the area, the stately architecture, one narrow building nearly abutting the next, gave my spirits a strange lift. And the promise of a bird or two, the pigeons cooing from their roosts in the caves, the two pin oaks at the edge of the street—these were all I wanted or needed of the natural world, I thought, ever again.

Inside, we climbed a spiral staircase to our loft. What may once have been a large, open space was now partitioned into boxlike rooms. The casement windows were covered with contemporary-looking Venetian blinds. I raised the blinds on the window in the front room and saw that our view was the three dark towers of the brewery, which sprawled across several city blocks. Taking my suitcase to one of the smaller cubicles, I heard Aunt DeeDee's voice echo around me, "Here we are, Lake. Home, sweet home. If we only had an elevator."

It didn't take us long to move in, we had so little. Most of it was Aunt DeeDee's clothes and shoes. The San Francisco apartment she'd rented was furnished. I finished unpacking while she took a shower. At the bottom of the last box was a collection of jars in various sizes—homemade plum jam, dusty and unopened, the jars that Mimi had given her sister each time she came to Wilders Ferry. I stooped over, and in the dust, with my forefinger, I wrote "Mimi" and then with my palm immediately rubbed it out.

The next morning Aunt DeeDee and I set up in the hall the small glass-enclosed bookcase she had taken from Mimi's room after removing Mimi's books and leaving them on her bed. Aunt DeeDee filled it with knickknacks; not a book was in it. Every time I glanced its way, I saw through the glass to the diary covered in painted linen. When I passed the bookcase on my way to my room, I tried not to look at it; it almost became a ritual.

I have to admit, though I missed my grandfather's odd company, it was easier to live somewhere else than in my mother's house; it was simply easier to bury my feelings. Aunt DeeDee had promised GranVinny that she would give the White Oak Lane address and enroll me in the high school she and Mimi had graduated from, and I was beginning to mark the days until the end of summer when I might, at last, begin to build a new life.

As the summer days shortened, Aunt DeeDee did her best to entice me into resuming our former exploration of the barren and rocky terrain of her love life. She clipped ads and tried to engage me in planning strategies, but more often than not, I'd nod politely and find an excuse to stay in my room. I knew, and I wonder now if she knew, something was different, something not entirely related to the losses we had suffered together. Whenever she met someone new, as soon as she got home she'd describe the encounter in detail, how they'd sip drinks with umbrellas and twisted slices of fresh fruit and arrive at concerts in strapless dress and tux. But these details no longer thrilled me, and responding now felt tedious, as if it were part of a job.

Although every Sunday GranVinny cooked us supper, usually something from a can, which we ate on a coffee table he'd moved into the guest room so we could keep company with GranPearl, GranVinny refused to visit the Loft.

"He just thinks old-maid daughters should live with their families until they rot. You know," Aunt DeeDee explained, lowering her voice to the conspiratorial, "that old Sicilian myth."

But I knew why he never came to see us. He was hurt. So many of his women had left him in one way or another.

One morning Aunt DeeDee, clipping the tags from another new pair of Gloria Vanderbilt jeans, said as matter-of-factly as she could, "It's time to celebrate the fact that we're alive. Mimi would have wanted us to." I wasn't so sure, but it was pointless to contradict her about her sister. "In fact," she said, "I think we *should* celebrate. We'll ask Art to join us. He's a headhunter," she added, her eyebrows arched. I knew she expected me to be impressed. I looked at her askance. She looked apologetic and with her finger removed what must have been a crumb near my upper lip. "A small dinner party. That's all."

That weekend, after our Sunday supper at White Oak Lane, DeeDee packed a shopping bag of GranPearl's cookbooks and *Emily Post* to take with us to the Loft. Then we rummaged through GranPearl's china cabinets and silverware and table linen drawers. She even got GranVinny to polish the silver pitcher. He collected a supply of soft rags, clean and folded, that he also used to clean his fishing tackle. Then, he reached into an empty vase on a tea cart and took out four tarnished silver napkin rings shaped like rose blossoms. When he turned them in his hand, I saw that they were engraved with the initial "R" in a fine Mediterranean script and "1943" on the inside. For a second I caught his eye. Aunt DeeDee took them from his palm and, without looking at them, tossed them on top of the tablecloth.

When we had amassed and shined everything we needed, GranVinny was already preparing his breakfast for the next day. "See you soon," I wrote on a paper napkin, but he waved the notion away, shook his head, and put a five-dollar bill into DeeDee's hand. She hugged him good-bye and whispered "I love you," though she knew he couldn't hear it.

Aunt DeeDee set the table for three—not a particularly festive number, I couldn't help thinking—and asked my opinion on the placement of every fork and knife. I was surprised that her experience with elegance was even more minimal than mine—or even Mimi's. (I recalled Passover meals, when Mimi uncovered from hiding all the china and silver she had received for Wedding Number One, the sparkle in the glassware, the gleam of the sterling.) One magazine DeeDee read suggested placing scented candles in tinted glass globes on the corners of the table, for "that romantic touch." I hated candlelight; my mother and her sister seemed to be so obsessed with it. But DeeDee was so happy that I just lit the candles dutifully, trying to memorize the layout of the table before the electric lights went out and I had to guess which end to locate the peas on.

Serving a multicourse dinner was a particular challenge to us since we weren't used to making more than one thing at any meal. I mapped out a schedule and set three timers. I spent the last hour or so alone in the kitchen while Aunt DeeDee "freshened up" and steamed up the Loft with one of her lingering showers. When I lifted a window, she said, "Don't. The air conditioner won't work if there's a window open." I closed one of the cookbooks and fanned myself, trying to look as supercilious as possible. Then I walked to the air conditioner and jabbed the "colder" button. The machine sputtered and stopped. I pushed every button, whispering "please, please" as if in desperate prayer, but nothing happened. I slumped in a chair until Aunt DeeDee, and a roomful of pent-up steam, materialized from the shower. When Art finally arrived we were as hot as we'd ever been—and exhausted.

All the while we were preparing the banquet, every one of Aunt DeeDee's sentences had begun either "Art this" or "Art that." When the man himself walked in, I was disappointed. He was, after all, the first man in my aunt's life I had actually met in the flesh, and I have to admit I had expectations about that flesh. I pictured him as one of the models in the magazines that she piled on every surface of the house. When I'd asked her what he looked like, she'd said, "Tall, I think."

I should have realized that Aunt DeeDee's notion of tall wasn't the same as the rest of the world's. As Art stood at the door, a foot and a half of air space separated the top of his balding head from the frame. Later, when Aunt DeeDee asked him to get the sugar cubes, which she kept on top of the refrigerator so she wouldn't be tempted, he had to stand on tiptoe. Otherwise, he may as well have been a teacher at Wilders Ferry Central School—nondescript, borderline homely—except that he was dressed with an eye toward success. A few strands of hair were carefully combed sideways over his pate, and he wore a tie clip with a fraternity pin. When he came in, he brought a "bouquet," two stems wrapped in clear plastic with fragments of a price sticker, so I knew he had picked it up at the local supermarket. Aunt DeeDee thanked him for it several times, during lulls in the conversation.

The menu, after hours of debate, was to be Rock Cornish game hen, Parker House rolls, Yorkshire pudding, Lyonnaise potatoes, and—our culinary capstone—baked Alaska. Apparently, I mused, we needed at least one capital letter in every course. The steam from the shower hung in the air, hovering near the ceiling and swirling in patterns that looked like skulls.

We politely seated our guest and then left him alone while we scurried around like the Keystone Cops; all we needed were nightsticks and helmets, Aunt DeeDee and I. Whenever a timer would buzz, one of us would fly into the cubicle kitchen, throw on an apron, and fiddle with the buzzer while trying to find our place in my byzantine outline of what to do when. When the headhunter thought no one was looking, he picked up one of GranPearl's Waterford goblets and, to examine it, brought it so close to his face he might have wiped his nose on it.

Dots of perspiration glistened on Aunt DeeDee's nose, and Art loosened his tie, removed his jacket, undid the collar button of his shirt. When we were in the kitchen, he furtively worked open a few more buttons, exposing the sweat-matted, graying hair around his breastbone. Between courses he dabbed at the back of his neck with a handkerchief, and every time he folded it on his lap, he said, "Pardon me."

"My, my," he kept repeating. "It sure is close in here." And he stretched his neck, lifted his chin from his shirt collar, and pointed it toward the ceiling as if to thrust his Adam's apple toward us. He looked like a box turtle.

The steam from the pudding blasted me full in the face. When I passed it to the headhunter, his glasses fogged, and he cleaned them on the tablecloth that GranPearl had hand-embroidered with satin-stitched apples and wheelbarrows while GranVinny was in Algeria sewing up the oozing wounds of soldiers.

Aunt DeeDee tried to use this act as an entrée for conversation. "My mother made that for my father when he was overseas during the war. I think he was in the Philippines."

"Africa and Europe," I corrected her.

"Whatever," she shrugged.

"So your father fought in the second War to End All Wars?" he said without irony. "That was the war when Americans could be proud to be Americans. Not like the last war. Hippies. Greasy kids trying to make us ashamed to make our country safe for democracy. Fight for world freedom."

"Oh," DeeDee interrupted, "did you fight in Vietnam?"

"Me? No," he said and guffawed, as if she had told a joke. "My eyes, you know." He pointed to his thick glasses lest we miss the point. "Those and the fact that my father's law partner was on the draft board." He gesticulated with his fork, then used it to carve a fluid line in the cheesy potatoes. He drew back from the steam. "Long-haired hippies."

I felt a strange ripple of resentment, something just under the skin; I stayed in the stifling kitchen for nearly half an hour, seeing in the rising vapors my father, his hair in a ponytail and tied away from his forehead with a bright-blue bandana. "Maybe we should just go out," the head-hunter was saying when I returned to the dining area.

Aunt DeeDee shot him a look that might have refrozen the ice in his water glass, and he quickly recouped. "I mean, you're going to so much trouble. We could go out for a while, have a couple drinks, come back when it's fixed."

Aunt DeeDee cranked up the broiler to brown the rolls, and suddenly the heat seemed suffocating. As we ate, the hot fog from the game hens and the pudding rose toward our faces as if in slow motion, and polite conversation all but stopped. I excused myself and nearly sprinted into the kitchen to stick my wrists under the faucet. When Aunt DeeDee came in I said in a stage whisper, "Let's bag the Alaska."

Aunt DeeDee and I watched from the living room window as he pulled away in his silver Honda, its air conditioner no doubt at full blast. We left all the dishes on the table, blew out the candles, one of which had already cracked one of the globe-shaped tinted glasses, and escaped to an all-night donut shop where we usually had to wear sweaters, they turned up the air-conditioning so high.

"He liked you," she said, swirling powdered cream into her coffee and emphasizing the "you" as if I were a contender. "Story of my life." She kept her eyes on her cup.

I was struck dumb. I didn't remember having spoken directly to Art the entire evening. And if I had let myself, even for a millisecond, the time it takes to nick your thumb on the razor edge of paper, I would have had to admit to feeling a hollowness, like the smooth tunnel of a silver flute.

meadowbrook high

As the gummy summer air thinned and we opened the door in the evenings to let the cicadas sing through the screens, the scalloped edges of the oak leaves on White Oak Lane began to curl the color of rust. Aunt DeeDee gave the White Oak Lane address to the school as promised, and she said she would drop me off at GranVinny's before work, and I'd walk down the lane and take the county bus system to and from Meadowbrook High School every day.

I spent so much time dressing for my first day of school that I was nearly late. Even before walking into the building that seemed to have more concrete, glass, and bricks than the entire set of storefronts off Main Street in Wilders Ferry, I felt hopelessly out of place. The parking lot was crammed with waxed cars. Kids hooted at each other from the backs of Corvette convertibles in powder blue and fire-engine red and from the windows of Mercedes-Benzes. The license plates were all personalized with initials and cutesy sayings—NO 1 and HE MAN and LOVE BUG. Despite these gestures toward individuation, everyone looked alike, except for the two or three chocolate-brown faces. All the girls carried leather purses with shoulder straps, and their earlobes were studded with diamond-like gems that looked as if they could be real. The secretary said, "Idaho, huh? We've never had one from Idaho before." I wondered if she knew where it was.

She sent me to the counseling center to get the scores of the tests I'd taken that summer to determine if I could pass into the tenth grade even though I'd missed school the spring before. I was afraid to ask for a map and spent about fifteen minutes wandering the halls. I passed a wall lined with glass cases of gleaming trophies and, near the ceiling, a row of framed photos, head shots, labeled with names, dates, and awards. All the students in these pictures wore suits, dresses, or high-collared blouses, and I was about to laugh at this display of historical nerdiness when I saw one face behind the glass that made my heart sink into my stomach. There she was, in a white blouse with a little round collar secured with a scarab stickpin that was so crooked it made her whole face look askew: Miriam Rose. She wore no makeup and was grinning at the camera. Under the photo a plaque read MOST LIKELY TO SUCCEED, 1964. For an instant I felt panicked that someone would notice a resemblance. Then I reassured myself. "Twenty years ago," I said aloud, but I felt a burning inside my chest. I doubled over and, while I caught my breath, pretended to be picking up a dropped pen.

I spent the rest of the day taking tests and talking to counselors. Meadowbrook had more counselors and psychologists and nurses and social workers than Wilders Ferry had teachers. The linoleum floors shone with wax and scuff marks from hard-soled shoes; the lockers were freshly painted a cheery blue, and all had locks that worked. The cafeteria was carpeted and air-conditioned. The corridors seemed to stretch farther than they did in fact, a lesson in perspective, pointing inward at the end, then turning perfectly into another equally long one. The students carried books to class, and not one backpack was in sight. Posters designed on word processors announced meetings of the National Honor Society and the Young Republicans. At the end of a corridor, I followed the odor of chlorine to an Olympic-size swimming pool. I had never before swum in chlorine, and when I swam in PE class for the first time, I took such a long shower to wash off the chemicals that I was late to class.

Meadowbrook had an honors program, and I'd made enough Number 2 pencil slashes between the right lines to test into it. From the first day, I knew they meant business. The rules had changed from those I had taken for granted at Wilders Ferry Central School. The game of school was won easily in Wilders Ferry, the goal being to manipulate as many teachers as possible during the day (and this tactic worked especially effectively on coaches who were assigned classes of English and history and math to justify their piece of the payroll) into swerving the focus of discussion to the last Friday's game with Coeur d'Alene or legalization of marijuana—anything so that we didn't have to lug books home. At Meadowbrook, at least in the classes I was tracked into, you won the game, I quickly learned, by getting the highest grades, being admitted to the most prestigious colleges (including the one my mother had graduated from), and ultimately, by making the most money.

In the afternoons, if the bus was even a few minutes late, I'd see GranVinny's olive-skinned face scanning the distance for me in one window or another, or if the weather wasn't too cold or rainy, he'd be working out in the yard, and as soon as he spotted me on the lane he'd stop, put down his watering can or rake, and lumber down the long drive to meet me. He'd carry my books into the kitchen, where he'd take out a pitcher of iced tea, or press the button on the coffee machine, which he'd already set. He would even buy little waxed containers of milk for me, though he never touched the stuff. We'd sit together at the glass table and not say anything for a while, and then I'd start talking to him as if he could hear every nuance in my speech; I couldn't help thinking of the way my mother had talked to her rabbit. He would look at me, taking in my whole face, the way I shaped my mouth around my words, the way I tensed and relaxed my lips, as if he wanted to understand everything I said, though sometimes his eyes would wander from my lips to my eyes, and his own would fill. Then I'd know to stop talking while he looked outside the window at some squirrel stealing his tomatoes, some still small and green on the vine, and he'd pick up the BB gun he kept at the back door, shoulder it, stalk out into the yard, and shoot at the squirrel thief until he had composed himself, long after it had fled into the spirea.

Every afternoon, we'd visit GranPearl in the guest room. She was getting stronger, the doctor said, but seemed to have no energy for us. I offered her perfumes and powders that Aunt DeeDee brought back from Neiman's, and sometimes she'd smile and say thank you, but mostly she just wanted to be left alone. GranVinny brought me books, old books, family books. I had seen many of the albums before, but now they were half empty, only a few photos in each plastic slot on each page. It seemed random at first, this pattern; it took me a few days to realize that he had meticulously removed all the images of his older daughter. I found many of these photos later, in the dim maze of his basement hideout. We'd pore over the half-empty albums, and I'd point to a face, and he'd either write down whose it was or shrug and point to his head with an extended forefinger and vertical thumb as if his hand were a revolver. Once, at a picture of my aunt as a toddler with a witch's hat and a diaper that was obviously soaking and weighted down to her dimpled kneecaps, he even laughed, a silent laughter in which only breaths were discernible, as if the sound were encased in convoluted layers of flannel.

Aunt DeeDee picked me up every night, sometimes only to leave me alone. When she was home, we'd play Monopoly or we'd try on clothes together. When I was ready to do homework, she'd say, "Just one more round" or "In just a few minutes." And when I'd shake my head, she'd pick up a magazine and thumb through it for a while and then pace around the room as if she were caged. I'd go into my room and shut the door and not appear until morning.

She didn't share my parents' passion for homework. Perhaps it was the fact that my social life was nil, and perhaps the fact that I had an inflamed desire to counteract the Idaho potato image that clung to everything I did, but I mined resources in myself I didn't know I had, and studied with a vengeance. When I closed the door to my room, Aunt DeeDee, clearly annoyed, would talk to me right outside my door in a voice just soft enough so I'd have to leave my desk and approach the door to hear what she said. I wouldn't give her the satisfaction of opening it, though, not even a crack.

Of all my classes, only English and Earth Science didn't make my stomach knot. At least at first. My father had brought home so many books that I didn't feel intimidated by the enormous amount of reading that Meadowbrook honors students were expected to do. I just wasn't used to thinking about what I read, at least not in a conscious way, particularly a way that manifested itself in ink marks that covered five pages a week. In Honors English students in pearl necklaces and gold chains and black penny loafers stuck their hands high in the air and spewed off a host of words like "trope," and "preternatural," and "cosmic irony."

I liked Earth Science because I knew a lot about it already. While my classmates had been staring at their TV's and lying on beaches in Fort Lauderdale, I had been backpacking in the Bitterroots and kicking around rocks; while their fathers were reading court cases and playing tennis at the country club, mine was poring over maps. The tests were objective, mostly rock identification, and I even memorized the textbook to maintain my edge. The only part that gave me pause was the day the book introduced the Idaho batholith.

I remembered the evening my father showed me on one of his maps where this notorious chunk of granite stretched from Idaho City north through McCall up into Grangeville. It formed the Salmon River Mountains, he told me, glacier-cut and rocky. I knew those mountains. We used to camp there with Dylan and Paris. My mind carried me back to the places where the whitebark pines stood as snags after they'd been burned. Dyl showed me how the young pines had begun to come up underneath, in the shadow of their elders, how they couldn't really grow up without shade, how we'd kick the rocks around their dark stumps. The granite in this book seemed so remote from the Idaho I knew, the granite made of quartz and feldspar and mica. I could see the real granite, not these slick pages of typeface and close-up diagrams of the way the rock should look. I could hear my mother's lilting voice explaining all the colors. How quartz takes on the color of something else, like a chameleon, but changes it a little. How feldspar has two colors: one milky, the other dark like the needles of the Douglas fir when it is coated with summer dust. Could hear my father tell me how feldspar was named for the fields where it is scattered. I could feel the warmth of our woodstove, the nights I'd spent reading with my father, the inlaid mica as transparent as glass, giving off an opalesque glow. And I could see the stones by the lake, how when we rolled them between our thumbs and forefingers, they reflected tiny mirrors of light. I could still feel the pieces of granite I'd pick up on the road and grip in my fist, the sharp edges blunted by age. Could almost feel that weighty chunk with the translucent scallops and pink stripes, my only gift to my only friend, how it made an imprint like a brand in my palm.

Once in a while, when I'd approach a locker, girls with Gucci bags and matching wallets and sapphire teardrop necklaces would politely say hello, and ask me if I had plans for the weekend, and I'd say, "Just family things," and they'd say, "Well, have fun," and turn away and talk about this or that party at this or that someone's house.

Between classes, I plastered a smile on my face, my still-unfamiliar lipstick sticking to my incisors, and threaded through the confetti of motion. All the bodies avoided eye contact with me, and when I passed them I thought I heard a giggle and a whisper, "Potato."

Looking for ways to hide, I discovered the library. It looked more like a reception hall than a high school library. It was organized into an L-shaped double room, spacious and carpeted in a cool-blue weave and lined with computers. In the center of the room directly off the hall, an antique globe rested on a marble pedestal. The first time I walked into the adjoining room I faced something that made my heart quiver against my ribs. In the center of this room was a piece of sculpture, a life-size statue of two men who, even cast in bronze, looked familiar. I walked all the way around it before glancing at the plate at its base on which was engraved their names: Meriwether Lewis, William Clark, the two names from history that every Idaho student, from the most inquisitive to the most obtuse, knew. I felt something elusive and irrational rise in my blood and lock my muscles.

I stared dumbly into the dark-gold hammered recesses of Clark's cape and struggled to come to terms with my own astonishment that St. Louis had laid claim to Idaho's first white heroes. Their clear severance from Idaho lore and grounding in the middle of the midwestern suburbs undercut my sense of the order of things. What did these insulated rich kids know about what Lewis and Clark really saw, the open spaces they explored and mapped, the details they documented? Could they picture Lewis and Clark building new canoes along the Clearwater? Did they know they could count the sands at the bed of the bright-green river that led them to the Columbia? How they gave colored beads to the Nez Perce, how perhaps one of their trinkets was a necklace that Clark laid around the neck of Graceanne's great-great-grandmother? How entire cities built in valleys between rocky hills carried the legacies of their names? I felt disoriented, but also annoyed at myself, astounded that I cared even an iota about which of my lives claimed historical figures 150 years dead.

I went straight to the shelves, piled books on a corner table, and after I had satisfied myself that St. Louis indeed had a right to Idaho's original pilgrims, I thumbed through a slim volume at the bottom of my stack. On a glossy page in the center, color drawings of familiar-looking plants drew my eye. They were cameo photos in purples and pinks and golds and red-oranges, flowers spreading luxuriantly through the forests and meadows and mountains I knew. Each was labeled with a Latin name, words I glossed over, but which I was sure I had seen before. And under them the vernacular. These, first identified more than a century ago two thousand miles from where I stood by the statue, bolted into my consciousness and plugged into something I knew well. I could hear them in my own voice, almost feel the shape of their names in my mouth. I copied them into a notebook and watched the clock until the end of the school day.

After school I waited for GranVinny to go outside to tend his gardens. As soon as he shut the door behind him, I ran down into the basement with my notebook and turned corners until I got to the makeshift greenhouse. I carefully checked the labels on the boxes against my list, both Latin and vernacular, and every time they matched, I smiled as if I were surprised. When I finished, I ripped out the page in my notebook, crunched it up, and stuffed it into my pocket. I listened for GranVinny, and when I heard nothing, I poked around in the corner, which was crowded with his gardening tools and old appliances dating from the fifties. I found the last piece of the puzzle with surprisingly little effort. At the back of an adjacent shelf was a neat stack of envelopes. I examined the top one and recognized GranVinny's name and address in Mimi's handwriting; the next paper was labeled the same. Every envelope contained an empty packet of wildflower seeds. A few of those on the bottom of the pile were beginning to yellow. Each was postmarked, and the pile was in chronological order. There were fifteen, one each year since the year I was born.

That night I stayed awake, thinking of Mimi digging up wildflowers and mailing their seeds to her father in an ingenious code. I wondered if GranPearl or Aunt DeeDee ever deciphered those wordless messages between my mother and grandfather, her cryptic invitations in the language he knew best for him to visit her in the West, compelling him to trace the path of the wildflowers that Lewis and Clark discovered on their revolutionary journey from St. Louis to northern Idaho.

Every afternoon, though I knew he couldn't hear me, I'd report to GranVinny the details of my day with a journalist's speed and precision while he studied my expressions and mimicked them with his own. When he was sure I had finished, he would disappear to the basement and reappear with another treasure, a journal, a scrapbook, Mimi's letters from camp, or just something he liked, like a glass ashtray printed with "Chez Paul" or a rusty Girl Scout knife, the sentimental import of which I could only guess. But he never mentioned the wildflowers; they must have been that private.

granvinny at war

The only time he has been separated from his beloved begins in the final month of 1942.

======

On the ship that takes him away from her, the throbbing of the engine shakes the table as he writes the first of the letters. His first package to her is from Casablanca, watercolors he has painted of the Moroccan landscape and an Arab woman. In Mostaganem, the roofs are flat and turreted. Keyhole-shaped open doorways separate houses from gardens. He pours plasma into burn patients from a crashed B-24.

They convoy by truck, these nomads, pass date trees and rosebushes. In his tent snakes nest under the bedside mat. It has been two months, and he has not heard a word from home. That night he scribbles by flashlight in his tent, first to her, then to himself, and then to his granddaughter, who will not be born for decades.

They move to a racetrack at the edge of the Mediterranean Sea.

The Arabs clear the track of hay, and the evacuation unit sets up its hospital in the grandstand, painting it with a large red cross and partitioning it into rooms for surgery and cots. He picks olives from their backyard.

He is sent into town with his buddies as part of a team to examine whores. He checks for sores and takes smears, saying nothing. Then the others take turns behind a beaded curtain in a makeshift examining room. They stay all afternoon, until the lowering sun through the slats of the shades stripes the couch. One woman in a black, high-necked blouse lies on her belly on a patterned carpet; it is edged with lions and lilies. Her bare buttocks make a half-globe on the floor, and he thinks of a charcoal drawing he wants to do of his wife. Vinny sits cross-legged next to her. She feeds him dates and figs with her fingers; he leans over to take them on his tongue. When the other men are done, they all have a party with champagne and hard-boiled eggs. It is already 1943.

Outside Oran, in a newly cut field of barley, he sets up "Bedside Manor." That night he is reading surgery journals by lantern light when shell fragments and shrapnel hail down, some piercing the canvas and the rest beating out a storm patter on the tin roof of the grandstand. He picks up his poker chips and helmet and heads for the foxhole. When the moonless sky is quiet again, he eats a tin of sardines his wife has sent him and he has secreted under his pillow. After washing his hands, he studies for the Italian lessons he has promised to give, to prepare the men for their move into Sicily. The fall of Tunis and Bizerte has left all of Africa in Allied hands.

Instructed to travel light, he mails home some of his clothes and a money order from his poker winnings. His sweetheart sends him cans of crab, and that night he celebrates by watching a Gene Tierney movie. Another day he knocks around town; guarding the front of the cathedral is a gilded statue of Joan of Arc. He buys sterling napkin rings from a vendor to send home for his beloved to have engraved with their names. A street artist does a quick pencil sketch of the young major, who is surprised that the face on the paper looks angry and mean.

The convoy travels inland, past herds of grazing camels and rocky hills, toward Constantine. He buys cantaloupes and melons and a tinkly bracelet from Arabs along the way. He dines on fried squirrel and boils eggs over a kerosene stove, drinks alcohol and lemon juice. He hammers nails into olive trees to hang his clothes. Flies and mosquitoes are thick, and bombers dip down toward his head as they speed to an airfield nearby. The unit pushes on, past miles of shell craters and tons of twisted steel that was once German and Italian tanks. At the harbor the men cheer at mangled Nazi planes.

Across the water they dock in Licata, off the south coast of Sicily. He brandishes a lobster to add to the sauce of his spaghetti dinner on the beach at Mondello. Up the north coast, in Palermo, rubble lines the streets. Women in long black dresses and hats cook with sticks over open flames and crowd open doorways to wait for rations. One of the women reminds him of his mother, and his eyes follow her; she moves fast, as if she knows he wants something. They set up a hospital in a medical school building. The injured pour in, chunks of flesh chewed off, skulls crushed, jagged bones jutting from bloody flaps of skin, muscles ripped away from shoulders and thighs. He sutures a hand, crisscrossing veins. A wave of bombers attacks. Flames leap up and lap at the air. His scalpel makes wavy incisions. For more than an hour he stares at a black cloud of smoke, then eats a glass of ice cream.

The Jeep takes two hours to Campobello. The stone house of his uncle is crammed with cousins, some from the clay hut next door. He brings the family snapshots of his beautiful, black-haired wife, which make them weep. His mother has written them that their new cousin is not Sicilian, so they don't ask about her family. "*Bella, bella,*" they say, arching their eyebrows and nodding. When he shows them the photos of his sister, Rosalia, and his parents in front of the restaurant, they clutch their hearts and rock back and forth in their chairs and on the dirt floor. He has carried one picture for many years. He doesn't tell them that the shiny black Ford and the white-banded hat are profits from bootlegging whiskey. He leaves them with licorice and cans of Spam.

A few weeks later, three of the men visit him. They bring him a chiffon-and-lace embroidered scarf, baskets of eggs and almond brittle, and a melon. He has little time to spend with them. He is supposed to attend a lecture on wounds. He knows his two years as an intern at County Hospital are not enough, and he has no other training. But he manages to get them a ride back and sends the scarf to Pearl along with some silk hose. The next day he sutures tendons, aspirates knees, and digs out bullets that have lacerated a liver and are lodged in a belly. At mail call he receives tins of film, his first in Kodachrome color. Later he reads *Anna Karenina* by lamplight.

They sail to Swansea. In England they wait for orders, know it's something big. He walks around London in a trench coat, smoking a pipe at Madame Tussaud's. They hang around until June, taking side trips to Edinburgh Castle and Stratford-upon-Avon. When they are told that they will be the first evacuation unit in the Invasion, his bowels gape and knot.

June 6. All night long planes drone overhead to the south. Two- and four-motored planes tow gliders by the hundreds. Dead silence greets every newscast. He sees *Whistling in Brooklyn* and is the last to leave an impromptu dance on a rough and sticky floor, with a Victrola and sandwiches. He washes his underwear, takes a shower, rubs impregnite on his shoes, and checks his gas mask. He sleeps with his clothes on and four days later sees the French coastline at dawn.

Thirty minutes before the unit lands, the Germans shell the shore. They are the first evacuation hospital on French soil, sent to clean up the early carnage. At nightfall they camp in a cow pasture, two miles from the front. While he digs his foxhole, shells whistle through the clouds. Artillery fire shoots into his ears and blocks out other sound. When he walks to the front, he sees smashed tanks and broken gliders. In the water float thousands of boats and cruisers and battleships, barrage balloons on every ship. Squadrons of bombers roar inland. Small-arms fire and mortar bursts blast the air; 88's whine; warships rain shells on the ground. In his ditch, he hugs the dirt, palms pressed to his ears against the eerie scream of plummeting bombs. Huge flashes of light illuminate the beach. Fallen silk parachutes drenched with blood dot the sand. Single bullets from snipers whiz by.

Later, waiting for sleep that never comes, he writes a letter to his beloved, which he folds and tucks into his socks. In the first twenty-four hours, 475 patients, strewn on the grass like bundles of discarded clothing, wait for him. They run six operating tables at once, but still they have to wait until the linen and instruments are ready again. Blasts from the inferno shake the operating room tent. He cuts and cleans and sews and washes with his helmet on, clenching his teeth at the diving planes, praying as best he knows how that the falling fragments will miss him and his patient one more time. He makes a pact with nobody in particular that if he is sent home alive, he will never leave her side.

Flares and smoke color the horizon a muddy red. Blood coats his clothes, the fresh thickening the dry. The chaplain scrubs to help him, pours plasma into soldiers in shock. Wounds from shell fragments and wooden bullets leave gaping holes in the chest and abdomen; limbs lie scattered about. For soldiers with only half a face, he searches for skin from thighs or buttocks to make a jaw. Into faces that are not mangled, he tries to jab a cigarette. Some have only the tongues visible. There is no news except what's in front of him.

They've had no time to put a canvas floor in the tent. In one week they perform 515 operations. In the first five days they run out of penicillin. His back aches from bending over bloodied bodies fourteen hours a day. They take turns trying to sleep. He stuffs surgical cotton into his ears. Then he pops Nembutals, washes them down with homemade gin, but the sky flashes all night, and the noise has entered his head.

They leave Normandy and its mounds of rubble, crumbled ruins, unburied and headless dead, woods shredded by shells, farmland dented with craters, tanks burnt, dead cows bloated and stiff. The weeds are knee-high. "I never dreamed of such destruction." That's what he says. "I never dreamed of such destruction." And that is before he enters Germany. Back at camp he sees Errol Flynn in *Uncertain Glory*. Planes circle; searchlights can't find them. Flak falls around him. Squadrons and squadrons of American bombers make their way to the tip of the peninsula. He gives blood sent from the States to Germans, and wonders if this might be the blood of his beloved, and if this soldier, who grabs him by the ankle to beg for relief from agony, has bayoneted one of her aunts off the train at Treblinka.

They bivouac at Guyancourt in a field of wheat and stubble in a piercing rain, set up hospital tents in the fields beside the Versailles woods. He uses a fish knife to rip away the muddy uniforms of the wounded. He binds charred feet and amputates legs purpled and stinking with gas gangrene.

He is trucked from battlefield to battlefield, and in April finds himself across the Rhine. He marches into Buchenwald and takes his first color pictures, pictures he never shows anyone. He brings them back, but keeps them in a safe-deposit box to which he has the only key. A shortage of coal has stopped the cremations just before they arrive, and the bodies are stacked on a truck trailer. On the way they pass a large warehouse in flames. A lone man crawls out of the blaze; he clutches bits of straw. When the fire is spent, the corpses smolder two and three deep. One of the thousands here could be a blood relation of his unborn daughters and his grand-daughter. He stalks off by himself, his hand over his nose at the stench, the final sparks the only sounds, and howls. He decides not to write about this.

It is May 8, Victory in Europe Day. May 8, nearly a quarter of a century later, will be the birthday of his only granddaughter. One minute after midnight, he finishes his diary on added pages and clips them to the book. He sends the book home to his wife. Their separation has lasted 950 days.

He honors his pact, never leaving her side, or St. Louis, again, not even to witness his grandchild's birth, not even to mourn his daughter's death. He never sees another bomber, but he hears them the rest of his days.

———

All that I know about GranVinny at war comforts me. If he could survive what he heard, what he saw, what he felt those two years and seven months, perhaps he could survive what I did.

first date

W ait 'til you meet Rushton. He's so shy I'm always afraid I'll intimidate him." She said "always" as if she saw him every night. "You know," she arched one brow knowingly. "The strong silent type."

Actually, I didn't know. All the strong men in Wilders Ferry had been loud. They'd knocked over chairs, and screamed obscenities over the screech of chain saws, and squealed pickup tires, and kicked up gravel into the metal of car doors, and polluted the air with the sudden thunder of shotguns. Dallas had been laconic, but I had no sense of his strength; I suppose even at the time he was more of a symbol than a person in my life.

My father had been quiet but not strong. When new shipments of books came in from publishers and impatient truckers dropped the boxes, sending them shaking onto the pavement in the alley behind the store, my father would call Mimi and wait for her to jog down to the store to help him carry them in. He'd open a box and get distracted, running his finger along the bindings to check for loosened threads and cheap glue, reading the jacket covers of the new hardbacks, the reviewers' quotes from the covers of the paper softcovers, while Mimi made methodical trip after trip from the alley.

At first Aunt DeeDee's attempts to have me meet Rushton were thwarted. She would choose a rendezvous place that had been closed for six months. Or she'd leave a message for him that he never received. Or her car wouldn't start. Once she even scheduled a meeting in the daytime, when I had school. It seems they had trouble communicating, this suitor and my aunt; I mean, even more trouble than she had with everybody else.

The first time she mentioned him, I was fooling around with the circuit breakers, trying to figure out what to do about the fact that half of the Loft was lit and the other half was in darkness.

When I asked Aunt DeeDee to help me, she said, "Rushton would know," she said. "Why don't you call him?"

"Who's Rushton?" I said, thinking, oh, no, not another one.

"This one's different," she said. "I met him the other night, at McGurk's. He was hanging out and drinking one of those fishbowls of beer, and my girlfriend knew him and waved hello, and well, I just have this feeling inside that he'll call."

As it turned out, of course, she called him, and I never did figure out how all this related to the circuit problem. I wondered if the conversation they had had at McGurk's was about plumbing and wiring because every time something went wrong with the Loft Aunt DeeDee would bring up his name. He took on the character of modern myth: I began to envision him as a savior with the body of a linebacker, wielding a larger-than-life vise-grip wrench in one fist and a toilet plunger in the other.

She couldn't just ask him to come over and assess our apartment for mechanical kinks, so she suggested we all go out for dinner. But I managed to convince her that she shouldn't be too eager on a first date to foist upon him the reality of her ward.

"Good point," she said, as if surprised. And I looked forward to an evening of not having to explain anything.

For their first date, she was supposed to meet him at the clock on the corner in front of Rosie and Milt's, a midtown restaurant considered "a place to be seen," one known for its bare floors, Formica tables, and noise level surely calculated to deafen the diners.

At the arranged meeting time she was still pawing through her wardrobe of umbrellas and verbally agonizing about which one to take. She left in a storm, one of those midwest spring humdingers, with those thick, hot raindrops sheeting down sideways. After her departure I put the rejected umbrellas back in the overstuffed stand and stood for a moment with my back leaning into the door as if I could barricade in the peace. By then I was used to having time alone, so I read, organized my room a bit, and was just plunking one of Aunt DeeDee's Phil Collins tapes into the cassette deck when the door swung open and she burst dramatically through.

She looked like a drowned virago, someone who belonged in an attic from a nineteenth-century novel, the hitherto coiffed hair plastered to the side of her face in flat strands and the bangs dripping into her eyes, the drops sliding off her nose into the carpet. Her umbrella—she had finally decided on the floral print to complement her shoes—was still half open and spotting the floor with a wet semicircle, and her new silk pumps, dyed scarlet for the occasion, bled onto the white rug.

"Aunt DeeDee, what happened?" I exclaimed. Her lips trembled, and she took off her raincoat, left it puddling in the entryway, ran down the hall, leaving a wet streak in her wake, and threw herself on her bed. I picked up her coat and shoes on the way and then entered the room.

"I was stood up," she gulped out.

"Not again," I said, and she began to cry, heaving sobs that shook the bed. They were so loud that I almost didn't hear the phone ring.

But I answered it, and when I heard the male voice, I realized who it must be. I astonished myself by wanting to yell at it, "What do you think you're doing, messing with her feelings like that?" But I merely thought the words, over and over, and the silence stretched out. And then came the laugh. I was so steamed I nearly slammed the phone down, but Aunt DeeDee grabbed it.

"Oh, it's you," she said, as if she didn't know. "Where were you?"

Disgusted, I went back into the living room and began to pick up the wet things dotting the floor and soaking into the rug.

They talked for the good part of the hour while I tried to look busy, but kept glaring at the stove clock and sighing as audibly as I could. Once in a while I'd hear a giggle, and finally I shut her door.

When she emerged, it was in her silk robe and carrying her plastic cosmetic bag with daisies printed on it. "I'm going to take a nice bubble bath and go to bed. It's been a long day," she announced.

"Aren't you going to tell me what happened?" I asked incredulously.

"Nothing to tell. Apparently there are two clocks at Rosie and Milt's. He waited under one, and I waited under the other. He's busy working the rest of the weekend, but we have a date for drinks next Friday. This time he'll pick me up. Then you can meet him, too." She smiled dreamily.

"Hope springs eternal," I said under my breath. But I was already planning my getaway strategy, since meeting another of my aunt's suitors was the last thing I wanted to do, and when Saturday came, I grabbed my toothbrush to spend the night at White Oak Lane.

When I returned the next morning, Aunt DeeDee was in the shower. She sang over the sound of the pelting water. Laid out on the bed was one of the outfits we shared, one that was tight even on my bony frame; a string of black glass beads, the kind that wound round and round; and dangly earrings that looked like black and silver darts. Aunt DeeDee's back, I thought; the Aunt DeeDee who meant business.

I walked to the library and returned at dusk. It was nearly midnight when I heard them on the stairs, a muted male voice, her throaty giggle, and "shhhh" in a sort of uncontrolled duet. I was in no mood to make ho-hum chitchat with one more suitor, especially one I had so recently been embarrassed by, so I clicked off my light. Then I believe I actually fell asleep.

The early morning passed uneventfully. I did my homework, walked to the corner market for bagels and cream cheese, and washed the dishes that had been sitting around for several days. (We usually used paper plates.) But about ten o'clock I caught myself sneaking peeks at the clock. At eleven, I began to make noise—slamming a cabinet door, turning up the stereo, that sort of thing.

At noon I walked into Aunt DeeDee's room. The curtains were wide open, and I wondered whether she had stayed up late to watch the moon, as I used to do from my curtainless room in Wilders Ferry on those long, otherworldly nights after Aunt DeeDee called and whispered the secrets of the world beyond. Lying with her hand tucked under her chin, she looked like a little girl in her pink nightgown with the lace collar. She took up only about a third of the bed, pillow to footboard; I often forgot how short she was. It struck me that I had rarely thought of my own mother, who wasn't much taller than her baby sister, as short, even after my eyes rose above her scalp and I could look down on her crown and see the silver highlights that had begun to appear.

Aunt DeeDee lay so still that panic shot through me like electric current, and I nearly dived toward her to put my ear to her heart. She stirred, smiled in her sleep, and stretched out her arms as if to embrace me, then rolled over, tucking her knees and elbows into her chest like a newborn.

I took a walk, and when I returned Aunt DeeDee was sitting at the kitchen table reading *People* magazine, her hair wrapped in a terry-cloth turban, and a warm fog filled the Loft again. I was beginning to wonder if I was living with Blanche DuBois.

"Hi, Sugar. Where'd you go?" She hated it when I didn't leave a note.

"Nowhere. Just passing the time." And when she didn't pick up on this flagrant hint at her selfish irresponsibility, I added, "I shopped, did the dishes, took your new shoes to be stretched while you slept the morning away."

"Honey, why all the hostility?" But before I could reply, she said, "It was so wonderful last night. Aren't you going to ask me what we did?"

"Did the earth move?" I asked, arching my brows.

"Not exactly," she said, and I wondered how literally she was taking this question, or if she understood the reference at all. "But this one's different." I guess she caught my cynical look because she added, "Really."

eye of the funnel

And in some ways neither of us could have foreseen, Aunt DeeDee was right: this man was different. The first difference was that I met him alone, without her, and during a tornado. DeeDee was to attend an overnight regional meeting in Chicago. The conference was called Aromarama, and we had worked on designing her display booth, for which she'd borrowed my tape recorder and Grateful Dead tapes and found a strobe light at an antique shop in the Central West End. I'd talked her into letting me stay alone; it was easier than I had anticipated. It was becoming increasingly depressing to spend time with my despondent grandparents, and I suppose I needed to prove something, to feel grown-up; or perhaps I simply missed the weightless feeling of casting about on my own. But that was indeed how I spent my first day alone, just casting about.

The day she was to return, I poked around and beyond the neighborhood. Heading toward Lafayette Square, I could sense the shift of ions in the air. I watched the sky close in on itself, envelop itself in darkness like the lining of a magician's cloak. The air itself rotated. Convolutions of blacks and grays, charcoal to obsidian. The ions charged the atmosphere, and the wind felt as if it were needling into my skin, into my hands, into my face. And there was something else. The smell. Usually the city smelled like the slaughterhouses and the Kroger Bakery, an occasional whiff of O. T. Hodges' Chili Parlor; and the highways, like gas and diesel fuel. But the wind had sucked the smell out of the city; the only odor was the wind itself. It filled my nostrils.

And it was quiet. The traffic wasn't backed up bumper to bumper, but instead, between one car and the next there was space. No horns blared. The tension, ironically, seemed lifted from the earth, as if the collection of life's individual tensions was nothing in the context of what was to come.

I headed toward home in the half-dark, but slowly, even after the first drops splashed onto my hair. The thought of being outside in the gray light of a storm excited me, made me shiver.

As soon as I entered the Loft, I turned on the television and the word "tornado" resonated in the emptiness, and I was on the spiraling periphery of something new, about to be swept into its vortex. I pictured Dorothy Gale, whom I suddenly saw as a midwestern kindred spirit, and the tornado that turned her life from black and white to Technicolor. And then I thought of Aunt DeeDee driving back from Chicago. I envisioned her fiddling with the dials on the car radio, turning up the volume to fight the static. A barely recognizable Top 40 song would be interrupted so that some sensationalist announcer could say the word that would chill the spines of all the excitement-crazed, addicted listeners, one of whom happened to be my aunt, who would doubtless just now notice the rolling darkness and the uncanny warmth of the wind, the imminent gathering of it from a radius of miles to make it form into the cone shape that could pull into its core the bricks and the glass and the artifacts by which people record their lives—my innocent Aunt DeeDee, who would panic, and pull over on the shoulder of the highway, paralyzed at the word.

Balls of yellow-tinged hail pelted the window and piled up on the ledge; I imagined the sound of them spattering onto the roof of Aunt DeeDee's car, quickening her heartbeats.

The phone rang, and I rushed to get it.

"Lake, are you all right?" She sounded so normal.

"Of course, I am," I said, immediately cupping my hand over the mouthpiece so she wouldn't hear the incessant sirens shrieking in the background. I had been set to reassure her, even though she didn't seem to need it. "Where are you?"

"Still in Chicago." I suddenly felt annoyed that I'd wasted time worrying. "I'm hot on a lead. It could mean big bucks." She paused and lowered her voice, so that I wondered where she was calling from. "And could mean something else. You know what I mean?"

"Hmmm," I said.

Her voice rose several decibels. "It's been rainy here. What's it like there?"

My God. She didn't know. "Looks like it's going to be a dark and stormy night."

"Sounds lonely," she said, missing my attempt at levity. "Anyway, I'm moving to the Hyatt, and I'll leave first thing in the morning. So at least I'll get some perks through all this. Do you want to go to GranVinny's for some company?"

"I can take care of myself for one more night, you know."

She laughed. "I know. Just let me be protective once in a while. After all, what could happen?" I smiled at her over the wires. "Oh, I forgot. Rusty was supposed to come over tonight and look at the dining area fixture. Would you mind calling him for me? Just tell him to come over tomorrow. I'll just call him when I get back."

Rusty, I thought. I should have known she'd eventually call him that; she was so insistent upon nicknames.

Then the operator interrupted.

"Whoops. Just ran out of change. Take care. You know, I worry about you sometimes, leaving you alone so much." She was probably waiting for me to say something nice—either that, or fingering the lining of her purse for loose change. At last she said, "I'll miss you. Will you miss me?"

It was a question Mimi had asked me many times, and I wished my aunt had been a few quarters short earlier. "Sure," I said, a response she seemed to find satisfactory. She made a kiss-kiss sound, causing me to hold the receiver away from my ear, and hung up.

"Wait," I called to the dial tone. I didn't remember Rusty's last name and knew I'd never find his number. She left addresses, phone numbers, and notes to herself in all her pockets and sometimes stashed them in drawers or even stuck them in the soil around the plants. I slammed down the receiver. The conversation had been disarming. She was worried about me to the point of being overprotective, and she wasn't worried about me enough. At sixteen I could tolerate neither alternative.

I was thumbing through the phone book in the hope that his name would pop out at me, when the door buzzer sounded. Taking the book with me, my finger still marking my place, I opened the door. I was not at all prepared for what I saw—a bearded young man in jeans, denim shirt, and windbreaker, one earlobe decorated with a silver earring shaped like a dove. He held what must have been a flower wrapped in waxy green paper in one hand, an umbrella in the other.

"Hello," he said. "I'm Rushton Pierce."

"That's it," I said, without thinking. "Pierce."

He laughed. "May I come in? I'm supposed to meet DeeDee here."

It still hadn't sunk in. I guess I expected one of her usual escorts, the guys who had nicked themselves shaving and still had a bit of Kleenex encrusted on a thin red line on the neck, or men in white shirts and corduroy sports jackets with a ballpoint pen clipped to the pocket. Since I may as well have been turned to stone, he said, "So you're Lake."

"So you're Rushton."

The corners of his mouth twitched a bit. "Your cousin sometimes calls me Rusty." I searched his face to see if he was kidding, or willing to correct his mistake. But his pleasant expression stayed fast. I stood there dumbly while it sank in that DeeDee had not told him I was her niece.

"There's a town in Idaho called Rusty. Actually, I think it's in Washington." When he looked blankly at me, I said, "They're very close together, you know." It struck me how boring this conversation was, and the blood rushed to my cheeks.

"To tell you the truth, I didn't," he smiled.

And suddenly I noticed that he was beautiful. His eyes were as blue as bachelor's buttons; his hair, the color of oak leaves in October. His beard curled around his mouth and up the sides of his face. His teeth were straight, and his eyes were not afraid to take in what presented itself. Two small scars crisscrossed his upper lip.

"What are you staring at?" he asked.

"Nothing."

"It doesn't matter really. I just want to know. Do I have spinach between my teeth?"

His eyes crinkled at the corners, and I laughed. He persevered. "So then, what are you staring at?"

"Your scars."

"I didn't know you could see them all." Mischievous. Not like the boys at school, with all that guile and giggling; just control. Now I'd call it manipulation. I was taken aback, but rose to the challenge.

"The scars on your upper lip, right side."

"What do you think?"

More games. "I don't know. Vietnam?"

He laughed. "I was only a mere babe in the sixties, but I'm glad I'm passing for mature. Anyway, I would have been a conscientious objector."

I was ready to throw in the towel; I wondered if Aunt DeeDee had told him *she* was no mere babe in the sixties.

"Well? So what's guess number two?"

"Do we have to play games?"

He must have picked up on my irritation because he said without hesitating, "A rosebush. I fell into one from my front porch when I was a kid. My mother had to pluck out the thorns. So you see, it's nothing glamorous, and I didn't know what else to talk to you about, so I prolonged this conversation. Sorry."

I was not used to a man of candor, even about such trivia, and for once had no handy retort.

"Well," he said, looking over my shoulder at the empty loft, "is my date ready?"

"Oh, my God," I said, feeling a new flush creep up my neck. "I'm sorry." When I formed those two words, I realized that they sounded foreign in my mouth.

"Nothing wrong, is there?" His face clouded. I was aware of the wind whipping at the window.

"My au— cousin called from Chicago. She can't make it in until tomorrow. I was just looking up your number to call you," I said weakly. He followed my eyes to the phone book that I was still pinching between my thumb and forefinger. He lifted it from me, and I stretched out and relaxed my fingers in relief.

"This is a fine kettle of carp." Just then a lightning flash trembled in the sky and illuminated a sheet of rain pouring down the windowpane. The lights flickered, then went out. The situation was doubtless beyond circuit breakers. A gray light settled onto the room. The wind took on a gnawing sound, as if it would eat right through the brick and glass.

"Look," he said, "I'd better go. It was nice to meet you." He zipped his windbreaker, pulled up the collar, and turned to leave.

I waited until he was halfway to the door before I said, "Wait. You can't go back out there now. Why don't you stay here? I mean, just until the storm lets up. That is, if you want to."

"I couldn't im—"

"Au— DeeDee would tell me I was rude if I didn't insist. Besides, it would be suicide to go out there now."

"Well, if you're sure. I'd hate for you to have that on your conscience."

"Here. Sit down. I'll find some candles."

He threw the jacket across a chair, sat on the couch, and when I peeked at him from the kitchen, where I was rummaging through drawers, I saw that he was squinting at the phone book in the gloom as if he were trying to read it. For a second in my mind, I saw my father reading in the dark of early evening, not bothering to turn on the lights. I shivered, then thought: this man Rushton does not deal well with unstructured time—a perception I have since wished, dearly wished, I had branded on the back of my hand.

"Can I help?" he called to me, and before I could answer, he was next to me, pawing through the kitchen drawers. Between the two of us we came up with five candles, all different sizes, and a book of matches. We lit the candles without ceremony, dripping wax onto saucers so that they would stand upright. It was darkening fast outside, not like before, when the dark had been generated from the eerie shifting of clouds, but naturally, the darkening that takes place in minuscule variations every day in the rite of passage from afternoon to evening.

I offered him some of Aunt DeeDee's wine and poured it into a glass. "Aren't you going to have some?" he asked, and something unnameable made me say yes.

I was just about to lift the glass to my lips when he raised his in a toast. I was too busy worrying about the logistics of sophistication, knowing there was already a strike against me because of my age, to be in a position to ask him to repeat it. Even today, when I replay this scene in my mind, sometimes I recall that he said, "To you!" and sometimes "To youth!" He looked into my eyes, and I felt the warmth of alcohol spread over my body even before I swallowed. It tasted different from the warm beer I used to share with Dallas in the Ford, and it felt different. Suddenly everything seemed hilarious, and I began to laugh.

"What?" he asked, amused.

"Everything. I mean nothing. I just thought of you and DeeDee waiting under different clocks in the rain. That's so typical."

We downed the glasses, and I poured another. We laughed at nothing.

"Tell me," he said after I don't know how much time had passed. "What do you do?"

To this day I still believe that if I had told the truth at this instant, nothing would have happened as it did. But I didn't hesitate for even a second. "I go to college."

He raised his eyebrows in approval, asked me where while he helped himself to more wine and drained the bottle into my glass.

I slurred the name of a community college I'd seen advertised on a billboard on the way home from GranVinny's and quickly asked, "You?"

"Washington U. Biology. I'm in grad school. Environmental stuff."

I was running my tongue around the rim of my empty glass, when suddenly he took it from me and lifted me onto the counter. My legs dangled, and I leaned back against the upper cabinets. I felt like a child, a sensation that struck me as unusual, alien.

"Stay there," he said. "I'll be right back. Count to one hundred, then close your eyes."

And he left to go back into the storm. The gusts shot in through the thread-thin cracks in the sills. The glass bowed in toward the room. I dutifully counted, anchoring myself to these numerals as if they would prevent me from being blown out through the windowpanes, from being whirled away past Aunt DeeDee pedaling on a bicycle like the Wicked Witch of the West, cackling and gathering momentum to change my life forever. And because this man, whom I didn't know, had barely talked to, and had resented for the vagaries of his connection to my vulnerable kin, had asked me to, I counted. I sat on that counter and closed my eyes, as if on display for my foolishness, exposed for my gullibility, mocking all the years I had spent encrusting myself against trust. I counted and closed my eyes—just because he wanted me to.

When I heard the door open, then click quietly closed, then heard the chain latch from inside, I realized those were exactly the sounds I expected to hear. I waited for the hello.

Instead, I felt a warm presence, as if it were the skin of his open palm, glide down the side of my face, a finger-length from my cheek. I shivered, and wondered if I should say something. More noises: a paper bag crunching; a drawer opening; the soft flick of material; a squeak, muted, on glass; then, as I opened my eyes, the unmistakable pop of a cork. It hit the ceiling and fell into the V between my legs on the counter.

"Where'd you get that?" I asked, handing him the cork.

"My car," he said. "I always keep a spare bottle in case of emergency."

I knew he must have brought it for him and Aunt DeeDee, but I laughed anyway.

And I continued to laugh. I laughed at the bubbles that overflowed the glasses. I laughed at the way they leaped up at my nose. I laughed at the way he wiped his moustache every few swallows.

We laughed and drank, me on the counter, him sitting at the table, and when my belly hurt from laughing, he asked, "So what are you studying?"

"Anything but art," I said and laughed to myself. "What do you like about biology?"

Before he told me, he shot me a sidelong glance, as if he were wondering if I was making a joke.

I concentrated on looking fascinated with what he said, and in truth I was fascinated, but not with what he said. As he spoke, his eyes never left my face. They were blue as I had first noticed, but moss-green spokes radiated from the pupils.

"So quit changing the subject and tell me about you," he said.

Since I felt caught in my unpolished ploy, I paused for a moment, pretending to examine the speckled countertop, and then I measured my words.

"I'm really studying human nature. And geology. I'm actually very boring. I like to read." I took stabs at topics to see what he wanted from me. But his expression went blank, and his gaze seemed removed, as if he were hearing something else, words I wasn't actually saying. I had the sense that I was blabbing on about a me I hadn't met yet, had merely imagined, and at that, neither consciously nor well.

When the silence began to seem heavy and unwieldy, and the terror of boring him rose to my throat, I added, "What else do you like?"

He slowly lifted both hands at once and reached toward me, then froze, fingers slightly spread, hands near my throat—froze as if he had just been turned to stone. "You," he said, not smiling. Over each candle arced a small halo, which dotted the dark room with rosy gold. The rich warmth of his voice, this word, the proximity of his touch gentled down my body with the champagne like the day's first light on the mountains.

Stop, I kept thinking; I should stop. It could be simple. But I could feel a hidden part of me open like a desert bloom in a Georgia O'Keeffe painting, like the core of a blood orange, like the violet heart of an iris. His hands moved to my throat and slowly unbuttoned the top button. And then my body forced my mind to shed its layers, and the rock of my control began to flow like lava, in oranges and scarlets, spreading the colors of flame inside, and I closed my thighs as if to prevent its entrance and exit. I pushed back a bit, hardly noticeably, just a tightening of the shoulder blades, a slight pull in the neck, and abruptly he said, "I'm sorry." And stopped.

I moved my hands to cover his and held them there, suspended between my mind and body, like a high-wire artist over a net of gosling down.

"It's okay," I said breathlessly, and realized I hadn't breathed for many seconds. He turned his back while I buttoned my blouse.

"Tell me about Idaho," he said, startling me a bit. Smiling, he walked to the refrigerator, took out a carton of eggs, and ferreted around in the cabinets. He plunked a mixing bowl and skillet onto the counter.

"Go on," he said. "I'm listening. I hear best above clanging pots and pans, especially when there's food on the horizon. I haven't eaten since lunch. First tell me how you like your eggs."

"Any way but with tofu."

And he laughed, and relief rippled through me.

I did tell him about Idaho. I told him about Jillian, Dyl, and Paris, and then about the boys on the school bus and Maybelle Purdy. I was careful to make them all sound older. I wasn't ready to tell him about Dallas, perhaps because Dallas had so easily faded as a presence in my life; and I couldn't tell him about my parents, as if merely mentioning them would make me lose my fragile control. The champagne was blurring my perceptions, and I was beginning to question my connection to Aunt DeeDee, convince myself that we might very well be cousins, but I didn't want to give any hints that evidence pointed to the other conclusion.

He cracked open six eggs on the side of the bowl and whipped them with a wooden spoon. Then he opened and shut cabinets and unearthed a couple of spice tins, threw in a dash of lemon rind and a dusting of nutmeg. Candle in hand, he stooped at the refrigerator, took out a container of cottage cheese, opened it, sniffed it, and plunked a glob of it into the bowl. I watched him, bemused. He poured the mixture into the skillet, turned up the gas, then laid the wooden spoon across my legs, using them for a spoon rest. The circle of flame from the stove looked azure in the dark. "What?" he said, noticing my face.

"I was just thinking how unlike DeeDee you are. She's so careful about following recipes; she just brings the wrong ones home. I think there's a recipe pool at work, and she gravitates toward the ones with Velveeta and canned soup."

Swishing the stuff around in the skillet, he leaned over and kissed my cheek. I shimmied toward the edge of the counter. "I'll set the table."

"No. Let me. You look cute there."

"Sure. Just don't make me close my eyes again. I think I've drunk so much now, I'd get dizzy."

"I'd like to go to Idaho sometime. Take a few pictures. I've heard it's beautiful."

I shrugged. "I guess so. I'm not sure how beautiful it is." I blundered on, waiting for him to interrupt. He didn't. "I mean, before I left, when I was much younger, of course, I hated it." He nodded. "So, if you really hate something it's not going to seem beautiful, is it?"

I wasn't used to talking so much at one time to someone who could hear what I was saying. He flipped the omelet onto a plate, found two forks, and handed me one.

I had figured he had forgotten all that I had said, and this much revelation in the woozy context of the alcohol and the gloom illuminated by small flames and the noise from the storm began to take on the relevance of a dream. So I was vaguely surprised when he said, as if he had been thinking about my words even as he served our supper, "No, and if you really like something, it is."

"Is what?" I asked, trying to pretend I was still coherent. He stood beside me at the counter and blew gently around the perimeter of the omelet. The soft circling of his breath brushed the skin of my face. The movement made me think how still the Loft was, how quiet, how isolated. Then he held the plate close to my chest, and I took a bite.

We ate in turns. First him, then me. Slowly, slowly, so as not to finish the night too soon. In the periphery of my vision, I thought I saw him watch the way I opened my mouth, how the fork slipped in smooth and triggered the taste buds to go wild with pleasure. I stared at the plate as the omelet diminished, wishing each bite could consume longer and longer measures of time—first hours, then weeks, then months, then years. Before I was done, I yearned for epochs and eons.

And when there was no more on the plate, I reached behind me to put my fork in the sink, but he caught my hand and brought it to his face, and gazing at me eye to eye, not even a wink, he put my fork in his mouth and licked it slowly clean.

"If you really like someone," he was saying while I imagined the soft, wet feel of his tongue against the silver prongs, "she is beautiful." He lifted me off the counter, held me in the air for a second before setting me down. Then he took a candle and said, "Where shall we go?"

Let's just stay inside this isolated place, anywhere inside this place, I thought, but couldn't find words to answer. Outside, a mile-wide funnel was gathering momentum. When I didn't answer, he led me by the hand to the least safe place in the Loft, the middle of the front room, put the candle on the table, and knelt in front of me. He circled me with his arms and pulled himself close; his beard pressed slowly into my ribs, and his leaf-colored hair covered my heart.

As he inched down to the floor, he whispered a word into my belly. I like to think this word was "beautiful."

The vertical cloud claims its territory in the hundreds of miles. Its toll on me I've yet to measure fully. As the funnel struck the surface of the earth, withdrew into the black clouds above, whirled around counter-clockwise, picked up speed, and then swooped down to strike the earth again, it scooped up all the objects in its wake and hurled them into chaos. People's belongings became dust and debris. The column twisted up air from around their houses and barns, their roofs and doors, from their staunch oaks and elms; it exploded from the inside out, dislodging their railroad cars on their tracks and overturning their Volkswagens and Cadillacs. Their war diaries and photo albums and the sanctity of their memories slammed open and shredded into detritus; their wallpaper peeled down from the ceilings. In the building next door the tornado ripped the window ledge and left a dusty pyramid of bricks in the dining room.

As the hissing crescendoed to its deafening pitch, I was thinking about anything but destruction, anything but danger. I was, for those long, life-altering moments, simply somewhere else. The implosion, only sheets of glass and a thickness of brick away, belonged in the life of someone else.

No one knows why tornadoes are; they just are. There is no asylum from randomness. Nothing is immune from the force of this demonic flight. It steals anything—witches on bicycles, paintings of a scarlet-skinned hairdresser, sterling forks licked clean—anything, even the rooted and the anchored. But being otherwise occupied with the business of changing the course of my life inexorably, I ignored this all.

In the late morning I awoke alone, to the barely discernible fragrance of a red rose that had been laid between my breasts.

sound of the river

The next time I met Rusty he was with DeeDee. When he saw me, he lowered his eyes and pressed his lips together, whether as a signal of surrender to the irrefutable truth or as a sign of secrecy I can't say.

"How are you this morning?" he asked.

"How are you?" I answered.

He looked serious. "DeeDee is grateful to you for giving me shelter in the storm, especially since you stayed up so late on a school night," he said, and I knew he knew me for the treacherous impostor I was.

I tried not to see him alone, and it was amazingly easy, given DeeDee's need for constant contact with one or the other of us. And often, it was both of us. In fact, we spent nearly every Friday night of the summer of 1985 as a threesome. I'd watch them holding hands and giggling and try not to think about his flat palm circling my nipples, first one and then the other. Saturday nights were theirs, and I'd ask them to drop me off at GranVinny's, where I'd lie in Mimi's bed, watching the fan rippling the ribbons of her pointe shoes.

Sometimes we'd go to the Washington University Little Symphony.

We'd spread a blanket outside in the quad, on the lawn between the brick walks. The night air was so thick with moisture that it was like trying to breathe at the bottom of a hot spring. We'd look out through the Gothic arch of Brookings Hall as if it were a keyhole, at the illuminated Gateway Arch and the riverfront, which glowed hot yellow from the lights of the jazz clubs. DeeDee would fuss over the paraphernalia she considered essential: the thermoses of ice, the insect repellent, the popcorn packed in sandwich bags. Once Rusty brought chocolate-covered cherries from Bissinger's, but they melted before she could open the grosgrain ribbon that tied the waxed box.

We'd lie next to each other on the blanket, and I'd concentrate on watching the musicians in the concert shell try to distract themselves from the sweat that collected under their starched collars and behind their bow ties. I imagined they played everything at top speed just to avoid the heat and go home a bit early. The stars would turn out, but they were nothing compared to the stars in Idaho, the grand smear of the Milky Way, the white on black, the thousands of diamond-colored pin-points that streaked across the obsidian sky. The sweat would gather at the nape of my neck and send rivers down my back, pooling in the indentations at the base of my spine. It burst into droplets on my nose and under my eyes. I'd squirm against the wet air, then against the damp burning of our bodies on the wool blanket.

"Just sit perfectly still," Rusty would say, and I would think, sometimes, when I would let myself, that he was moving infinitesimally closer to me with every measure of Mozart or Brahms or Bartôk, and I'd listen to the ghost of the ephemeral harmony between us instead of their arpeggios and chords, and would hear only the beat of his pulse.

In the stark afternoons, I felt him in the heat that rippled up from the asphalt. I conflated the heat of his presence with the summer he had brought and with the hot, moist, uncareful coupling of male and female parts. The mere memory of the feel of him, the stretch of his skin over his shoulder blades, the small ridges of his teeth—all the details I longed to cast away—churned together in the oceans of my imaginings and clung to me like a wet skirt. In his most mundane touch, in the brush of his arm against mine, in his fingertips as he handed me change for a soda pop he had bought at my request, in all his touches, I felt the indisputable resonance, like the sound of the sea in a conch, of that single night. Sometimes, in the dark, I caught myself whispering his name over and over—Rushton,

Rushton, Rushton—and hearing from my mouth the sound of the river in April.

One Friday night Rusty took us to the heart of the northern end of downtown, to Crown Candy Kitchen.

"I thought we ought to show Lake what a real city experience is like. No renovations. Nothing upscale. Something bona fide," he said.

"I'm up for the bona fide," I said from the backseat behind him. DeeDee turned her head away from us and stared out the window. As we crisscrossed the city and passed the bombed-out-looking buildings and the litter on the streets swept up with the stale wind, DeeDee set her jaw grimly. The name on a street sign caught my attention. "Cass," I said. "Didn't GranVinny and GranPearl once live on Cass?"

DeeDee shrugged. The streetlights cast the entire block in eerie shades of yellow and gray.

"Is that where they met?" Rusty asked.

"I think it was, actually. Did I tell you that before?" I thought back to our only conversation alone together. I didn't remember what I had said. The words themselves had evaporated.

"I guess you must have," he laughed. "Or else we're getting to know each other so well, we don't need to talk."

DeeDee's head jerked to the side. "They met on Cass," she said.

"I meant all of us, of course," he said quietly.

"Cass," she said and jabbed the button for the radio, which blared at us until we pulled into a parking space.

A black man clutching a paper bag to his heart leaned on the meter. The stench of grocery store wine and stale sweat surrounded him like an evil aura. He grinned and held out his hand. DeeDee gripped Rusty's arm, crowding me closer to him in spite of the heat, and rushed forward. I walked behind them. "Hey, folks. Only a quarter. Park all night," he called after us.

We turned onto St. Louis Avenue. "You know," I said, "I think GranVinny asked GranPearl to marry him here."

Rusty looked back at me. "Where?"

"Here. Crown Candy Kitchen. I thought the name was familiar."

"How do you know?" she snapped, and before I could answer she stepped up her pace, flung open the door before us, and strode inside.

Rusty and I glanced at each other and followed her through the door. It was the first time I recall that she didn't expect me to know every detail about her life, to have subsumed or absorbed her memories, and more—the first time she didn't want to imprison me in her sensibilities. It struck me just how circumscribed my life had been—from the purple house to White Oak Lane to the Loft.

I stopped in the entrance, my system suddenly on overload. I scanned the room to take in the riot of decoration. Something about the imagination of this place spoke to me, as it might have to GranVinny half a century before. From the sculpted ceiling hung milk-glass lamps on chains. Ceiling fans revolved. Gadgets and curiosities and memorabilia and doodads were wedged and hung wherever possible. Painted trays advertising Coca-Cola from 1917 to 1942 lined a long wall like a historical display; engraved bronze plaques under each gave the date. A pine-framed poster in an upper corner presented two women poised on a red-draped seat as if suspended from the sky, pointed toes dangling in the blue. The old-fashioned woman, labeled "1886," was dressed innocently in a sailor dress and matching blue bonnet; the "modern" woman (1936) wore a silk camisole that buttoned at the crotch. Stained glass stretched across the top of the soda fountain. On the counter a glass bowl was piled with mottled bananas. Three tiers of candies enticed like tinted baubles behind a walnut-and-glass case topped by a row of clear canisters crammed with confections. Each booth had a tabletop jukebox and a small mirror. The names of ice cream concoctions and prices were painted on each mirror in a brick-red script, fading at the serifs, as if someone had scratched the letters away with a fingernail.

DeeDee and Rusty had squeezed into a bench of a booth. DeeDee's face was buried in the menu, and she didn't raise her head when I sat down. On the Formica table Rusty tapped out the rhythm of Madonna's "Like a Virgin," which pulsated from the jukebox, and tried to catch the eye of the waitress. DeeDee closed her menu and fixed her gaze on the melting ice cubes in her water glass.

After we ordered, I excused myself. In no hurry to return to the tension, I lingered at the counter, and then I wandered alongside the case that housed the confections: salt-water taffy twisted in waxed paper; blue gummy sharks; pin-striped marshmallows; tiny tarts like muted pastel beads; gumdrops molded into strawberries with plastic stems, sliced into tangerine sections dusted with white sugar, shaped into pineapples and dipped in coconut; shoestring licorice; hard candies wrapped in blue foil; shiny peppermints of orange and yellow and green; tar-black sen-

sens and jelly beans; chocolate rum raisins; frosted almonds. At the far end of the case, in the corner, a mound of translucent rock candy glittered like lake-washed quartz. Mimi would have loved them, I thought. Beauty with no purpose. I ran my fingertips over them, and my prints left a spiral on the glass.

Threading my way back to my seat, I caught a glimpse of the two of them that made me hesitate a few booths away. Although they were facing me, they didn't look my way. Her head was nearly obscured by the tall, tulip-shaped glass of ice cream in front of her. He was laughing, and one hand was wrapped protectively around her shoulders. With the other hand, he fed her with a silver-plated spoon. A cherry-colored glob fell onto her shirt. She reached for her napkin, but he stayed her wrist, and I thought I could read his lips, "No. Let me." He wiped the spot from her blouse, then sank his spoon into her sundae and lifted it near her lips. She opened her mouth, and the spoon entered carefully. She swallowed, the cold taste making her shiver. The sauce dripped onto her chin, and laughing, he scraped it up and back into her lips with a spoon. Her arms at her side, hands in her lap, she may as well have been his prisoner. All traces of anxiety were wiped clean from her face; even the wrinkles seemed to have disappeared. I continued to watch, knowing they were not wondering where I was, not even seeing that I was so close, while my own ice cream melted under its layer of molten caramely fudge. When they finished, she put her head on his shoulder, and I saw what he couldn't see—on her otherwise submissive face, a triumphant little smile. His face was empty of expression, like a mask. On the mirror just over their heads was scrawled "Lover's Delight."

Later that night, she came into my room.

"Are you asleep?" she whispered.

"Not anymore." But I hadn't been asleep, and I knew I might lie awake all night. I imagine she must have thought it was like old times, her slipping into my sleeping hours like this.

"I'm just so happy," she said.

"You didn't seem to be earlier in the evening," I said into the pillow.

She pretended she didn't hear. "I was just thinking. About how he makes me feel."

She waited while I listened to the fan and watched the hot, circulating air stir the dried rose hanging from my dresser mirror.

"You know," she continued. And I was afraid I did.

The night July passed into August, and the heat still held us in its sultry stranglehold, I dreamed about a garden. GranVinny was kneeling in the turned earth and planting bulbs. He raised them one by one to his ears: the ones on his right to his right ear; the ones on his left to his left ear. Each one sang to him in turns. They gave him rounds and ditties and airs and arias. He was smiling, and his eyes were wet with pleasure. He leaned toward the earth, and when he felt the damp ground around the rim of his ear, both forefingers rose toward the sky, and he conducted the music and closed his eyes to hear it more clearly and fully, so as not to be distracted by the dew and thick leaves of grass, and he heard them in a choral symphony. From my sleep I strained to hear, too, to discern which symphony, and knew I was near to hearing the singing with him, to feeling the vibrations of the chords, vibrations that came trembling from the ground and shaking the earth. Then I realized the shaking wasn't a dream. I popped open my eyes expecting an earthquake, expecting the ceiling to wobble, the windows to rattle and crack, my bed to toss me to the floor, when I saw that it was my aunt, kneeling at my bed and bouncing lightly on the mattress next to my face.

"Did I wake you?" she asked, an inch from my nose.

"I was just trying to dream," I said, flipping over my pillow and turning my back.

"I wanted you to be the first to know." The silent symphony faded from perception forever. "I proposed."

I felt something viscous—like fog, or steam—seep into my head. "Does anyone actually still propose?"

"You're not hearing me, Honey." She leaned into the bed. She was right. I wasn't hearing her. I wasn't hearing anything. "We're getting married. Rusty and I." She stopped talking but didn't move, waiting for me to say something, anything. "Now we can be a real family," she said at last.

After she left, I lay awake, eyes fixed on the blank ceiling, until the alarm filled the dreamless silence in my head.

another wedding

The next night we drove to White Oak Lane. The house was dark except for a single light in his basement study. DeeDee stumbled on the front porch, and the key grated against the doorknob while I fumbled to find the lock. When we finally let ourselves in, she flicked on all the lights on the first story while I went downstairs to get him. I paused at the threshold of his study. He hadn't felt the vibrations of my footsteps on the stairs and didn't turn to acknowledge me. He was seated in his overstuffed chair, his head bent in a book. I recognized it as one of his own, a volume he'd reinforced with masking tape over the binding, and labeled "1946." I waited for him to sense my presence, so I wouldn't frighten him, but more than that, I simply wanted to watch him. Salt-and-pepper hairs coated his arms and his muscular calves. He was wearing denim cutoffs and the T-shirt I had given him for his birthday. It was red and green, the colors of the Italian flag. The back was printed with an onion that had a face, legs, and arms. It was flexing its biceps. On the front the shirt read, VINNY, THE ITALIAN SCALLION. His eyes had crinkled up, and he'd worn it every time I had seen him since. It always smelled like fabric softener and had the same sharp creases over both nipples, as if he laundered and folded it every day.

Sometimes he nodded; sometimes his gaze rested on a line, and his eyes bored through the page at the invisible, as if he were fleshing out the notes and sentences in his head; sometimes his body shook with soundless laughter. He flipped the pages loudly and snorted and belched, and still I eavesdropped.

Suddenly he jerked up and saw me there. He stood, stepped toward me, and drew me to his chest. I leaned into him to press my cheek to his, and something compelled me to cling to him for another second or two after he pulled away. "Forgive me," I whispered into his dead ear. At the time I believed that intruding on his private world would be the most heinous crime for which I would ever need to ask his forgiveness.

DeeDee's voice sounded hollow on the way down the uncarpeted steps. "Sweeeeetheart," she called, and we walked slowly up to meet her.

They embraced hello, a kiss on each cheek, and for a while we simply stood at the door to the basement. He glanced from her to me and back, puzzled.

"Is Mama in bed?" she asked, as if she weren't usually in bed. He nodded. "I have good news," she continued, upping her volume, her jaw opening and lips stretching to make sure he understood. He looked to me to explain, and she tapped his hand to get back his attention. She motioned for him to follow her, and she sat down at the kitchen table, opened her purse, and took out her little notebook with the gold pen. I hadn't seen it in years. She leafed through it until she came to a few blank pages at the end. As the pages shuffled by like an incoherent cartoon, I recognized my childish printing.

She took the pen and wrote, "Papa—Good news! I'm getting married. I want you to give me away." And she handed him the notebook as if she were handing him a winning lottery ticket. Her eyes stayed on his face. She was expectant; I think she actually thought he might cast off his tragic mask and light up like the Fourth of July, and we would together tear off our inner shrouds and life would be glorious for us all. His eyes darted to the guest room, as if for direction, or support.

I sat on the long side of the table and they at each end. He drummed his fingers on the glass tabletop, the noise loud and intrusive. But his face remained impassive, as if the page in the notebook were still blank.

DeeDee drew in her lips and pressed them together. She reached for the notebook and wrote, her fist tight around the little pen. "Be happy for me, Papa."

I passed it to him. He merely glanced at it, the beat of his fingers now faster.

She grabbed it this time and scribbled furiously, "Say something. Write something. Anything."

And he extended his hand toward the pen as if his hand were made of granite and wrote a couple of words and put down the pen so vehemently that it made a loud clink against the glass and I was afraid it might chip. As I passed the message to DeeDee, I read upside down. "It's too soon."

DeeDee's face turned a reddish purple from the neck up. Her left eyelid blinked open and shut out of her control. "What do you mean too soon? What are you talking about?"

My grandfather stood up and turned around to face the west wall, the wall lined with GranPearl's cookbooks and framed recipes in her own mother's script. His shoulders sagged, and his arms hung lifeless at his sides, as if he were waiting for the emotional charge from the other side of the table to dissipate. I noticed for the first time how aged he looked. My heart skittered.

"He means—" I began to explain.

"Quit telling me what he means," she screamed, and he turned toward the vibrations. "You have no idea what he means. He's just a selfish old man." His eyes widened and registered fear at the sight of her narrowed lids and heaving chest, and I thought I could hear his heart pump in starts, and stop.

DeeDee fumbled with the notebook and her purse. Her hands shook as she zipped it shut, and she hit her hip on the corner of the table as she strode out of the room.

At the front door she called back. "Are you coming, or not?" He looked at me in despair, shaking his head when I rose to go.

On the drive home we said nothing. She bore down on the accelerator with her spike heel and skidded onto the highway, while I clutched the armrest. With the windows rolled up tight, the only thing audible, besides the shrieking horns of irate drivers, was the sound of her shallow breathing.

When she pulled into the garage and the car jerked to a halt, we sat in the dark for a moment.

"I don't think he wanted to—"

"Please don't speak for him." Her voice was unnaturally even and subdued. The taut control frightened me, and I unbuckled my seat belt and reached for the door handle. "He's perfectly capable of speaking for himself," she added, glaring straight ahead through the windshield to the murky back wall of the garage.

As I squeezed the door handle and it made its little click, she said, her tone measured and low, "I've been thinking. It's best if you come straight home after school in the fall." I said nothing. "He's crazy, you know," she added, and I opened the door. As I walked toward the Loft, I heard the slam of the car door and then her choked voice, "All he thinks about is his Miriam. His precious Mimi. They can both go to hell."

When I did what I did, not a moontide later, her words rang out in my head, like an echo blocking out all other waves of sound. But there was no other continuous stretch of time, no other week, or year, when I grieved as much as I did in that single moment.

The next morning I woke up wary, listening for signs of her black mood, but I heard only the shower and then rustling. I read the *Post-Dispatch* in bed, waiting for the slam of the garage door and the revving of the car motor, but at nine o'clock I could no longer stand the suspense and walked into the kitchen. Her hair coiled in a towel, she sat at the table reading *Bride's* magazine. Several pages were marked with orchid Post-its. A full pot of weak-looking coffee was on the table, and she was humming "Daisy," one of her favorites in GranPearl's repertoire.

"Did Neiman's declare a holiday today to show solidarity with the Gramm-Rudman bill?" I asked, dumping the watery brown coffee down the sink.

She laughed, and I wondered if our visit to White Oak Lane hadn't been just another nightmare. "Where do you come up with all those funny things to say, Lake? As a matter of fact, I stayed home today so you and I could have the whole day together."

I reached for the filters, dipped the measuring cup into the coffee, and filled the pot with water. The pot was still under the faucet when she added, "I mean, I'll need more than just a day of shopping with my little maid of honor, won't I?"

The water ran over the pot, over my hand, and splashed onto the linoleum.

"Let's start with Saks and work our way up. I can't wait to see you in black."

And black it was. In fact, she wanted everything in black—Black Hills gold rings, black china at the reception, black velvet bows to bundle the balloons in the aisle, and black-eyed Susans in the bouquets. Whether or not the color was chosen subconsciously to pacify GranVinny, who might never be ready to come out of mourning, I didn't know.

We used several of her vacation days and several times that of her sick days and every night except Saturdays, which she spent with Rusty, engrossed in wedding plans. The Friday night threesome was tacitly disbanded, and she met with one or the other of us individually to effect her master plan.

First we shopped. I let DeeDee choose my dress. It was georgette and voile, and low-cut, though not quite as low as hers, which V'd down her chest to the breastbone.

Then we called churches, interviewing them over the phone. I found the minister, of course—under letter "G" for "Good"—the Church of Good Feelings. He was an amiable sort, who was attached to no particular denomination and had no fixed feelings whatsoever, so we could stand before whatever tribe we could dredge up in a rented room in the Forest Park Hotel and comply with my aunt's insistence on a proper ceremony without overreliance on God. The Forest Park Hotel was my idea, and I suggested it at first just as a joke. That was where GranPearl and GranVinny had been married close to half a century before, where both a priest and a rabbi officiated, and as in their firstborn's wedding twenty-eight years later, the Jews ate all the mostaccioli and the Sicilians ate all the bagels and lox. I was sure DeeDee would think the Forest Park was a terrible idea, and eventually view it as a way for me to express my anger at my enforced estrangement from GranVinny, so her response surprised me. "That sounds like just the place," she said. It occurred to me that she realized neither the symbolic nor the historical significance of this place, and I left her in her ignorance. The hotel was in the Central West End, only two blocks from where my parents had been married for the first time. We made a pilgrimage to check it out.

We parked the car on McPherson and decided to stroll around the area to window-shop in the boutiques and antique stores. We were about to turn toward the hotel when forest-green letters painted in a window caught my eye: LEFT BANK BOOKS. I felt a pang of something haunting, like the familiarity of the dream of someone else. We crossed the street, and I walked through the door, leaving DeeDee outside reading the want ads tacked to the corkboard framed in blue molding. I browsed unnoticed. A Vivaldi flute concerto tinkled from speakers in the corner near the ceiling. It was a recording my father had often played on Sunday mornings while he was sweeping the floor, or reading from the pile of magazines he'd borrowed from Left Bank Books West over the weekends.

I knelt by the unstained pine bookshelves that looked so much like the shelves in his bookstore in Wilders Ferry, and pictured my father stooping in this very spot, excitement at being in the company of all these books just waiting to be opened and embraced flushing through his nervous system. It wasn't until I walked out the front door that I noticed the store had an oval window. The oval window on a city street . . . the clustered blossoms of hawthorn trees . . . the beveled glass . . . the blond wood—I saw clearly and in conjunction the simple images of two of my lives.

On the way home I felt hollowed out. It was impossible not to envision Left Bank Books West, the shelves empty and splintery, and the ghost of my father looking at it forlornly.

"Small but fancy," DeeDee was saying, as if I had been following her thoughts all along. "That's what we'll aim for, won't we? As long as we can have caviar and ice sculptures, and lace tablecloths under all the gifts."

I thought of the photos of Wedding Number One I'd gawked at while I waited for disease to finish with me and take its leave.

"I thought you hated caviar," I said, staring out the windshield.

"It's the *idea* of caviar, Honeylamb. Where's your imagination?"

The details of the wedding consumed our days and nights, her lunch hours and her coffee breaks. Her orchestrations took a Barnum-and-Bailey turn, and as her ideas expanded into the outré, I stood apart like a voyeur waiting for increasingly intense hits of sensation, fascinated with such foolishness. The invitations were to be engraved, the cake to be studded with black plastic swans, the aisle to be dusted with rose petals and potpourri, the rice to be bundled in yellow cellophane and net, the champagne to flow from a fountain, the tables to be swathed in chiffon, the ritual to begin with a procession around Lafayette Square Park, the napkins to be embossed with "Rushton and Diane"—an artist's vision gone awry. Perhaps all this wouldn't have been unusual for a younger bride, but although DeeDee always hedged about her age, I knew it had to be over thirty. And, besides, I wondered whom she would invite to participate in all this folderol. When she had told GranPearl, the rhythm of her mother's rocking had hesitated only the slightest bit.

And yet . . . and yet, for one month I did as I was told. There was something reassuring in suspending the raw feelings that threatened to cascade around and drown me. I went through the motions, and the wet heat that permeated every gesture, every act, made these motions seem surreal. If you could see the heat rising in vertical waves from the pavement, surely everything must be illusion, and safe enough.

Every time I thought I could steal away to visit GranVinny, DeeDee would find something for me to do. The countless errands one runs before weddings—dyeing silk shoes, checking with the bakery on the cake, addressing announcements, counting and recounting with the caterers, negotiating with the organist—all these came under my bailiwick as maid of honor, however reluctant. When DeeDee needed something, she would drive to White Oak Lane and return with a check, but I was never asked to perform this errand. My sense of isolation increasingly encased me, and I began to play a game, counting the hours, and eventually the days, how long I could go without uttering an intelligible word.

DeeDee was in the shower when the door buzzed and I walked downstairs to answer it. It was Rusty. The moment I saw him I turned and walked away. It was the first time we had been alone together since the night of the tornado. He followed me.

"So what's the plan today?" I asked, my back to him still.

"Rings," he said.

"What'll it be? Matching swans that attach to each other around those long, Freudian necks?"

"Lake," he said, touching my shoulders. I drew away. "What's wrong?"

I turned around. "Why are you doing this?" I blurted out.

"Doing what?"

"Marrying her."

He came toward me, and I took a step back. "Don't," he said, the pain in his face aging him, and I imagined him an old man, feeding his wizened wife with a plastic spoon.

"Because she needs me," he said at last.

"That's it?"

He shrugged.

I have since considered my complicity in all this. To what degree was I the liaison, was I the enabler, was I perhaps even the spoils? And how much did this charade of a ceremony have to do with Mimi? But something in his tone, something in the absence of his opinion in the machinations, in the way he looked at me, made me more than just a witness. It was as if he had joined me at my stance behind the bleachers, enjoying the thrill of the three-ring acts and knowing that after the cotton candy and hot dogs, after the applause, we'd all go home to our other lives. It struck me that Rusty might not actually believe this marriage would ever materialize. He seemed to have disappeared, superfluous to the ceremony and, I began to suspect, to life in general. The wedding had burgeoned like an uncontrollable vine in some monster movie. Now I see that the spectacle overshadowed all sense of any marriage that would follow, all vision of the years and decades ahead—all the dirty dishes, light-bulb changes, checkbook reconciliations, stained laundry, moves with piles of cardboard boxes, and even the nights of damp, heartrending love.

I went to my room, leaving him alone to wait for her. As they were about to leave the apartment, DeeDee called back, "Oh, I forgot. Could you check with the caterers about the canapés? We're running late."

I opened my door a shoulder's width. "I'm running late myself," I said. DeeDee's face washed over with unpleasant surprise. She blinked. "Well, excuse me," she said and trotted out, her heels making sharp, fast clicks all the way to the bottom of the stairs. Rusty lingered in the doorway as if he were waiting for me to explain, then opened his hand in a wave, and I nodded good-bye. As soon as they left, I cracked the front window to let out the steam from her shower, turned on the air conditioner full blast, grabbed DeeDee's car keys from the shelf, and left for GranVinny's.

The house was dark, and his car was gone. I walked into the guest room. My grandmother was asleep, and I tucked the sheet up to her chin. I sat next to her for a while, listening to her snore. The noise made me restless. I knew GranVinny wouldn't be gone for long, but I paced around and found myself following the stairs down to the basement. I pushed cans aside on shelves, opened a footlocker to look inside. The tackle box that looked like Mimi's paint box caught my eye, and I pulled open the locks. It was neat and orderly, the flies and hooks and fishwire sorted into separate sections. I was about to shut the lid when I saw something that looked like paper wedged into the corner of the lower tier. I edged it out. It was a letter, addressed to Mimi in Wilders Ferry in my grandmother's handwriting. It had been taped shut and reopened, and over the address, in capital letters, were the words "Return to Sender" in my mother's printing.

Dear Miriam,

It's after midnight. So many things cross a mother's mind at night. You and little Lake have been gone for ten hours, and still, our argument is with me. I feel exhausted but am unable to sleep. I know we haven't been close, and I regret this more than I can ever tell you. Right now I'm thinking back to those long, hot evenings when you were an infant and I would take you out in the carriage to cool you off, when your father was a resident sleeping on a cot at County Hospital between emergencies. You don't know this, but every night he was gone I would whisper to you from above your carriage and rock it to my words to help you feel them since you couldn't yet understand them. I promised you then that you would have everything. You wouldn't have to live on a dirt floor like your grandparents, you would never have to be ashamed of the way you talk or dress, you would not have to turn down a scholarship to college like I had to because I couldn't afford books, you would get the best education possible. (I wanted to send you to private school, but your father insisted if we moved into Meadowbrook you'd get the best of both worlds in a public education.) I swore in every way I could, whispered right into your tiny little ears, that you would never, ever feel the pain of wanting. I watched you grow and become all I dreamed for you. You were beautiful, and brilliant at everything—not only your schoolwork, but your art lessons, and piano lessons, and ballet lessons. We were glad to let you choose your own college, so proud that you were accepted into one of the Seven Sisters. I tell you this now not to get credit or acceptance. I know it's hard for you to give them to me. I hope someday you see all our differences as little ones, normal ones between a determined mother and her spirited daughter . . .

Feeling like a spy, I laid the letter down. My eyes felt hot. Why couldn't Mimi have accepted all this love and selflessness? I felt too weighted down to read on. I was about to return the letter guiltily to its envelope when a line in the final paragraph caught my eye. I skimmed down to the bottom of the page.

I tell you this now because I want you to know why I felt so deter-mined that you should not marry a dropout. I knew in my heart that Kirk was wrong for you, and I know it still. And I admit I thought it was wrong for you to have his child. It wasn't so much the shame of getting pregnant out of wedlock, as you seem to insist I felt. . . . It's just not fair to have brought a life into the world without being able to give it the things it needs. If you had only let us help. . . . But I knew you wouldn't; you've always been so stubborn.

And now, to know you are living the way you do, with no furni-ture and no central heat and no telephone, with an unambitious husband who can't really support you. I want, Miriam, for you to consider letting us raise Lake in St. Louis. You know we can give her the best in education, music and dance lessons—art lessons, too—all the things she'll never get from the kind of life you live in Idaho. Show her you truly love her. It's time to stop being selfish . . .

Before I left the house, I folded the letter carefully, noticing how the creases were worn, as if they had been smoothed out and folded count-less times before.

The heat wave remained with us through Labor Day and into the week-end of the wedding. Every night, my wet skin snapped me awake, and I'd lie in the semidark in the stagnant air waiting for the morning, the win-dow fan blocking out the noise of the city. Sometimes I could feel my aunt prowling around, and I knew that in the morning there would be a note with another assignment for me, the details of this barbaric ritual having taken over even her sleep.

The night before the wedding the thermometer registered ninety-eight degrees when the moon was on its way down. DeeDee had taken a sleeping pill. I couldn't sleep and didn't even try, just sat at my desk, my T-shirt clinging to the skin over my breastbone. At 4 AM the phone rang, and I leaped up to answer it. At the telephone table in the hall, no longer in reach of the fan or the living room air conditioner, I felt my skin swell with the heat.

"Hello," I whispered.

No one answered. I sat there holding the phone. "Rusty?" No response. No sound. "Do you want to talk to DeeDee?" The person didn't hang up, just breathed evenly and naturally, and for several minutes we just held the phone, as we had the first time, before we met. The receiver made damp circles over my ear and at the side of my jaw. It felt strangely comfortable, this connection, and suddenly I wanted to sleep. "Sleep well," I whispered. Then I cradled the receiver softly, went to bed, and didn't wake until noon.

All afternoon the sun bore down. I went with DeeDee to get her hair done, but the curls fell in the sticky weather. By the time I put on my dress, it stuck to the small of my back, and my hair dripped into my face. DeeDee had orchestrated it so that we would form a caravan from the Loft to the church, perhaps a holdout nostalgia for homecoming parades. The minister would lead the procession; then she would follow, chauffeured by the best man, a friend of Rusty's whom neither of us had ever met, a waspish-looking young man who was pleasant enough but winked at me so often that I thought he had a nervous tic.

We all stayed indoors near the air conditioner until the very last minute. I was to signal to Rusty, waiting in the Loft as if he were a monk practicing being solitary but ready to take his vows. The minister was a quarter of an hour late and didn't bother to apologize. DeeDee paced at the door in the corridor at the bottom of the stairs and every few minutes stood on tiptoe to peek out the window to the street. As soon as she saw the reverend pull up, she said, "Let's go," as if she were a drill sergeant.

I helped her into the car, stuffing in the layers of her gown so it wouldn't get stuck in the door. "Tell Rusty," she directed. "Turn north onto Kingshighway," and she smiled as she blew me kisses. I was about to shut the door when she leaned toward me and said, "We're all going to be so happy together." A river of perspiration ran between my breasts. I slammed the door. The minister pulled up a few yards so that the groom's car could follow but at a safe, invisible distance. I signaled Rusty to come down, and as he got into the car in the driver's seat beside me, I fixed my gaze on her license plate, the double "D" for "DeeDee," and we pulled behind them onto the road.

And this is what I see today: Her dress takes up most of the front seat. The groomsman driving has to feel for the gearshift among the layers of moiré and voile; in her lap she holds a smart pillbox hat with a pearl stickpin, stiffened chiffon gathered around the rim in a half-veil. Every few minutes she licks her lips nervously and pulls down the visor to look in the mirror.

We wend our way past McGurk's, redbrick storefronts, shops with awnings, and then the old city hospital as we start up Lafayette. At Schwarz Studio we form a caravan around the park. We drive by three-story manses with tiled mansard roofs and balconies where riverboat captains used to retire for their evening cigars. Turrets are trimmed in lilacs and indigos. Behind the park's cast-iron fence with the fleur-de-lis peaks are beds of English perennials. The shade under the persimmon trees and catalpas is shaped like giant daisy petals. At the gate with the ball-topped stone pillars, we turn north onto Mississippi. Then west onto Park, where sycamores line the curb; there is no breeze, and their leaves are absolutely still. Then another left turn, a perfect right angle, onto Missouri. From the heart of the park, the bronze statue of Thomas Hart Benton stares blindly through us. DeeDee waves at the picnickers and bag ladies, the open-palmed, slow sweep of a princess. Then we follow Jefferson to Highway 40.

We parade up the hill, curving over the bridge, past the Missouri Boiler and Tank Company. Sometimes she waves, but to the car and not to any of us in particular, lest she inadvertently view her groom; and we stay back. An American flag hangs limp in the dead air. The cityscape spreads out on the right, the sun ricocheting off the Arch, and we duck under the arrow for Highway 40. We whoosh by signs for Forest Park Boulevard, Boyle Avenue, Forest Park Community College, billboards for Budweiser and KMOX radio. At the sign that says Kingshighway North, Highway 40 ribbons to our left.

The last memories I have of this procession are of that highway, spiraling into the distance like the lake at Wilders Ferry. All the rest of my memories of this procession are not my own. I have not been able to afford them. I can see only what DeeDee saw on her wedding day on the way to the Forest Park Hotel.

———————

She speeds ahead of them in the traffic, envisioning the black velvet bows around the white balloons, seeing herself float down the aisle as if it were a magic carpet. As she exits at Kingshighway North and yields to the right, she glances one more time in the mirror and, not immediately spotting the antenna with the white crepe paper bow that matches the one she tied in the same place on her car, she has her driver turn into the street to Barnes Medical Center to let them catch up. There is something of the Lot myth here, for she turns and looks back, swivels around, first her chin and neck and then her shoulders. For a while she waits, squinting at one car at a time across as much of the horizon as stretches behind her. Cars jockey for room around her, horns screeching. She grips the back of the seat, her fingernails, polished to match her lipstick, digging into the upholstery. She scans the road for some sign of the white car, closing one eye at a time for sharper focus, still trusting her niece and her husband-to-be more than her own vision. Then she gathers the folds of moiré and voile and scoots around the other way, nearly kneeling on the seat to get a closer perspective. With her hand she shields her eyes from the relentless light. Then she digs around in her purse and puts on her glasses. Finally she faces straight ahead. The afternoon sun glances off the copper facade of the Medical Building and shoots back into her eyes, blinding her. She takes what she wishes was an endless breath before she screams, "Stop!"

exile

And so, for the third time in my life, I disappeared—this time with the single-minded determination of a criminal to escape. I knew my mother and I had that much in common. We both could do the unspeakable.

We drove until we ran out of money, stopping only to buy food at truck stops, zigzagging from freeways to back roads as if we were being pursued, and pulling off onto the shoulders to sleep in the car, or in a farmer's field after dark. When we got tired of driving, we stopped in a city whose name I tried not to learn.

When he rented the furnished apartment, he stopped me in the corridor at the entrance, and my heart opened up at the core, readying itself to let in panic. I was afraid he would carry me over the threshold, and the recognition of what that meant scratched on my consciousness like a dagger tip. But instead, he removed a handkerchief from his pocket and blindfolded me and led me in by the hand. It was a long oblong of a place, four rooms off a narrow corridor that got the sun only in the late afternoon and was lit by one bulb, which was burned out when we entered and we never bothered to replace. In the twilight we would take turns hiding behind a door, ready to spring out at the other one of us who was walking up or down the corridor anticipating the flesh that any minute would make each raw nerve sing, and not noticing how the balls of dust that collected in the interstices along the wood floor resembled small, grounded clouds. Lunch hours, we would find new uses for the furniture, bending over the curved backs of the sofa, draping ourselves on the frayed arms of overstuffed chairs, curling belly to back around the upper arc of an oval rug, sitting spread-legged on the edge of the dresser, its mirror throwing the reflection of a bare back into the room. And midnights, we sprawled out on the chilly steel webbing of the fire escape, the darkened ground rendering the height invisible.

For thirteen months I didn't look at a map, didn't listen to the radio or the television, lest I awake to the feeling I knew would come to imprison me for life. It was extraordinarily easy. We found jobs wherever we could, but changed them often, as if to protect ourselves from becoming allied with the real world, from getting to know people, hearing what they had to say, being drawn into their lives and therefore out of our own.

I sentenced myself to fantasy. It wasn't enough to fantasize that each of the people who might be searching for us was gone, for I did imagine them far away, on Orcas Island or on the Baja Peninsula; I always gave them pleasures in their exile, the way I always gave them to myself. In some visions these people glided in orange catamarans on oceans that shot back starbursts of light, the sun and wind smacking their faces, faces with expressions that I could never allow myself to see. In other versions they slept on their folded arms on white dunes and took the yellow light under their skin. In the winter they skated in the woods, crossing hands and cutting crazy eights in the ice. Always, always they were with each other, or a partner, someone faithful, someone to take care of them.

But it was not enough to see them happy and far away. I convinced myself that I lived nowhere. As long as I was nowhere, I was doing nothing wrong; as long as I was nowhere, I was hurting no one. I drew images of Rusty around me always, a screen that let in shape and light and kept out everything else, like a translucent shade pulled tight over my eyes. When he was away, working at whatever job he had for the month—clerking or waiting tables or checking in library cards—or even when he walked down the block to pick up a can of soup or tuna fish, I saw him behind my eyes. His image took up all the space on the back of my lids, and there was room for nothing else.

I insulated myself with illusion and imagined myself happy. I was con-demned to my joy: to the ways we made love, to the ways we hid from each other, to the meaninglessness of our words and phrases, which slipped from our mouths like empty air. There was a sameness in all this, in a world where all texture came from the confines of our own skin, in the dreaminess of something that should never have been. We woke up and went to work, and that was the extent of our real life. We merged our days and our nights, one blending into the other seamlessly, in the same ways we blended into each other, pumping until we were numb. The notion of our lives as "mine" or "his" was eradicated, washed away, like the thin top layer of sand where the beach joins the sea. Place and time dissolved. We were sucked away in the vacuum of an endless today. The only sense of to-morrow came in the moist whisperings of fantasies into each other's ears, all desire taking the shape of our bodies and what we could make them do.

No knowledge. No remorse. No guilt. No pain.

When pain did reenter my life, it was not my own. One day, at the café where I served greasy hamburgers to truckers and garbage collectors, I found myself walking out the back door at break time. This door led into an alley. I studied the boarded-up windows across it and was hardly aware at first of the sound of whimpering. I lowered my gaze. Squeezed between two metal garbage cans was a stooped figure, head bent down, a cigarette dangling in one hand. I vaguely recognized her hair. It was bleached and piled high on the head, and anchored with gold hairpins. She was the woman who took a smoke break every half hour nearly to the second, and blew smoke rings with her head tilted up into the sky, I suppose in an effort not to offend the other employees. For a few minutes I simply watched her. Suddenly, her head shot up and she spat at me, "What the hell are you staring at, you goddam little snob?"

I pivoted and headed for the door. "Go ahead," she called. "Just walk away. That's it." And then she stood up and kicked the garbage can and kept kicking. I could feel the numbness lift from me, and slowly, as if through a thick fog, I walked toward her, grabbed the can by its metal handles, and dragged it out of her reach. For a moment she just stood, gasping, shoulders tensed, arms stiff at her sides, eyes narrowed and fo-cused on the can just beyond the length of her legs. She was tall, like some latter-day Viking or Amazon, her beehive hairdo giving her a tow-ering effect. The laminated tag pinned to the pocket of her salmon-col-ored uniform spelled out "Doreen," and until now it hadn't registered that that was her name, or that she even had a name. In fact, as her upper torso heaved next to me, I began to catch glimpses of who she was. She was the one who said, "Pardon me for living," under her breath when the customers demanded quicker service or called her "Honey." Until that moment I wouldn't have been able to offer any of the details of her life; I simply hadn't seen her.

Now not only did I see her, but I saw something else in her. There were so many glimpses of the familiar about her. Her size brought the image of Graceanne to the brink of awareness, just a little inkling, like the scent of alfalfa on a June breeze. Her clenched fists made me see Paris, the fists I had to open to give her my last, and only, gift. The silent heaves brought back my grandfather, mourning the death of his daughter. And her vulnerability, exposed and fragile, shielded only by evanescent anger, suggested something, or someone, still beyond my sight.

I asked her to talk, and she did, though she stood rigid and kept her fingers pressed to her palms. Her story was one I knew, one that most of us know. A man. A younger woman, whom he'd taken to for her tight skin and free spirit. He'd moved out, leaving Doreen first choice of the furniture. Since they were never married, they needed no divorce. No ugly ends that didn't come together, except of course for her insides, which were rent and shredded. We stayed out there long after the cook yelled at us to come in. I walked her toward the back door of the café.

"After you," she said, in mock chivalry, holding open the door.

"I think I'll just go home."

"See you tomorrow?"

"Sure," I said, and smiled, although I knew I would never see her again.

After my shift, I hung my uniform on a hanger on the outside door to the café. Before I could think, I returned to the apartment and on a grocery bag wrote a note to Rusty. I scribbled furiously, covering the brown paper. Now I wonder if I weren't half waiting for him to come home from work early, to rescue me and bring me back to the painless life of pretense we had assumed for too long. But he didn't come back, and before I left, I took the bag with me, all but the last word, which I ripped from one of the bottom lines: "shame." I left the brown scrap on the counter. I took nothing else with me; I wanted to leave the same way I had come. Before I walked out the door, I placed my key under his pillow.

turns

I made my way back to Idaho on a Greyhound, over the roads my parents must have taken when they emigrated in their painted school bus to a land neither of them and no one they knew had seen. As the bus sped west, then north, topping already snowy mountain passes and curving around glittering rivers, I tried to envision my return, but saw only the landscape. At the pinnacle of Lookout Pass, where the time changes and Montana ends, the bus pulled to the side. I stared down at the woods spiraling into Idaho, and it struck me that from this view the trees had the shape of the forest painted on the school bus.

Even when about a hundred miles later, past plowed fields and stacks of hay bales, I saw the small signboard that said WILDERS FERRY, POP. 508, I knew that it was no longer the same place I had described to Rusty during the tornado. Behind the sign was a small complex of buildings, the largest of which said SEARS. Fronting one building was a sign fashioned in blue neon. We drove down Main Street and rounded the corner. The Satellite had a new addition, which stuck out into the alley. The bus stopped in front of the Hoot Owl, and I peeked in the window. They had removed the lunch counter; in its place were racks of T-shirts. I imagine they all said "Idaho."

Early-morning haze hung over the lake, and I knew the wives of the mill hands had been up since before dawn, lighting fires in their woodstoves to remove the chill from the breakfast spoons. The haze shadowed the mountains across the water. The shadows gave them shape against the sky, and the purples changed from moment to moment, lavenders deepening to the royal shades of queens' robes. The small crimson berries of goose currant dotted the side of the road, and the huckleberry bushes, thigh-high, ran claret banners up the hills. The yellow triangles of tamaracks pointed toward the cusp of the fading moon.

Shivering in the autumn air, I stood at the end of the dock and watched the haze burn off the lake. The water was many colors: amber at the edges, myrtle-green at the shallows, lapis farther out. The pale rays silvered on the water, throwing out stars of light, the ripples fanning out from the middle and twinkling with diamonds. Aspen winding with the stream that fed the lake flashed a reflection of their fragilely connected sun-colored leaves into the water, and I saw, as I never had before, how Yellow Creek got its name.

I noticed how the gravel gets progressively smaller close to shore. I scooped up the small fragments, stooped at its edge. The sand caught the light like tiny mirrors. Purple quartz, rose quartz, smoky quartz, ground by glaciers and waves, sifted through my fingers. Bits of mica sparkled gold and silver in turns. I knew I was seeing through an artist's eye. And like a discriminating artist, I, for the first time in my life, felt ready to make considered choices.

I count whatever triumph I can claim in what I did not do. I did not sit at a barstool at the Short Branch waiting for a blond logger, did not go to Wilders Ferry Central School or stop in the Satellite or Left Bank Books West to gawk at the changes. Instead, I saved all the intensity of closure for a single person, a person whom I had so painstakingly *not* considered for so long.

I headed down the street toward Alice's Hair Art. I held my breath, praying that it would still be there. On the way I passed people who looked familiar, but no one person I knew by name. A few of them nodded or smiled. They all looked at me curiously, as if I were still some kind of freak. It struck me that our impact on the community—the paintings on display in Sandpoint, the painter's model with access to all the secrets of the town, the soap-opera quality of the schoolgirl disappearing one spring, the rumor of her being orphaned, the sudden drama of the plane crash, no funeral—must have been explosive. I suddenly felt exposed. A myriad of feelings churned in and rose from my belly as if from Pandora's box. One feeling at a time, I told myself.

I turned left at the corner, and there it was. I looked in the window as I had when I was a child.

She was facing away from the window, and I stared at her broad back the way I had years ago in the lion claw bathtub. She was rolling someone's hair in purple plastic rollers, and I could see the lips of the customer move in profile and knew Graceanne was doing what she did best—not styling hair, but listening.

I took a step back and waited on the sidewalk. I almost felt as if I were invisible, an intruder. To become visible would alter the dynamics, imperceptibly change the pattern of the fall of dominoes that make up another person's life. Suddenly I couldn't do it one more time. I watched Graceanne's face as she listened. She rolled the hair slowly, as if pacing herself to the tempo of the other woman's story, and her face dipped and squiggled and opened, absorbed. Watching this scene without sound, I was mesmerized. This is the knowledge GranVinny has, I thought, and hearing myself think his name made me shiver. Another minute and I'll leave; I'll walk to the Hoot Owl and climb on the bus and drive east and not look back. Another minute.

And then she shifted her position and spotted me outside the pane. For a second she froze, holding a strand of wet hair vertically from the head of her client and a square of tissue paper squeezed between her lips; then she nodded, an odd nod, curt and polite as if to a sparring opponent. She took the tissue from her lips, folded it over the strand, and rolled down tight.

When I opened the door, the cowbell clanged. Without looking up she said, "It'll take me about another half hour."

"I can wait," I said, and sat on the red plastic chair I had waited on years ago, picked up a magazine, and pretended to read.

When the woman was safely under the dryer, Graceanne removed her rubber gloves and motioned me into a back room lined with plastic bottles. We sat at a card table covered with a beach towel. She made us a cup of tea with a plug-in hot coil. It wasn't until we sat down that I really looked at her. Her hair was short, cut as if with pinking shears slanted up so that it looked like fringe. Her hands shook around the teacup. In spite of her height, she looked frail, and her wrist bones protruded like door-knobs.

She stared at me for nearly a minute, as if I were a ghost, or someone she couldn't quite place. "What did you want?" she asked. Her voice still brought back the waterfall.

"Just to talk," I said.

"Go ahead. Talk."

"I mean I want you to talk."

The corners of her mouth turned up slightly. "That's a new one."

"I want to listen." She looked at me as if I were a speck of lint on the chair. Then she glanced at a clock on the wall. "I need to hear about"—I hesitated—"my mother."

She looked down at her hands, lifted them from the table, and spread her fingers. They opened slowly, like a swallowtail uncurling from a co-coon.

"Is that all?" she asked with a trace of irony. "You look like her, you know." She reached toward my face as if to touch it, but drew back. Her hand hovered for a second, then disappeared under the table.

"I wondered if you'd left Wilders Ferry," I said.

"Where would I go?"

"Just . . . away."

She stirred the tea with the handle of a plastic fork, her lips tight in a half-smile, her eyes focused on an object in a reverie. I was about to in-terrupt, remind her I was there, when she said, "I did go away."

She said it with the sudden inspiration of a poet, and I realized that once I would have responded with a hard-edged comeback. But I settled back into my chair and said nothing.

"I spent two years listening to people talk about her. Sometimes just to hear themselves talk. But when they saw that I wasn't listening, they'd hush. It kinda closed me off, I guess."

That notion struck me as odd; I had always thought of her as closed off anyway.

"When I was a little girl, my parents used to take me to the Ada County Fair. They'd buy me cotton candy, and I'd bury my face in it and twirl it around my tongue and take as much as I could into my mouth and feel the little wisps melt into sugar, and suck my fingers to get all the sweet stuff into my mouth where it belonged. And the rest of the night I'd spend doubled over with a bellyache. But still, all I could think of was how beautiful that pink spun sugar looked towering up out of the paper cone, and how it felt in my mouth."

I had never heard her say so much about herself and listened to the whirring of the clock while I turned over things to say in response. In some ways she had said it all.

"You lived with both your parents then? And they're still living?"

"They live in Boise. My mother's taking courses at Boise State and my father's an accountant." The ends of her lips stretched up, as if in a smile. "You're as nosy as your mother." I couldn't bear to ask whether or not she knew a river-runner. I was beginning to feel relief, perhaps from the real-life details that were filtering back into my life. The amorphous feelings that we fabricate are so much more powerful, so much more tyrannical, than the gritty truth. But something inside me, one of my Rose genes, pulled me back into the murky, unpredictable world of the dramatic.

"I never grieved for my mother," I said, and saying it, I knew it was true.

"You didn't need to, honey. I grieved enough for you, too." And she laughed from deep in her throat. Then she added, softly, the vertical current of the waterfall resonating in her voice, "She loved you more than she ever loved anyone."

"Right," I said.

She squared her shoulders. "She wrote her own funeral service, you know."

My heart fluttered like the wings of a crazed moth.

"I found it in that fishing tackle box she used as a paint box. Sorry I kept it so long." She looked right into my eyes.

And then I saw my hand reach toward hers on the table, saw it as if in slow motion, saw that it was as pale as a seagull wing and that, as it came closer to Graceanne's, it seemed to grow paler still. It rested on her hand, and I gripped it hard, could feel metal biting into my palm like a brand, and I knew it was a ring, a silver rattler with a garnet eye. She slowly brought her other hand from her lap and blanketed mine with it. The familiarity made me want to weep.

"I thought when you came here, you needed to ask me something," she said. I loosened my hold on her hand, rubbed my eyes, and thought for a long time.

"I wondered if you'd heard anything about Karl?" I said finally.

"Who's Karl?" she asked.

Today I dig deep, claw around for visions of my mother with this woman, and as much as I clear space for them to come, they never appear.

I think she knew what I really came for. The question I thought I should ask, the one I must have intended to ask, that must have been a filter for everything I saw and smelled and heard and touched, I chose not to. It is a matter of privacy, precious privacy, that allows us to be anything we want. Our choice. And at last, my choices about the composition and shape, the textures and tints of my life were beginning to take form. I left the mystery in Wilders Ferry where it belonged, and I took with me the remnants of my illusions as if they were a kaleidoscope, gorgeous, extraordinary, eternally changing, but contained. Something I could pick up and view—or not.

The metallic handle of my mother's paint box biting into my hand, I took the lake road to the house I had planned never to view again. A fringe-winged hawk sailed over the roof, then drifted out of sight. The purple paint had peeled in places and discolored, and the first-floor windows were boarded shut.

I slowed down and tried to peer through the cracks between the boards. In these few years the hawthorn tree had grown so that its branches reached to the bottom bevel of my oval window. The school bus was still parked in back. The evergreen forest and rising sun were scratched with graffiti, and weeds and bear grass pierced the rusted belly.

Between the boards, I saw clear through the walls to the kitchen and to my mother, baking bread.

She mixes it and stands on a stool to knead it, smiling at the pleasure in the colors, in its speckles of grain, in the malleable feel of it on the heels of her hands, and the thud it makes when she plunks it onto the slab of the cutting board.

She is my age, to the day, and naked. Flour dusts her chest, and she has a flour smudge like unfinished war paint under her left eye. She is taking comfort in the sun entering her breasts, in their freedom to move and be warmed by the light. She is thinking about the smell this dough will make as it heats, how it will change all its molecules, and then change the house; and she is contemplating the silky warmth of a woman who will need her, the woman she would never know in her daughter, perhaps even if she had lived to know that daughter as a woman. She turns to face me as if she sees I'm there, her expression beatific like a madonna in a Raphael painting, as if she has just delivered a child, painless, to the world. Her lips curve up, and she spreads her hands out on top of the stove, as if its warmth were entering every cell of her skin, as if in a blessing.

final words

For more than a thousand miles, that funeral service, a page torn from a sketchbook and rolled into a scroll like the one I had imagined giving Graceanne, sat unread in a metal box on my lap. Through the streaked windows of the Greyhound I stared through timberland and buttes and barren plateaus and sage-dotted plains, and carried my mother's legacy back into the heart of the country. At a hundred times the speed of Lewis and Clark, we crossed the border into Missouri and whizzed by miles of corn stubble and groves of rust-leaved oaks. I wondered if the century-old trees that shaded the house at White Oak Lane had begun to drop their scalloped leaves, turn the lawn the color of something precious and irretrievable. Oak leaves in October. Rusty's hair. Even naming this color, thinking his name, stabbed me deep, carved me out from the inside.

Grief pecked at my inner eyes, leaving burning wounds throughout my head, and I panicked that the very act of reading would became impossible, part of the penance. As the bus neared St. Louis, I unlatched the box.

Discovering the service, retrieving it, reading it—it was all so painful

I wanted to scream. But I fought against blaming myself, or Graceanne, who had for reasons of her own kept my mother's final message to me a secret.

Given Mimi's passion for ceremony, the service she wrote seemed sketchy and short. I wondered if she really expected to die, or if this were simply another entry in her sketchbook, some inkling to breathe life into and leave as legacy. The instructions were straightforward. There were her favorite poems, the Shaker hymn "Simple Gifts," and a succession of conventional farewells, a layered litany: first, her husband, Dyl, Paris, and Jillian, all at once—all the people who had left Wilders Ferry, never to return; second, Graceanne; third, her sister; fourth, her father and mother. No mention of Karl. And then came a cryptic part—these words: "Goodbye to all those I have loved, with or without wisdom." That seemed to cover the gamut. It wasn't until the last line, about two-thirds of the way down the page, that my name was mentioned. And here is what she left for me: "My last words are for my daughter, the only real art I have ever made."

That was it. Whether or not those were the last words themselves, the only words she had for me, or whether she meant to add to them will remain a fragment of the mysteries I inherited.

Just before the bus pulled into the terminal, it crossed Cass Avenue, where my grandparents had met and courted so long ago. As I emerged onto the street, no one caught my eye; I was noticed in no one's periphery. I felt I had become invisible.

I crept back into survival in increments; rented a room in the north of the city; got a job in an office. The room had a small desk by a single casement window, and from it I watched the winter come to the street.

I removed the café curtains from the rod and let myself see nothing beyond the gravel-pitted snow at the curbs. I shivered at the window. The radiator became so cold to the touch that I covered it with a wool blanket. I suppose I could have asked the landlady to turn up the heat, but I preferred to take the cold into my bones. I sat on my hands to keep them warm and every few minutes massaged my fingers to keep them from becoming numb. I did, some weeks into February, look up my aunt in the phone book, but she was no longer listed. I was paralyzed at the task of imagining her happy in another place. I passed weekend afternoons doing little else but walking. The icy slush seeped into my boots and then my socks and then my skin. My feet tingled, and the wet wool rubbed the heels raw. This was the shape my mourning took, and I gave myself to it bit by bit.

The first hints of spring—the forsythia and purple crocuses—brought with them a sadness as I tried hard to keep out images of the suburbs not twenty miles away. One night, after opening the window to let in the warm air, I had the following dream. I saw my grandfather crouching in his garden.

His veined fingers are pollen-stained like a splash of pale-yellow paint, and he is patting soil around the daylilies. His knuckles are knotted, arthritic, and he puts down his spade every few flowers and rubs the swollen places. When he bends into the lilies' orange tongues, he turns his head just a bit to the right, toward the sundial, and I notice an engorged place on his neck. I touch it; it is hard. He doesn't see me, or feel my hand, and of course doesn't hear my gasp, but he knows I'm there and isn't startled, as if he has expected me all along. He finishes the row and struggles to stand upright, but his spine is bent like a weeping willow, and he remains stooped. I reach down to help him, but my fingers skitter through him as if through a ghost.

The next afternoon, when I asked the cab driver to let me out at the street sign painted with oak trees and a sorrel horse, the sign that read WHITE OAK LANE, the sun hit it head-on. I walked up the long drive.

The house looked deserted. I still had my key and let myself in the back door. I half expected him to have changed the locks. Inside it was silent, and it struck me that this was the way GranVinny always heard it now. My first thought as I took in the furniture and pillows and vases and bowls and sculpture was that nothing had changed over the year and a half of my absence. I walked to the living room. I searched the room for the albums or diaries that used to be scattered about the house, and found none. Perhaps by now he had put the photos back in the albums, or perhaps he had emptied them entirely, removing all of his hapless bloodline from his sight.

Moving into the hall, I ran my finger over the railing of the banister, and the dust formed a gray disk on my fingertip. The mahogany on the chair arms and the knickknack shelves was dull and unpolished. I pictured the way he used to shine the newel post with his monogrammed handkerchief and knew that this was only one of the things I must have done to him. I knew dust had also made gray rings around the lathed posters of my mother's cherry wood–bed. I tried not to look too carefully as I wove my way through the furniture to the basement. So certain was I of my specterlike anonymity, I didn't even bother to close the basement door behind me.

I walked past the shelves still stacked neatly with shoe boxes, all still carefully labeled, boxes of dirt, kept for years. They resembled small caskets waiting for vampires or other spirits to return and fill them again. And I hoped for his sake a spirit would return to him, even if he could never see it, or hear it. If only he had been able to hear the gorgeous names of the plants in his daughter's voice. On the bottom shelf was his tackle box, the replica of his daughter's paint box.

I opened the door to the garage and pulled the string that switched on the bulb. I blinked. At first what was wrong didn't register. I simply knew it: something was wrong with this picture. There were not one, but two cars in the garage, and one of them had a license plate marked with the double D. My blood quickened, and I was afraid that wherever she was in the house she could hear it thudding. I left by the garage door and walked stealthily from the side yard to the front.

And suddenly he appeared, tending a flower bed in front of the living room window where he used to make faces at his granddaughter in her sickbed years ago. He raked at the small buds just visible over the top of the earth, speckling the lawn with shades of blue and green.

I watched from a safe distance, waiting for him to turn his profile so I could see the shape of his neck. I gripped the scroll in my fist, half hoping he would see me and not recognize me, so that I could disappear and be with him at the same time. But he kept his head down, studying his fledgling plantings, and walked around to the flower bed in the backyard. I followed a distance behind him and stopped where he had stood. I gazed into the living room. I squinted at the glare of the glass, and when my eyes had adjusted to the light, I saw two faces, one superimposed on the other.

One was my own phantomlike reflection, looking like parts of me I had never seen before. Rather, I had seen these features, but not on me. They belonged to my aunt when she used to lead me into the cellar by candlelight. I never noticed how our cheekbones angled back, how our eyelids hooded our pupils, how our chins were shaped like upside-down hearts. And behind my reflection, almost congruent with it, was a figure that made my heart beat like the wings of the dragonflies over the lilies.

At first I thought it was the ghost of my mother. And then I knew who it was, and that it was no ghost. I stared at both of us. Her eyes were wide, and her chest expanded visibly with every shallow breath. I shook my head to rid me of my fantasies, and when I looked again, the figure had vanished into the house. Listening to the screech of the blue jays, I waited for her to return, but although a shadow passed behind the shades in the upstairs window, she did not come down to the living room.

I found him again, kneeling alongside his cactus garden. He saw me coming, froze as if cast in bronze, gripping his sandy spade like a dagger. I came to him slowly, hoping with all the powers I could gather that each step would thaw his heart. I knelt next to him and ran my hand slowly along both sides of his neck. When I felt only the flat slope to the collarbone, only the soft, wrinkly skin, no swelling or lump, a lifetime of tears sprang up. He laid down his spade, removed my hand from his neck, and brought my fingers to his lips, unsmiling. I embraced him with all my strength. He held me and rubbed his scratchy cheek against mine.

And then I pulled away as fast as I could, regret already knotting and unknotting inside me, and ran around to the front and to the winding drive, which would forever rid them of me and the pain I embodied. I was halfway down the slope of the lawn when I looked one more time toward the house, and I saw the new flower bed that GranVinny had been tending when I had first spotted him. The speckles of color belonged to wildflowers, and they merged and blurred in my wet eyes like a kaleidoscope, fragments of beauty with no purpose, and in that vision I saw the lapis and myrtle-greens and star-and-diamond whites—the refracted colors recalling the lake at Wilders Ferry. The pattern of the just-born plants confused me; it seemed so unlike him, this random arrangement, and I shivered at the thought that this randomness was the product of a decaying sensibility.

I was about to turn a final time when I noticed in the blooms a right angle, like the one on a right triangle. I followed both lines of the angle out and saw that they were straight and careful and that they formed a definite pattern—a single letter—L. I glanced over my shoulder and saw him walking steadily toward me. And suddenly I knew, knew even without looking, what letter was next. And next after that. Something I could barely recognize as pleasure washed over me. And I made one last well-considered turn, toward redemption, toward the threshold that would take me to her.